"You must see the benefits of this engagement. It may not be what either of us want, but we can use this to our mutual advantage."

The battle within her must have shown on her face, because Bastien took a step closer and said quietly, "We only have to pretend just for a little while. Once we have visited the queen, much of the furor will die down and we can quietly break the betrothal."

She pulled her gaze from him and stared out over the garden. The earnestness in Bastien's voice couldn't be ignored. She knew how badly he wanted to gain his rightful place in society. He deserved that.

Hadn't he come to her defense all those years when she was a mere servant in his father's house? Didn't she owe it to him to make his path as smooth as possible as he had once done for her?

Lilas stared unseeingly around her. Though she hated the bind she found herself in, she knew that they would have to succumb to the dictates of society for now.

"Very well. I'll help you."

Author Note

Some critics of romance say of the genre that it's bad escapism. Others say it gives its readers unrealistic expectations.

I beg to differ. I grew up reading Harlequin. No matter what the real world presented, I could escape to a world where love conquered all. Was it escapism? Yes, for romance reminds us of the power of love—of one's self, and of each other.

It's a dream come true to be able to write for them. When I got the call from my editor, Carly, I was so flustered, I started talking about cooking. There wasn't even a segue. Just bam! Cooking. Poor Carly! She had the most extraordinary look on her face. She was used to my rambling and verbal twisting about (I talk a lot), but even that went overboard. How exciting to see where this new journey in my writing career will take me.

I hope you enjoy Bastien and Lilas's story. Exploring pre-Revolutionary France in a Cinderella story was a lot of fun. Lilas, our defiant maid turned popular artist, and Bastien, our devilish Prince Charming.

If you'd like to get in touch, I can be reached at parker@parkerjcole.com, through my publisher, Facebook or Twitter @parkerjcole.

Carpe diem!

PARKER J. COLE

—

The Duke's Defiant Cinderella

ISBN-13: 978-1-335-72346-8

The Duke's Defiant Cinderella

Copyright © 2022 by Parker J. Cole

Recycling programs for this product may not exist in your area.

For questions and comments about the quality of this book, please contact us at CustomerService@Harlequin.com.

Harlequin Enterprises ULC
22 Adelaide St. West, 41st Floor
Toronto, Ontario M5H 4E3, Canada
www.Harlequin.com

Printed in U.S.A.

Parker J. Cole is an author, speaker and radio host with a fanatical obsession with the Lord, *Star Trek*, K-dramas, anime, romance books, old movies, speculative fiction and knitting. She lives in Detroit, Michigan, with her family. To find out any and everything about her, visit ParkerJCole.com.

Books by Parker J. Cole

The Duke's Defiant Cinderella
is Parker J. Cole's debut title for
Harlequin Historical.

Look out for more books from Parker J. Cole
Coming soon!

Visit the Author Profile page
at Harlequin.com.

To Michelle Styles.

You wouldn't let me quit. You wouldn't
let me give up. You wouldn't let me stop.
You wouldn't let me stop believing in myself.
This book would not have been written if it
wasn't for you. I wouldn't be here if it wasn't for
you. "Thank you" is far too inadequate,
but until something better comes along,
it'll have to do.

To Carly.

Thank you for the countless hours you've
poured into me. You didn't have to, but you did.
Thank you for making me a better writer.

Chapter One

Château de Velay, Languedoc, South of France,
April 1771

Ivy rippled in gentle waves along the stone wall of the enclosed *potager*. The waxy leaves brushed against the bowed-down, mob-capped head of the servant girl. She sat huddled in the corner, her shoulders shaking, her cries muffled and her sorrow palpable.

Bastien St Clare, Marquis de Velay, stood a mere foot away from the girl. He called out softly, 'Lilas?'

The servant's head jerked up. Her eyes widened, showing him they were the colour of dew-tipped lilacs. Tears trickled down cheeks almost as dark as his own.

'Monsieur le Marquis!' Hastily she wiped the moisture from her eyes and scrambled to her feet. *'Pardonnez-moi, monsieur.'* She gave a quick curtsy. 'I did not see you there.'

The pleasure of seeing her warred with his concern for her distress. 'Lilas, why are you crying? Is there something I can do?'

Her mouth opened as if she was about to tell him. He

leaned forward a little, waiting for her reply. Then wariness appeared in her eyes, and she closed it once more.

'It's nothing, *monsieur*.'

Alarm riddled every part of his body. For the first time since he'd known her Lilas was holding secrets back from him.

This would not do.

'Lilas, you know you can tell me what's wrong.'

'Can I?' An incredulous tone lined her words.

His eyebrows drew together in the centre of his forehead. 'What do you mean by that?' The words came out harsher than he'd planned.

'*Pardonnez-moi, monsieur.*' She stepped back and curtsied. 'I have forgotten my place.'

Bastien raised his eyebrows. 'I must have struck my head on the gate before I arrived. You've never acted like a servant with me before when we are alone.'

Her eyes flared like twin flames. 'I'm sure I don't know what you mean, *monsieur*.'

The tension that had gripped his shoulders was released in a single motion. At least he knew the real Lilas was still there under that ill-suiting servitude.

It still begged the question: Why was she acting like this? Master's son and servant they might be, but he had always come to her aid over the years. He'd always protected her whenever the servants of his father's house had mistreated her for some perceived slight.

'I am not leaving until you tell me what is wrong, Lilas.'

'I can't do that, *monsieur*.' Her high voice sent any pretence of submission to the winds. 'Can't you see that?'

He shook his head. 'I can't,' he answered quietly.

Her eyes fastened on some invisible object. 'It has

nothing to do with you.' Her teeth sank into the corner of her bottom lip. 'At least, I don't believe it has.'

Bastien moved until he stood in front of her, capturing her gaze. 'You're talking about mysteries, Lilas. What is it? What has happened?'

She took in a deep breath. 'The Duc de Languedoc has summoned me. I am to go to his study within a half hour.'

Bastien took a step back. 'Père? What would Père want with you?'

An unnatural stillness came over her. 'You do not know?'

He gave an ungentlemanly snort. 'My father doesn't see fit to make me aware of his plans, Lilas. He simply ensures I obey them.' His hard voice softened slightly. 'I understand how you are feeling.'

'Do you? What could you know about it?'

Bastien's chest expanded. 'More than you think.'

At the scoffing sound she made, he lowered his brows over his eyes. 'You doubt my words? Do you think we are so different?'

'*Aren't* we, Monsieur le Marquis?'

Mockery and cynicism tinged the use of his formal title. A strained silence followed.

Then Bastien chuckled, shaking his head. 'This is why I have always liked you.'

Lilas's mouth fell open. '*Monsieur...?*'

'I have known you for the past ten years. You obey not because you must, but because you choose to.' He drew nearer, standing in front of her. 'Do you think I have forgotten the *fille des cendres* with the ash-smudged cheeks *ma mère* introduced to the household?' Without conscious thought, he lifted his finger and trailed it along the side of her face.

Lilas gave a violent jolt, but she didn't move away.

Her startled eyes lifted to his, their depths filled with inquisitiveness. An arc of awareness went through him. This was the first time that he had ever touched her. It felt as natural as breathing.

Was her skin really this soft and warm? Or was it simply the newness of this interaction? Unable to tear his eyes away from the sight of his dark finger against her brown skin, he continued to stroke her lightly.

'That same *fille des cendres* used those ashes to create beautiful works of art.'

He reached out and gripped her wrists. Those clear eyes met his own. Her tears ceased, and she regained her usual witty and headstrong disposition. The pads of his thumbs discovered the hint of flesh along the insides of her wrists not quite covered up by her sleeves.

His eyes roamed over her. 'Never hide from me, Lilas. Not your secrets or yourself.'

Lilas's head tilted to one side. 'Can I ever really do such a thing with you, *monsieur*?'

'I don't intend either of us to find out.'

Her lips curved into a smile. 'How wicked you are.'

'I am,' he agreed.

His thumb moved in a circle along the skin of her inner wrist. It was just as soft there as it was along her temple. Seeing Lilas like this, touching her like this, only added to his ever-changing discovery of her.

Theirs had been a curious relationship ever since she'd been employed in his family's service when he was ten and two years of age. Had she been a woman of nobility, this…friendship between them would never have developed. But over the years, he'd been thankful for its existence.

The starched uniform rested upon her person in an ill fashion. Lilas lacked the carriage of a submissive servant. When they'd first met, her thin, starved eight-year-old frame had stood erect, and her violet-hued eyes had boldly met his. That little square chin had been thrust out even as it had trembled.

Through the years she'd performed her duties admirably, but within the depths of her dark violet gaze flamed tongues of rebellion. Maybe that infernal boldness was what drew him to champion her cause whenever he could. Such inherent fire deserved a free rein, even if she was a servant.

Today, something about her brought him a perception unknown before. What it was, he didn't know, but touching her had opened his eyes to her as a woman.

Her attire left everything to the imagination, but he noticed for the first time her unblemished brown skin, that delicate retroussé nose with its narrow nostrils, and the plump, brownish-pink mouth with its upper lip slightly fuller than her lower one.

Bastien shook his head, trying to rid himself of those thoughts. Lilas was a servant in his father's house. Bastien had never seen her or any of the others who served his family as objects for conquest.

He wasn't going to do so now either.

Bastien unclasped his hold from her wrists, feeling bereft once more. 'Tell me what is on your mind, Lilas? Why were you crying?'

She rubbed at her wrist. His stomach knotted in an odd way. Was she trying to smooth away the sensation of his touch?

'I believe I know the reason why I've been summoned.'

Drawing his gaze away from her hands, he asked, 'And what is that?'

'I believe your father is going to dismiss me.'

'Dismiss you?'

Bastien's disbelieving voice eased the weight on Lilas's heart. His reaction showed he had nothing to do with her suspicions. Which only left one possibility. The cook, Madame Fournier, had gone to the Duc de Languedoc yet again.

'I believe so.'

'Why?'

'I think Madame Fournier must have complained about me.'

'I'll have her thrown into the streets,' he snarled through gritted teeth.

Despite the future swirling before her like a dark mist, Lilas felt her heart lighten further. For a few horrible hours she'd believed Bastien had something to do with the summons to his father's study. She should have known better.

'It would do little good. The Duc de Languedoc is lord here. His word is final. Perhaps this is the best way.'

'Why do you say that?' He lowered his brows over his golden eyes. 'What do you mean?'

Lilas said nothing, spellbound. Bastien St Clare's golden gaze was filled with something she'd never seen before. Once or twice, her sorrow at the mistreatment she'd received from the other servants had sent her fleeing into his arms, seeking the kind of comfort an older brother could provide. But she couldn't ignore that he'd touched her *like this* for the first time since they'd known each other.

As she'd grown up, Lilas had often been reminded of their positions in life. Though he might defend her like one, Bastien St Clare was *not* her brother. He was her master's son. A man she must obey. When she'd come to terms with this, she'd ceased seeking out his comfort.

Today was different.

His gaze hadn't been at all brother-like.

But Lilas didn't want to believe Bastien had looked at her as if he were aware of her as someone other than the cinder girl he usually protected.

'Lilas, what do you mean?' he repeated.

'I have no desire to excel at my duties of washing vegetables, *monsieur.*'

'Oh?'

'Ever since my arrival from the orphanage I have cleaned your home, washed your clothes and served your meals. In all things I've shown deference and humility. I have been careful to be a servant who serves a proud and prestigious house.'

He made a sound in his throat. 'And?'

'No matter what I do, it's never enough. I am still only the *mulâtresse* foundling.'

'Your life could have been worse,' he said, not unkindly.

'I am grateful I escaped a more dismal future,' she agreed with a nod. If the Duchesse de Languedoc hadn't taken pity on her that day when she'd come to do her good works at the orphanage, who knew what trials she would have suffered?

'Many children die in the orphanage long before they reach eight years of age. The nuns were not cruel, but neither were they overly attached to me.'

Frequently accompanied by starvation, sickness and poverty, Lilas had known she had something within her that had kept her from succumbing to the same fate as hundreds of orphans before her. Her burning desire for more had refused to be doused. Instead, it had bloomed into a full-fledged fire.

That unquenchable fire still smouldered within her.

'I will always be thankful that the Duchesse de Languedoc took me away from that place. But should I fall to my knees and thank St Martha that I have become accomplished at making beds? Washing clothes? Do I pray to the Virgin that I might attain Madame Fournier's position as cook in the household and thus wreak vengeance upon her?'

He caught her wrist again. 'Is that what you want? Tell me, and I'll have her thrown out this instant.'

A part of her knew that if she were to truly demand the cook's dismissal Bastien would see to it post-haste.

He increased the slight pressure of his thumb on her inner wrist. Every part of her became riveted to the spot, making the hairs on her skin rise and brush the underside of the material of her clothes. It made her itch in an inexplicable way she couldn't understand. An itch demanding to be scratched and stroked at the same time.

'I don't want that,' she said truthfully. She really should pull her hand away... 'Madame Fournier and all those who disdain me only see a servant who has gained favour with the master's son. They believe I presume to be above my station.' The flames inside her leapt as she finally expressed what she'd never before dared to say aloud. 'They don't realise I *am* above their station.'

Swiftly, she lifted her eyes to Bastien's. There was no mockery or disdain in his gaze. His thumb circled around the distended vein and an involuntary shiver took hold of her.

'Are you?' he murmured.

'They are content to be servants for the rest of their lives. I am not. That is why dismissal from the Duc may be a blessing from the Virgin herself.'

Silence reigned once more. She felt the heat of Bastien's hooded gaze as surely as his thumb that rested on her.

Without warning, he released her. She gasped at the sudden loss. The sun darted behind the clouds. A gust of wind ripped at her clothes, cooling her as if the removal of his touch had ushered in an odd chill.

Shaking her head at the idea, she listened as he spoke. 'I understand your plight. Do you think that among the nobility one such as I is truly accepted?'

Lilas frowned. 'You are the son of a *duc* who himself comes from a long line of noble descendants, *monsieur.*'

A hard edge tinged his words. 'My uncle, the Comte de Clareville, says my father destroyed generations of noble blood when he married my mother. In his eyes, my father not only wedded a commoner, but one with a different heritage—which my uncle could not tolerate.'

The bulge in the centre of his throat bobbed.

'Que Dieu repose son âme.'

His sombre words dampened the mood like drops of invisible rain. Wanting to send away the melancholy of his mother's passing two years ago, Lilas reached out and touched his arm in sympathy. It flexed under her fingers. *'Oui, monsieur.* May God rest her soul.'

His eyes drifted deliberately to her hand on his arm. She jerked it away.

He frowned. 'If you are dismissed, what will you do?'

Would he laugh at her decision? Of course not. She trusted Bastien as she did no one else. Abandoned by her parents, ignored by her religious caretakers and ostracised by the other servants, she had no cause to put her faith in humanity.

Gazing out at the rows of box hedges that enclosed many plots of herbs, vegetables and fruits, she rested her eyes on a fruit tree studded with budding new life.

'I'll capture the dawn and hold still the night.'

'You mean you will pursue your art?'

A feeling of wild abandon crept over her. 'I'm not a woman when I paint. Or even a person.'

When she painted, that infernal fire within her abated for as long as she became at one with her work. It was the only time she felt free.

'What are you, then?' he asked softly.

'I am wielded by my art. When I paint, I obey its will. It never restricts me. When I leave, my life will be my own. I'll have no master to obey.'

'Have I been such a terrible lord, Lilas?'

She shook her head. 'You have been my master's son and my friend.'

'Whatever happens you must hone your skill. Become an artist in your own right.'

'How? I am hardly likely to gain an apprenticeship.'

'I will do what I can to ensure that you do.' His golden eyes were unwavering in their regard. 'I will not abandon you, Lilas.'

'Why are you doing this? I am no one.'

'Have I ever treated you as if you are no one?'

'Never.'

He stepped closer to her. 'Have I ever looked at you as if you are no one?'

He gripped her hand once more and rubbed his thumb along the back of it. Her eyes almost drifted shut at the pleasure. She could easily get used to that.

'You have the softest skin,' Bastien murmured. 'Why have I just discovered this on the day you are leaving? I could have—'

'*Pardonne moi*, Mademoiselle Villemarette.'

They jumped and turned, seeing a bland-faced manservant behind them. If he saw their clasped hands, he gave no sign.

She tried to tug her hand away, but Bastien clamped down on it. When he refused to let go, she swallowed to moisten a dry throat. *'Oui, monsieur?'*

'The Duc de Languedoc wishes to see you now.'

Her heart fell to her feet. She opened her mouth but Bastien interjected.

'Mademoiselle Villemarette will be there soon.'

The manservant gave a deliberate cough. 'The Duc de Languedoc has expressed the urgency of his request.'

'You've delivered your message. Now go,' Bastien dismissed him with a curt nod.

The manservant bowed and left.

'I won't let anything happen to you, Lilas.'

His golden eyes stared down into hers with a throbbing intensity. She felt something stir between them. Reminiscent of a fledgling bird flapping its new wings. Cautious, so very cautious, and yet still eager.

Lilas tried again to pull away, but he said, 'Don't move.'

She stilled. *'Monsieur...?'*

'I said, don't move.'

His voice slid along her spine. Her mind blanked as his head bent. A fine trembling racked her body as his face came closer.

Mon Dieu, was he going to kiss her?

Her eyes shifted to his mouth, seeing its fullness. What would it be like to feel his lips upon hers?

Just as her eyes fluttered closed, he angled his mouth over to the side of her head. His lips brushed the ruffled flap of her mob-cap, skidded along her temple and against the cusp of her ear. She barely suppressed a shudder as he spoke.

'You will be a brilliant artist, Lilas. I will not accept less from you. I expect to have the wedding portrait of my future wife and myself painted only by you, for an exorbitant fee.'

Her chest caved in and her eyes smarted. Of course he hadn't planned on kissing her. She choked on an unsteady laugh and shoved away the nonsense of a half-formed wispy dream. '*Monsieur*, I shall do my best to diminish your fortune.'

Bastien let go of her. 'Come. We must meet my father now.'

An imp of mischief prompted her to say, 'I'm not the one who delayed us.'

Angry bees buzzed in Lilas's brain. They dug their stingers into her mind with an unbearable tenacity. She could barely believe the words she was hearing. This could not be real.

Clearing her throat, she squeezed her upper arms. 'My father…is coming here?'

'*Oui, mademoiselle.*' The Duc de Languedoc spoke in soft tones, at odds with his military bearing. 'I know it must come as a shock to you, but I've received a message from your father, who is my dear friend. His name is Louis Moreau, the Comte de la Baux. He is coming here to see you within a few days.'

'*Incroyable…*' she breathed, and collapsed onto the plush ottoman.

A father. She had a father!

Her mind whirled with the knowledge. Glancing up at Bastien, she saw her shock mirrored in his eyes. And something else…but she was too befuddled to think about what it was. All she could think was that she wasn't an orphan after all. She had a father and…

'What about my mother?'

The Duc de Languedoc shook his head. 'It's all rather puzzling, Mademoiselle Moreau.'

Lilas started. How quickly the Duc de Languedoc had used her new name. The nuns at the orphanage had given her the name Villemarette. That wasn't her name. Not any more.

She cleared her mind to continue listening to the Duc de Languedoc as he said, 'Your mother died in childbirth, and we thought her child had died, too.'

With an intent regard just like his son's, the Duc de Languedoc sat on the settee across from her.

'Your mother's name was Atalyia. She was a beautiful woman whom your father loved very much. Her death was a bitter loss to the Comte de la Baux, but in time he married a widow with a son, who are also most eager to make your acquaintance.'

Lilas shuddered. A family. She had a family! A father, a stepmother and stepbrother. It was almost too much to bear. Despite the wave of euphoria washing through her, torrential rains of curiosity still assaulted her. So many questions that they threatened to drown her.

'Monsieur le Duc, how did I end up at the orphanage? Why did—?'

'Unfortunately, my dear, I do not have any of the answers to your questions. Your father, from his letter, is just as perplexed by the turn of events as you are. All I know is that he recently received a letter from an unnamed source telling him you had resided at the orphanage near here since you were a baby. When he investigated further, he discovered to his great relief that you were here. I know the Comte de la Baux very well, and I can assure you he will not rest until he unearths all the circumstances behind your disappearance eighteen years ago.'

Too many emotions crowded in on her. A family, a father, the mystery of her birth and her disappearance… How could she make sense of it all?

Did she need to make sense of it right this instant? No. For now, she would push everything else to the back of her mind and focus on the most important aspect—she was going to meet her family!

Dazed, she looked at Bastien again. He still stared at her, but his shock had passed and the expression on his face baffled her anew. Instead of looking pleased for her good fortune, she sensed he was full of consternation. His silence bore a heavy air.

But why?

'I'll tell you what I can, Mademoiselle Moreau, and when your father arrives he can hopefully answer some of your other questions.'

'When will he be here?'

'Within a fortnight—if not sooner.'

A fortnight. Fourteen days until she could meet the man who'd sired her.

'Forgive my impertinence, Monsieur le Duc, but please… Tell me what you know about my family.'

She was like a sponge desperate for moisture! This new knowledge of who she was…she wanted every drop of it.

A faraway gaze entered the Duc de Languedoc's eyes. 'We—that is Louis, myself and my wife, Carmen—had travelled to Colonie de Saint-Domingue to visit Carmen's family and were on our way back to France.'

'The Duchesse de Languedoc?'

'My goddess…' the Duc breathed in a reverent tone. 'She was a free woman whom I had met there while I was visiting a friend's plantation. My eyes had never seen such beauty until I gazed into hers…'

His voice trailed off, and it was a few moments before he started to speak again.

'We were on our way home when a freakish storm suddenly struck. The waves tore our small vessel into pieces and the few crew members who had sailed with us were killed.'

'How awful!'

'It was.' His mouth tightened at the corners. 'I was terrified I would lose my wife of less than two years, but a Maroon boat came to our aid and took us to their island.

'When we landed, we were dragged from the boat and surrounded by Maroon Guards. I was certain they were going to kill us, but Carmen threw herself upon me, protecting me with her body.' His throat bobbed. 'I will always believe her presence was what saved us. The Maroons had no reason to trust white men—their hatred of the British was strong, even though the conflict between them was over. She spoke a few words of their language, and whatever she said gave them pause. They tied us up—even my wife—and led us deep into the mountains of the island.'

The Duc de Languedoc continued, telling Lilas of how the Maroons had imprisoned them all, except for his wife, who had been sent before the Queen Nanny of the Maroons, their leader and a powerful *obeah* woman. Through her talking with Carmen, she had learned that he and Louis weren't British, but French.

'Several times I thought we would be killed. During that time Atalyia, your mother, came to where we were held prisoner and tended to Louis, who had suffered injury from being shipwrecked. Throughout those weeks the bond between them grew, even though I could see the disapproval of the other Maroon people.'

The Duc cut a look at her.

'But Atalyia was a blood descendant of the Queen Nanny, and as such had a certain sway with the people. I believe that's what kept us alive. By the time Louis had healed, the suspicion against us had waned—thanks to Atalyia—and we were given a vessel to set sail once more. When we left, Atalyia came with us, and soon after we returned to France she became Louis's wife.'

Lilas's breath shuddered out of her. Listening to the story, she couldn't believe it. Hearing about her mother and father meeting each other just whetted her appetite for more. She wanted to know about her mother's people, her father's people—and more. So much more!

Warmth flushed her face as she glanced at Bastien again.

Bastien shook his head. 'And we thought you were going to be dismissed.'

'Dismissed? Hardly that. In fact, there's something else I need to tell you both. I'm sure Louis wouldn't mind my saying this.' A pleased smile creased his face. 'Lilas is your betrothed, Bastien.'

Bastien stared at his father. 'What did you say?' The words came out hoarsely. 'I didn't quite—'

'Mademoiselle Lilas Moreau...' his father nodded to the stone-still figure, sitting there '...is your betrothed, *mon fils.*'

Blood pounded against his temples. Bastien couldn't prevent his voice from going up an octave. 'When did this happen?'

His father gave him a sidelong glance. The soft, understanding expression he had shown to Lilas as he'd told her parents' story had vanished. 'Some time ago.'

'When, exactly?' he snapped.

'When you were small.' His father relented. 'We wanted a marriage to combine our houses. When we discovered Atalyia was with child we penned a contract that said in the event of a daughter's birth we would bring you two together.'

Bastien seethed behind his clenched teeth. The Duc's overbearing ways had caused more rifts between father and son than all of France's wars.

Though he loved his father as any son would, the Duc had always kept a tight rein on Bastien's actions, making sure he never crossed the line into indecency or impropriety. Due to his mixed blood, Bastien had always had to behave better, work harder and remain above reproach.

But didn't he have the right to live his life as he chose? Must he always be so conscious of his station and status as the *mulâtre* son of a *duc*?

'Why would you do this without my consent, Father?'

His father's gaze hardened. 'I don't need your consent. You are my son, and you'll do as you're told.'

'I am not horseflesh for you to breed.'

The Duc folded his arms. '*Mon fils,* Louis was like a brother to me as we were growing up—closer even than my own siblings. What better way to solidify our friendship than through marriage?'

Bastien had no desire to marry, although he knew he must eventually. The agony of his mother's death had caused him and his father to drift apart. Château de Velay had become a mausoleum, and Bastien longed to escape its sorrowful confines.

After several months of discussion his father had finally agreed to allow him to travel on what the British nobility called a 'Grand Tour'. Besides travelling to areas of interest in his home country, he wanted to go elsewhere in Europe too. Due to his father's tightly fisted grip, Bastien had barely stepped outside the borders of France!

'You gave me permission to leave for my Grand Tour.'

'Bastien, you cannot leave now.'

His fists curled. 'You cannot dictate my whole life this way, Père.'

His father blew out a frustrated breath. 'Don't you understand, *mon fils*? We had both taken women who were not noble Frenchwomen as our wives. To some in society, I had married a common woman of a supposedly inferior race.'

'Like my uncle?' Years of listening to the Comte de Clareville's vitriolic opinion of his mixed blood sounded in Bastien's mind.

His father gave a careless shrug. 'Ignore that idiot.'

Bastien's lips thinned. It was his father's answer to everything. Just ignore it.

'Had I wanted your mother for my mistress,' his father was saying, with venom, 'and sired a dozen *bâtards* from her womb, no one would have objected. But I did the unthinkable and gave her the humble honour of my name.'

The Duc had loved his wife with a fierce intensity. So much so that even now, after two years, the pangs of Carmen's death still pierced him like a thousand needles.

His father slashed the air with his hand. 'Society couldn't understand why I would marry her—' Philippe's voice broke. 'But I did marry her, and likewise Louis married Atalyia, and it brought us closer together than ever before. We wanted a marriage between our children to be the ultimate seal on our friendship, but we thought the chance lost for ever. Now, through a miracle, it is possible once more—and you want to deny us our dearest wish?'

'Père, I will choose my own wife.'

A few seconds passed before his father gathered himself, and then he nodded towards Lilas, his composure intact once more. 'You already have one.'

Bastien's fist clenched and shook. 'You married a woman of your own choosing. Why can't I?'

'Monsieur le Duc?'

Lilas's tiny voice broke through the argument. The Duc glared at Bastien, but directed his words to Lilas. 'Mademoiselle Moreau?'

'May I speak with Monsieur le Marquis in private?'

The Duc's chest expanded. *'Bien sûr.* Perhaps when I come back I will hear good news and I will finally have the opportunity to share with Louis the joining of our houses.'

His father walked out the room, leaving them in silence.

Bastien blew out a breath as his gaze landed on Lilas. She looked the same, yet the knowledge of her lineage had already altered her demeanour. A new confidence sat upon her shoulders.

Rare was the day a servant discovered she was the daughter of a *comte*, with wealth and status attached to her name. And, pleased for her good fortune though he was, a part of him grew wary. Suddenly she wasn't below him in station any more.

Bastien sighed. 'Lilas, you must believe me—I did not know about this.'

Lilas's eyes were dark as an indigo sky. 'There is a silver lining, *monsieur*. I will have to depend on you for my refinement and introduction into society.'

The open vulnerability in her eyes frightened him

in a way he hadn't expected. She looked as if he were Solomon himself, able to solve the problem of their predicament.

But did she see it as a predicament?

He shook his head. 'Lilas, I am confident of your successful entry into society, but I won't be there to see it.'

Colour leached from her face. 'You won't?'

'No one dictates my future. Least of all my father.'

He pulled back a chair and sat down before her. This close, he found himself unable to look away. Lilas wasn't an uncomely girl. Far from it. Thoughts of those moments in the *potager*, touching her warm soft skin and being beset by a powerful urge to kiss her, flooded his mind.

Lilas possessed the kind of beauty that would only grow as she matured. In time, given her new circumstances, she would rival the most sought-after women in Paris with just a look from her uncommon violet eyes.

If his father hadn't been so interfering, maybe…

But no, Lilas was his father's choice, and not his own. It was just another way to control him and he would not bow down.

'We have shared many confidences over the years, haven't we?' he asked.

She nodded.

'The reason I asked my father for permission to make a Grand Tour, as the English do, is because what I want above all else is to experience life for myself. Along with my freedom. And I also aim to tempt a highborn lady of breeding to marry me.'

A fleeting look crossed Lilas's face. 'With what?'

Bastien laughed. 'With what? You wound me, Lilas. Surely you can tell? I'm surprised you even have to ask.'

Some women had no compunction about his mixed

blood ancestry. He was particular about whom he bedded, but he'd had his share of liaisons.

Lilas's eyes roved over him in a leisurely fashion. No stranger to feminine interest, he saw her eyes gleam as she studied him. He wasn't sure why this hint of womanly appreciation from her should make his throat dry. Nor why the fact that Lilas was no longer unattainable and in fact was a potential match for him should send the most damnable sensation of...*something* coursing through him.

'And I must do this before I am forced to marry you.'

'Forced?'

He dragged his fingers through his hair. 'Don't you see, Lilas? My father has controlled my life for far too long. Now he wants me to marry the woman he's chosen for me. Am I so inept that I need my father to lead me to the marriage bed?'

Her throat worked up and down. 'Is marrying me so terrible a fate, then, *monsieur*?'

'Marrying you isn't a part of my plan, Lilas.'

'What do you mean?'

'When I marry, I need a highborn woman with an impeccable reputation. Not one who used to be a servant girl.'

As soon as he spoke he wanted to pluck the blunt words from the air and stuff them back down his throat.

Lilas flinched as if he'd struck her.

'Servant girl?' she repeated slowly. 'You lied in the *potager*, then? I thought you...' Her voice trailed away.

A muscle leapt in his jaw. 'No secrets between us, remember?'

Moisture filled her eyes. 'I thought you cared about me.'

Something twisted in his chest.

A hidden truth pierced through the barrier he was trying so hard to maintain.

Bastien inhaled a deep breath. He did care about Lilas. In what way, he wasn't sure—he'd never delved deeply enough into his own feelings. If he had, he'd have had to acknowledge something he wasn't ready for.

'I do care, Lilas,' he replied measuredly.

Even though she hadn't moved, it was as if an invisible chasm separated them. She blinked, and the sheen in her eyes disappeared. 'There is nothing to explain, Monsieur le Marquis. I am still not good enough for you.'

'Lilas, please try to understand.'

The chasm grew wider. He could practically see the abyss appearing between them.

'I do. All too well.'

'Lilas—'

She held up her hand, her face blank. 'I trusted you, Bastien.'

His mouth fell open. She'd never called him by his name. The familiarity stroked a tingling sensation down his back.

She stood. 'If there is some way to break the contract, rest assured I will find it.' She turned and headed for the door.

He had to stop her and tell her...

What?

Lilas gripped the door handle and stood there for a long moment. Then she looked over her shoulder at him.

The pain in her violet eyes scorched his brain like fire.

'I never want to see you again. *Adieu*, Monsieur le Marquis.'

Bastien knew he'd hurt her beyond all repair.

He bowed in farewell, his stomach churning. 'As you wish, *mademoiselle. Adieu.*'

Chapter Two

Faubourg Saint-Germain Quartier, Paris, May 1775

The rain-soaked cobblestones of Rue de St Dominique gleamed under the dancing firelight of the street lanterns. Low stone walls guarded the neighbouring *hôtels particuliers*, the lavish townhomes of the nobility. Their towering edifices pierced the heavens as if to claim co-dominion.

The Duc de Languedoc's horse-drawn carriage clopped down its hallowed path, its plush interior cushioning Bastien's upright figure. He brooded on the tall houses. Was it possible to travel up to the stars and escape everything?

Estienne St Clare, Vicomte de Vivarais, shifted in the seat across from him. 'Are you certain you know what you are doing?'

Bastien spared his cousin a glance before returning his attention to the scenery outside. 'I'm quite certain, Estienne. Père is dead.' His stomach knotted and he could barely breathe. It was a moment before he croaked out, 'There is no need to tie myself to a marital contract neither Lilas nor I wanted.'

'It's been four years since you last saw her. We can always move forward with the formalities instead. I can approach the Comte de la Baux, as protocol dictates. Tell him you wish to make your betrothal to Mademoiselle Moreau official.'

'That won't be necessary.'

'Our Grand Tour lasted four years, Bastien. During that time Mademoiselle Moreau could have provided you with written confirmation that she wished to break the engagement as per the contract.'

'C'est vrai,' Bastien acknowledged with a nod.

It was a point of reason Bastien had difficulty explaining away. After their last meeting, he'd expected Lilas to immediately cut up the blasted contract and burn it in the fireplace. Yet, when his father had died, three months ago, the family solicitor had related that the contract between their families was still valid unless it was rescinded by Lilas.

'Doesn't that mean she wants you to marry her?'

'What Mademoiselle Moreau wants and what she will receive are two different things.' The corners of his lips curved downward. 'I will not be…' His voice trailed off.

What was the proper term? Coerced? Forced? Lured?

He cleared his throat. 'I will not be…*forced* into matrimony.'

'But your father—'

A muscle leapt in his jaw. 'You can be silent now, Estienne.'

At the note of command Estienne leaned back in his seat, while Bastien inhaled a sharp breath and eased it out slowly. Most days he appreciated his cousin's support, even though he was the son of the uncle he despised. The Comte de Clareville had tried to drive them apart, but Estienne had refused to fall for his father's trickery. They were as close as brothers.

The sudden halt in the carriage's movement drew Bastien from his introspection. The raucous din of activity outside beat against his ears.

Estienne glanced out of the window. 'All Paris must be here. We're two hours beyond the time on the invitation and we're still unable to get close.'

Alarm wormed along Bastien's spine as he peered out. Against the backdrop of the evening sky, Hôtel de la Baux stood silhouetted like a graceful dowager receiving her guests.

Carriages lined the street like a desert caravan. Elegantly dressed horses pawed at the ground. Livery men darted up and down, relaying news to the occupants of the loitering conveyances.

'Surely, a *vieille fille*'s coming out doesn't merit an attendance such as this?'

Estienne groaned. 'Bastien, I told you earlier…' His words died away. '*Sacré bleu!* You're calling your fiancée a spinster? Bastien, she's your betrothed!'

'Only for a short duration.'

Estienne lifted his shoulders. 'Till then…'

'Don't,' Bastien warned.

A chuckle escaped his cousin's mouth. 'Haven't you been paying attention to the news about your fiancée?'

'I have not,' he stated bluntly.

He'd done everything in his power to avoid hearing anything about Lilas over the past four years. Tried his best not to think about her at all. The Grand Tour had taken him to Austria, Italy, England and Germany, and his travels had helped keep Lilas out of his thoughts.

'That is to your disadvantage, cousin. This is not a

coming out ball. Mademoiselle Moreau has taken Paris by storm as an artist of singular talent.'

A jolt went through him. 'An artist?'

Estienne grinned. 'A very popular one.'

It should not come as a surprise to learn that Lilas had become a popular artist. After all, he knew how talented she was.

He remembered once some years ago she had told him that he was her only patron.

Things had certainly changed in that regard.

Their carriage inched along at a snail's pace. Estienne made a commentary Bastien scarcely heard. Tonight he'd endure the vapid, glittering company of the Parisian elite and then he'd return home.

Half an hour later they arrived at the entrance. Attentive servants drew open the carriage doors. Bastien hopped out and studied the well-dressed attendees of a society he'd once thought meant everything.

Women adorned in flowing gowns of intricate patterns tittered behind silk fans. Powdered hair, tall and topped with ornate headdresses of sweeping plumes and lace, added a certain regality to their profiles. The men matched them in magnificence, in jewelled hues of coat, waistcoat and breeches. Most had foregone the wearing of a wig and had pulled their dusted hair into a neat *queue*.

Following the throng of people waiting to greet Mademoiselle Lilas Moreau, Bastien stood with Estienne and fiddled with the cuff of his coat.

What kind of reception would he receive? When the invitation had arrived he'd toyed with not responding. Involving himself in Lilas's life was not in the plan he had for his future.

He ground his teeth together. Even in death, it seemed

his father would not let him live his own life. But tonight he would get Lilas's notice to dissolve the marriage contract once and for all.

Richly attired servants opened the doors and he stepped into a crowded, well-lit entrance hall lined with gold trimming.

'Well, every unhappiness to you, Bastien,' Estienne quipped. 'Your broken engagement awaits.'

Bastien smoothed the material of his coat. '*Oui*, Estienne. My broken engagement awaits.'

The teardrop crystal chandelier cast a magical glow over the great room.

'Shall we call this a resounding success, Mademoiselle Moreau?' a low, smooth voice said from behind her.

Face flushed, Lilas turned to meet her stepbrother's pleased brown gaze.

'I think so, Baron des Deux Collines.' She fanned herself, looking around the room. Golden light pervaded the room like the glory of an angel. 'I think so.'

'I told you not to call me that,' Pierre said with a snort, even though his eyes gleamed with amusement. 'It is *ma mère* who is obsessed with titles, not I. Monsieur Damiani will do.'

Grinning at his insistence on being referred to by his father's name, Lilas shook her head and glanced around, basking in the success of the evening.

People hovered around easels upon which paintings depicted landscapes, still-life, biblical scenes and portraits of several prominent members of the aristocracy.

Four years' toil had resulted in this. Not only that, but the newly crowned Queen had given Lilas her patronage. She'd not yet received a summons from Court, but it was only a matter of when—not if!

'I'm surprised so many have attended.' Her stepbrother grinned. 'I wonder if they're here to see the paintings, or you.'

'Do behave yourself, Pierre.' She playfully smacked his arm with her fan.

Pierre pushed his spectacles further up his nose. 'I am!'

One moment Lilas was sharing in her stepbrother's mirth. The next, foreboding traced icy fingers down her spine and her scalp prickled. What was wrong? Her eyes glanced around the room, trying to discover the source of her unease.

'Mademoiselle Moreau?'

Lilas whirled around at the querulous tones behind her. '*Monsieur* and *madame*—how pleasant it is to see you.' She gave the guests a brief nod of acknowledgement, still searching for the source of her discomfort.

'I hope you haven't offended them,' Pierre said as the couple, stiff with affront, stalked away.

'You can't offend marble, can you?'

As she continued to greet other attendees, her unease increased. Trying not to draw attention, she kept on sweeping her gaze around the room. Something was happening. Or had happened. Or was going to happen.

But what?

The hairs along the back of her neck stood erect. A sudden clamminess of her hands made the material of her gloves stick in the creases of her palms.

'Oh, dear…' Pierre muttered unhappily, angling himself towards her.

'What is it?' Lilas asked. Pierre's distress was like hers. Thankfully, that uneasy feeling had dissipated. Perhaps she was imagining things.

'Mère is trying to lure me across the room to that rather plain woman she's talking to.'

Though Pierre was her stepbrother, Lilas felt as close to him as a sibling in truth. Since she'd joined the family as the legitimate daughter of the Comte de la Baux he'd accepted her, often escorting her in society.

Lilas hid her laugh behind a fan. 'Your mother is only trying to find a match for you.'

A mixture of mirth and pain appeared in his eyes. 'Her prospects lately have been getting less and less attractive.'

'But loftier in title,' she reminded him, unable to keep the teasing out of her voice. Her stepmother's penchant for trying to match her son with women of high status was an ongoing source of amusement to them both. 'Surely that is some compensation?'

She followed his anguished gaze and winced in sympathy, seeing her stepmother talking with a woman who, as anyone's idea of beauty, even the kindest, failed miserably. Yet the sparkling jewels and ornate gown spoke of her wealth.

'I can barely look at her, much less feel any desire to kiss her.'

At that moment, the Comtesse de la Baux gestured to Pierre.

'She's summoning me.' Pierre's eyes widened behind the spectacles.

'You do not have to go to her if you don't wish to.'

Pierre shook his head, laughing softly. 'It is far too late to develop a will against my mother now, Lilas.'

Though he spoke in a self-deprecating way, Lilas knew Pierre and the Comtesse de la Baux shared a strong bond.

Lilas gave him a gentle push. 'If you suffer now, you won't have to later.'

He grinned. 'Only you could be so practical.'

He thrust his shoulders back, took in a deep breath and marched forward with an almost military bearing. As he walked away, Lilas felt that feeling of unease return. She frowned and glanced around the room again. She couldn't see anything. But some primal part of her was reacting in an odd way, warning her of…

Danger? No, not danger in a lethal sense.

Calamity? Surely not that either, as this was the best evening of her life.

Then what?

Shaking her head at her own foolishness, she pasted on a smile and greeted the next couple who came up to her.

A few minutes later, as she directed another guest towards a painting, she heard a voice say from behind her, '*Bonsoir*, Mademoiselle Moreau.'

Lilas's body jerked violently. Her gloved fingers fumbled, almost dropping the ivory-handled fan. Within the cavity of her chest, her heart threatened to escape.

That sixth sense had been warning her of this!

The past had come back to haunt her in the form of Bastien St Clare.

On the heels of that came another thought. What was he doing here?

'*Ça fait longtemps.*'

Yes, it had been a long time. Yet that unforgettable voice, with its dark, mesmeric tone, still affected her senses.

How could he be here? Why?

Setting everything else aside, Lilas thrust her shoulders back and tamped down with an iron will the flittering sensations within her. She pirouetted in a graceful movement and gave a curtsy of respect, her purple gown billowing out.

'*Bonsoir*, Monsieur le Marquis,' she greeted him.

Lilas hesitated to look up into Bastien's face. His presence made the air crackle. He exuded waves of restrained energy like the calm before a storm.

On an instinctual level she knew that with one glance into his lion eyes she'd never be the same again. Easier to begin at the bottom. To take in the shiny square-tipped black shoes that shod his large feet. Study how the white knee-length stockings strained over his bulging calves. The way the tight, dark velvet breeches hugged his muscular thighs with an almost lover-like fit.

An odd breathlessness took hold of her. The striped waistcoat accentuated his narrow, trim waist. The pleated edges of his sleeves peeked over the wrists of the long black evening coat. She rested her gaze on his hands, remembering how they'd touched her skin long ago.

Would they feel the same if he stroked her now?

Lilas snorted. Why was she thinking that way? It wasn't as if he would ever have another opportunity to touch her. Yet still she saw how the frills at his collar bloomed, drawing attention to the cedar-like column of his throat.

When she gazed into his face she could barely believe it was the same person she had once known.

Four years ago he'd been handsome. Now he was devastating.

His skin had darkened from a warm chestnut to a rich, deep carob. Wavy black hair shone like onyx under the firelight, smoothed down and tied at his nape into a *queue*.

Her eyes collided with his golden-hued ones under their winged black brows, and the primal force exuding from him stole her breath away. The room and all the other occupants disappeared in a muted haze. Every raw nerve of awareness screamed as his lion eyes ensnared her.

Those were the eyes of a man she had once believed was her friend.

Now they were the eyes of a familiar stranger.

'It's a pleasure to see you again,' she lied in a cool voice.

She saw Bastien's lips twist. He clearly knew she was lying, but he was too much of a gentleman, or too wicked, to say so.

'It's the Duc de Languedoc now, Mademoiselle Moreau.'

His father had died? Her face burned with embarrassment at her ignorance, and she let her lashes shield her eyes. 'Monsieur le Duc, my condolences on the passing of your father. I had not heard.'

She'd done everything she could to avoid news of the St Clare family.

Bastien cleared his throat. 'Enough of sorrow. May I offer my congratulations? I find it gratifying to see that you have succeeded in your artistic pursuits.'

'*Merci,*' Lilas replied in a dutiful tone.

He became brisk. 'Mademoiselle Moreau, may I have a moment of your time in private? There is a matter I wish to discuss with you.'

Her heart fluttered like the desperate beating wings of a bird attempting to escape its cage. She knew what that matter was—the marital contract between their families.

Fanning herself, she said languidly, 'As you can see, *monsieur*, I am occupied and unable to leave my guests. Should you wish to call upon me within the next few days, I shall be more than happy to receive you.'

His golden eyes glowed. 'That is not acceptable. This matter is of an urgent nature.'

The deep voice had a slight bite to it. The sound of it transported her straight back to childhood. She could hear that same voice raging at the servants who had attempted to belittle her.

Even then he'd had little tolerance for anyone who went against his will or desire. He had known who and what he was. As a young girl, she'd been thankful that the force of his anger hadn't ever been directed at her.

The nervousness that had plagued her left. She drew herself up to her full height. Once upon a time Bastien had been her master's son. She refused to deny it. But, though she still wasn't quite his equal, as a *comte*'s daughter she did not have to obey him as she once had.

'That's unfortunate, Monsieur le Duc, as I cannot accommodate your request.'

His eyes narrowed. 'Are you putting on airs with me, Lilas?'

Though apprehension spiked down her back, this battle of wills invigorated her, making her feel reckless. What could Bastien do about it? In the past she would have never openly defied him. But things had changed.

Lilas thrust out her chin. '*Mademoiselle* Moreau to you.'

A vein throbbed along his temple.

Feeling triumphant, she pasted a bright smile onto her lips as she saw more guests coming to greet her. '*Madame!* I'm so glad you—'

Hard fingers grasped her hand. Lightning darted through her, reminding her of that one other time when he had touched her.

She gasped at this breach of polite conduct, her face

flaming as Bastien raised her gloved hand to his mouth. The heat of his lips through the thin material burned.

She should make a fuss, or object to his insolent behaviour, but she couldn't open her mouth.

His lion eyes gleamed as he murmured, 'Until later, Mademoiselle Moreau.'

She heard his true message as if he had spoken it aloud. There was no escape.

Her heart hammered in her chest as Bastien finally let go. Bowing, he walked away, leaving the imprint of his lips on her like a brand.

Bastien's jaw clenched as he walked away from Lilas Moreau. He'd received small satisfaction for going against protocol, but he'd wanted to get past her reserve.

Was it because she had defied him? Or because he'd been floored by the change in her?

Four years ago she'd stood before him as a servant, on the brink of womanhood, her body slender with youthful curves and budding maturity.

The woman who defied him now had completely swept away that youthful persona. Like a caterpillar metamorphosing into a brilliant butterfly.

The pressure along his jawline eased. His mind's eye travelled over her body once more. Her servant's uniform had hidden much of it, in more ways than one. Now the fashions of the day allowed an observer to view her in the full bloom of beauty.

She'd forgone the use of the lead-based make-up most of the women in society wore. The Armagnac hue of her skin shone through, clear and smooth. Her unpainted full lips added a naturalness that was unusual, but refreshing in a sea of white, garishly painted faces.

From the top of her purple-beribboned powdered *pouf*

with its characteristic ringlet curls to the slender length of her neck, she bore a certain regality not even the new Queen possessed. The ruffled neckline and tapered style of her gown revealed the wide expanse of her voluptuous décolletage and accentuated her tiny waist.

Lilas Moreau's poise and grace rivalled any of the well-bred attendees in the room. Even more striking was the level of confidence she bore. Her defiance might be unwanted as she attempted to stop him from achieving his goal, but it drew him to her as well. Seeing Lilas now was to recognise the woman she was always meant to be.

Hadn't she said years ago that she wasn't meant to be a servant? The veil of servitude she'd worn for ten years of her life had never sat upon her comfortably. The cloak of a lady lay upon her shoulders much better. And, despite his irritation, he'd liked seeing her that way.

Candlelight had reflected in her eyes, giving them a luminous sheen as anger made them look almost purple. She still reminded him of the girl who used to bring out all those odd protective instincts in him. But tonight she'd brought out other instincts. A man's curiosity over a woman who'd captured his interest. Lilas was both familiar and strange—a combination that was invigorating and yet dangerous.

Bastien remembered her reaction to his kiss. A slight tremble had overtaken her when he'd pressed his mouth to that silken-clad hand.

A hint of lavender had wafted to his nostrils, mixed with a womanly fragrance of her own. Despite himself, he'd inhaled that sweet scent deep into his nostrils, as if to lock it away.

He'd clasped her fingers as one would cradle a young, fragile bird. When their eyes had met, her violet gaze had darkened to a deep lilac. Only then had he relinquished his hold on her.

He frowned as another thought came. Why was she being so evasive about that ridiculous marital contract?

Someone bumped into him, and he glanced up to see he'd happened upon a sizeable gathering in front of a large mural in three panels.

Entitled *Almost Eve*, it detailed a scene of a sun-drenched Adam embracing Eve in a garden of Eden flourishing with symbols of sensuality—bold blossoming flowers, plump ripe fruit and long grasping vines.

A little dog, representing fidelity, barked at a shadowy nude woman who faced away from the couple. The shadowed woman drew the eye more than the entwined Adam and Eve. Her face was bathed in darkness from the thick crop of trees overhanging her, except for the downward curve of a rather seductive mouth, which carried jealousy along its line. Supple flesh and the curve of a generous backside with pearlescent skin completed the look. The shadowy woman's hands caressed a bright apple with long fingers, while the silhouette of a blue-eyed snake could be seen above her.

Bastien stared at the mural, caught up in the story it depicted. Lilas's technique gave the impression that one might enter that garden and be privy to it. He found himself in awe of her skill. She'd always been talented, but truly she had improved almost beyond recognition.

Bastien narrowed his eyes on the painting again. There was a hidden message in it, he was certain. He stepped back, seeing other elements lending deeper meaning to the picture. Things only someone well acquainted with the painter would know.

He'd once believed that no one knew Lilas better than he did.

Was that still true?

'What do you think, Monsieur le Duc?'

The light from the crystal chandelier fell on Lilas in a cascade of gold, giving her visage an ethereal façade. Could any man be master over such exquisite beauty? Unlikely. Rather, a man would be enslaved by it.

She drew him away from the crowd, and he followed her to a somewhat secluded corner.

'*Magnifique*, Mademoiselle Moreau,' Bastien said truthfully. 'Your talent has come to fruition.'

'Hardly,' she said with a wry smile. 'I see many imperfections. But perhaps those are what keep us from believing we have nothing more to learn.'

He nodded. 'Perhaps.' He took a step closer. 'I thought you were busy with your guests?' he said in a pointed tone.

Her violet eyes flicked in his direction. 'What do you think of the story of Adam's rejection of Lilith, his first wife?'

'That painting is not about Lilith.'

A shrewd look dominated her face. 'Oh?'

He shook his head.

'Please, tell me what you think it is about, *monsieur*?'

Bastien took a step towards her. 'On one condition.'

'*Oui?*'

'If I am accurate in my interpretation, we will cease this tiresome game and you will meet with me in private to discuss the contract.'

She stilled in an unnatural way. 'And if you are not accurate?'

'Then I will meet with you about this matter at a time of your own choosing.'

Bastien waited for her response. It was as if they were cocooned in their own world, and the rest of society had disappeared. A fanciful thought he wished were true. This new Lilas intrigued him.

'Very well.' She gave a single nod. 'Tell me what your interpretation is.'

'It's about you.'

A visible start shook her body, and he knew he'd guessed accurately. Her tongue darted out and licked at the seam of her mouth. He followed the action with his eyes, transfixed by it.

'What made you come to that conclusion?'

'There are no secrets between us, Mademoiselle Moreau.'

Her chin dipped down as she averted her gaze.

'Lilith embodies all the rejection you have ever felt.'

Her violet gaze drifted towards him again.

'Her nakedness represents your birth and lack of family when you were sent to the orphanage. The darkness overshadowing her face and the light on her body depicts your mixed blood. Those fingers, caressing the apple, tell of your desire to take knowledge away from Eve and keep it for yourself. She isn't good enough for the apple, but you are.'

Her face had taken on a stony façade while her violet eyes glittered like amethysts.

'Do I need to go on?' He couldn't keep the mocking tone out of his voice.

'Bastien!'

Pleased that she'd forgotten herself enough to call him by name, and not his title, he said, 'There is one strange oddity I can't account for, which is the serpent's blue eyes shining in the darkness. But it isn't as important as the rest.'

Lilas's nostrils flared like a horse's as she glared at him.

'Should I draw forth the true meaning behind the painting?' he asked. 'Adam isn't rejecting his first wife.'

'Stop it,' she said tightly.

Mercilessly, he went on. 'He is rejecting his daughter. Unlike Eve, born from Adam's rib, Lilith was born from the same clay as her father.'

The silence between them pulsed more vibrantly than the chatter of the attendees. Tension of a different sort wavered between them.

Bastien dipped his chin. *'Ai-je raison?'*

Was he right? Of course he was! Why had she even challenged him?

The need to escape prodded her. 'My guests—'

'Mademoiselle Moreau, our *tête-à-tête* will not take long. But it will happen.'

Those determined golden eyes refused to take no for an answer. Why had she thought she could escape him?

'Mademoiselle, won't you accompany me to where we can talk in private?'

'Are you mad? Without a chaperone?'

'I assure you, your chastity isn't at risk.'

'Only my reputation. Women of my rank do not go anywhere alone with a man. You've already caused enough of a stir by kissing my hand in front of all these people.'

A devilish light appeared in his golden eyes. 'Just a stir among these attendees? Or in you?'

Heat seared her cheeks at his words. How could he say such a scandalous thing? And how dared he bear that knowing expression, as if he were aware of the fact she could still feel the imprint of his lips through the thin material of her glove?

'You once told me, *mademoiselle*, that your art made

you more than a servant and a woman. Be that way with me now. We have much to say to each other. Remember, there are no secrets between us.'

Did she want to? She wanted to get away from the memory of his desertion that still hovered at the front of her mind. But when was the last time her blood had warmed with excitement like this when she hadn't been painting?

'Very well.' She motioned with her chin to a secluded exit. 'We'll go out that way.'

He held out his arm in a gallant gesture. *'Mademoiselle?'*

She glanced at his arm. How strangely Bastien was acting. He knew as well as she did that modesty, at least outwardly, mattered to these members of good French society. They weren't like the English, with their more frequent physical contact between the sexes. Yet, he refused to put his arm down, almost challenging her to take it.

And she… She allowed herself to defy convention.

She placed her hand over his arm. The hard muscle tensed under her fingers. She swallowed, wondering why she should have such a strange, breathless reaction to that sign of strength and masculinity.

They walked, their gait leisurely. Would her act of defiance affect the guests' view of her? She waited with bated breath, but besides one or two curious looks no one appeared too offended at this uncharacteristic display of intimacy.

Perhaps it had to do with their being a *métis*—a mixed noble couple. Neither of them looked less than stately. Hours of rigorous comportment lessons had lent that assurance to her. Her eyes slid to Bastien's tall form. Born into his station, how well he wore his nobility, with the refined bearing expected of the elite.

Had he found the highborn lady he wanted to marry? Some blonde, innocent beauty just out of the school-room? A raven-haired impoverished yet highborn lady? Whoever it was, she wouldn't be a former *fille des cendres* like her.

'Where are you going, Lilas?'

She whirled around to see Pierre coming towards them. His warm brown gaze twinkled. She squirmed inside as his head tilted down with a pointed look at her hand resting on Bastien's arm.

'Monsieur le Duc, my stepbrother, Monsieur le Baron des Deux Collines.'

Pierre cut his eyes at her but while the men exchanged greetings, she used a few precious seconds to pull herself together.

'Where are you and Monsieur le Duc going, Lilas?' Pierre lowered his voice. 'Alone?'

Once again, her cheeks warmed at the impropriety of the moment, but Bastien's unconcerned expression gave her the impetus to lift her chin and say, 'Away from here. Won't you join us?'

Part of her experienced relief at Pierre's presence. For the past four years she'd obeyed her stepmother's every admonition of proper behaviour. Been so careful in her new position as her father's daughter.

And now, within less than an hour of meeting him, Bastien's presence had caused that fire within her to flame.

They exited the exhibition room without any further interruptions, and made their way to the small, secluded dining room she'd prepared for select guests she wished to court.

Her gaze skimmed over the table, already made up

and decorated with a bright white cloth and immaculately polished silverware.

It wasn't that long ago when she would have been one of the numerous maids who had spent hours preparing this very room. How pleasant to be standing here with Bastien, receiving him as a guest.

'Monsieur le Baron, I am grateful for your escort, but I request to speak to Mademoiselle Moreau in private.'

Though Bastien spoke the words as a request, it was a dismissal.

'In private? Without a chaperone?' Pierre's eyes opened wide with mock horror. 'Perhaps you have been abroad too long, Monsieur le Duc. How can I trust that an inch of your coat won't edge onto Lilas's gown?'

'Really, Pierre…' Lilas fanned herself. Being alone with Bastien would test all her skill to remain as unaffected as possible. She didn't need her stepbrother's teasing about social etiquette, of which he was particularly scornful.

'I trust you to behave yourselves.'

Pierre left and Bastien closed the door, leaning against it in a languid manner. Beneath the casual pose his golden-eyed gleam remained ever reminiscent of a lion…lazy but alert.

Anger welled inside her as he stood there, so triumphant over his interpretation of her painting. Not even Pierre had guessed at anything more than what the work seemed to portray. Yet Bastien had immediately seen the hidden messages.

How could he be so insightful in one area and yet so obtuse in another? Didn't he know how badly he had scarred her when he'd left? How could he not grasp that being in the same room with him was a struggle for her?

The past and the present warred inside her like two soldiers locked in battle, fighting for dominance.

Snapping her fan open, she fixed her gaze on him. 'You are almost correct in your interpretation of the painting.'

He stepped forward, looming like some dark, golden-eyed warrior angel. 'Pray, what did I get wrong?'

'Unlike Lilith, who knew her father, I never knew mine.'

His forehead creased. 'What do you mean? You met him four years ago.'

'I did not. He died before I ever had the chance to do so.'

He stiffened at her words. She felt the painful memories rise in her mind as she tugged on the edge of her gloves.

'After you'd left your father's study we waited for a fortnight for the Comte's arrival. And then several more days. Then, a day before the Duc de Languedoc was to send a messenger, one came to us with the news that my father had perished in a carriage accident. On his way to meet us.'

'Mon Dieu!' Bastien exclaimed in an appalled undertone. 'I did not know this.'

'How could you?' It was impossible to keep the bitterness out of her voice. 'You'd gone on your Grand Tour, abandoning me without a backward glance.'

The whole sordid story came pouring out then. The Comte's title and entailed estate being held in trust under the care of her late father's solicitor until she married. A generous allowance granting her more wealth than she could have ever dreamed of. Her removal from Château de Velay to Hôtel de la Baux in Paris.

'It wasn't only the loss of my father I had to cope with.

He was also my last hope of knowing my mother. The last opportunity for me to discover how I ended up in an orphanage when I know both my parents wanted me and loved me. You knew your family, and you still left them. I didn't get a chance to know mine at all.'

Bastien stared down at her. Along the side of his jaw a muscle ticked. For a moment she almost felt sorry for him. His father had passed away probably fairly recently, as she'd not heard of it. Now he'd learned his father's dear friend had passed away long ago.

Then she remembered how selfishly he'd acted when he'd left, and she swallowed her sympathy. 'I felt like an orphan all over again.'

Her words punched his gut. Bastien could hardly imagine the anguish she must have gone through. To have a father so briefly, after eighteen years alone, only to have him snatched away before even meeting him.

He knew the feeling of loss all too well.

A bulge swelled in his throat. 'Mademoiselle Moreau, *je suis désolé.*'

'Are you sorry?' Her eyes narrowed. 'How can you be? Not once in your time away did you even think to write to me, to enquire about my well-being.'

'I didn't write to anyone.'

A suspiciously moist gleam dampened the fire in her eyes. 'Was that fair? You weren't supposed to just abandon me! Your father hardly had time to comfort me before my father's widow, the Comtesse de la Baux, whisked me away to a whole new life I barely comprehended. Why weren't you there? Didn't you know how much I needed you? Trusted you? And you were gone. I was alone, without a father or a friend.'

The hurt choking her voice compounded the guilt in his chest. How could he have been so badly mistaken?

But of course she couldn't understand the necessity of his leaving. When she'd lived as a servant in his home she'd had no comprehension of the prison that had been his life. He'd tried to explain it to her once, but she wouldn't hear it.

So certain of his privilege as the son of a *duc* had she been, so steadfast in her belief that a gilded cage wasn't a real cage, she hadn't been able to understand the driving force guiding him down a path created by his father, not himself.

She wouldn't understand it now either. Nothing he could say would change that.

Ignoring the heaviness in his stomach, he stepped away from her. 'I can't begin to understand your pain, *mademoiselle*. Nor to apologise for the harm you believe I've caused you. The marriage contract between our families—what do you wish to do about it?'

She blinked. 'Have you found your highborn lady?'

The question was unexpected, but he shook his head. 'I couldn't in good conscience offer myself to any woman when we had yet to settle this matter between us.'

'I see.'

'And you, Mademoiselle Moreau? Have you found a man to lay claim to you?'

She glanced away. 'Does it matter?'

'I want to know,' he pressed.

'Why?'

'There are no secrets between us.'

'So you say. Once that was true, Monsieur le Duc,' she clipped out, using his full title as a barrier—a wall, even. 'But it is no longer the case. You forfeited the privilege of knowing my innermost thoughts when you left.'

He flinched. 'Did I?'

'I release you from the contract. Only ourselves and those few confidantes of our families know of the agreement so there should be no scandal.'

Looking at her, he couldn't believe this was the end. But he had to accept it and it was what he'd wanted. Wasn't it?

'Very well.'

'I must attend to my guests. Please excuse me.'

He opened the door and let her pass. His eyes followed Lilas Moreau as she kept her head lifted and her shoulders back, heading as far and as fast as she could away from her former betrothed.

Chapter Three

'Dead?'

'That is correct,' Bastien said grimly. 'Four years ago.'

Estienne's blue eyes widened in the darkness of the carriage. 'I can't believe it. My father never spoke of it to me.'

'The Comte de Clareville would find great pleasure in my father's plans being curtailed by death.'

His cousin moved uncomfortably, but he didn't defend his sire. After an awkward hush, Estienne coughed. 'Are you going to go through with the marriage? Seeing as how your father and the Comte de la Baux would have wished for it?'

'I am not.'

Another pause. 'Shall I wish you joy on your broken engagement, then?'

Bastien tugged his gaze away from the scenery. The sway of the carriage as it left Hôtel de la Baux was lulling him as he supposed a woman lulled a child. A recalcitrant child. One who had no desire to feel the comfort of her arms as she rocked him.

'Bastien?'

He started, aware that he'd been staring at his cousin

without seeing him for a few moments. '*Oui*, congratulate me.'

Estienne eyed him. 'You don't look at all happy about it.'

Bastien couldn't fault his cousin for his confusion. After all he had learned, how could he feel anything remotely related to joy even though he'd achieved what he'd said he wanted?

'Shall we turn our minds to other things, Estienne?'

His cousin leapt at that invitation, prattling on about a woman he'd met at the exhibition while Bastien brooded in the darkness.

'You forfeited the privilege of knowing my innermost thoughts when you left.'

That had rankled more than he expected it to. It *had* been a privilege to be Lilas's confidante. Whenever his uncle had made his cruel remarks about Bastien's mixed blood, and others had followed the man in the same vein, while his father did nothing to defend him, Lilas's company had been a soothing balm.

She alone had treated him as a friend, and he'd revelled in that. As she'd matured, perhaps sensing the social divide between them, her confidences had grown less, but they had never fully ceased.

When she'd stood there in that tiny room tonight, he'd had a difficult time reading her. Once, she'd been like a well-read book, her facial expressions open and honest. Now she bore the placid mask of a lady, and he'd been unable to penetrate too deeply beneath her calm exterior.

He didn't like that at all.

After their conversation, his eyes had followed her for the rest of the night. He'd found her in the distinctive purple gown, surrounded by men and women alike.

Her bewigged head had risen higher than anyone else's, as if to proclaim her as royalty.

How well shc'd blended in. She handled the intricacies of society perfectly. If they had married, she wouldn't have been an embarrassment to him. Not that he would have ever considered her an embarrassment.

But Lilas wasn't his ideal wife. This vague figure in his head, whoever she was, was the woman he needed to seek.

His father's recent death had passed the ducal title on to Bastien's shoulders, elevating his position among the elite, and yet he was as much on the outside as he ever had been.

Four years ago he'd sought freedom from his father's control and had begun to seriously think about marrying the ideal woman in order to further his own plans. Now, as the new Duc de Languedoc, he could finally live a life free from his father's shadow. Eventually he'd find the proper wife to help strengthen that position, and he'd be fully accepted into society instead of mocked for his heritage.

The carriage pulled up in front of his town house. He exited the carriage and stood still for a moment. The silhouette of Hôtel de Languedoc against the backdrop of the night sky towered above the world like a cold, empty shell.

He swallowed hard. He was an orphan now.

Once they entered the house, Estienne hurried to his bed, pleading an early-morning appointment. Relieved, Bastien sent his manservant away, wanting his own company. With an unsteady breath, he made his way down the corridor, going towards his father's study.

No, *his* study now.

A fist clenched against the organ centred in his chest

as he entered the candlelit room. Seeing the crimson furniture and ornate trappings, Bastien let his gaze land on the high red velvet chair near the far window. He recalled the last time he'd seen his father sitting there.

He heard anew the wistful tone in his father's voice. 'I was married to a goddess for nearly twenty years. Why interest myself with mere mortals after that?'

Because one of those mere mortals was your son.

On a cold January morning, after a long wasting-away, his mother had been buried in the family catacombs, leaving a devastated husband and child to mourn her. If there was a better mother, she had yet to be found.

She'd anchored his soul.

Much in the same way Lilas had this evening.

Bastien drew himself up short. Could that be right?

He couldn't ignore the feeling of homecoming that had settled on him when they'd been reunited. Despite the separation of four years, the moment he'd seen her again he had indeed felt anchored.

He rubbed at his forehead, the thought chafing at his brain. Bastien had no wish to have such a feeling as that. It would be like discovering one was in love with a woman.

Tugging the ribbon from around his hair, he dragged his fingers through the long strands. Why should any man love a woman when it would hurt so dreadfully if something happened to her?

'Bastien, you're finally home.'

He turned his head to see a womanly figure gliding towards him. A smile lifted the corner of his mouth as he stared down into a beautiful face. 'Cousin, what are you doing up? I thought you were leaving tomorrow?'

Guerline DuValier laughed—a husky sound that pleased the male ear. 'Are you in such a hurry for me to leave? What would my aunt have thought of you, rushing me away?'

That musical lilt of her accent eased the tension from his shoulders. His mother's niece always made a dark day bright again. It could be because she possessed similar traits to his mother. And in the right light she physically resembled Carmen quite a lot. They both had mahogany skin, and shapely figures—albeit that Guerline, only a year past her eighteenth birthday, still carried the effervescence of youth.

He chuckled. 'She'd probably have scolded me. You may stay as long as you wish. But I would have thought you'd want to rest for your trip home.'

Guerline's bright copper eyes dulled. 'I am well-rested. There is nothing to do here since your father passed away.'

It was Guerline who had finally breached the wall of silence between Bastien and his father. She'd obtained knowledge of her cousin's last known place of residence and sent Bastien a message, telling him that his father was seriously ill and had taken a turn for the worse.

You must come. I do not know how long he will last.

Until then, he'd no idea that his father had even asked Guerline to come and nurse him. She'd been doing so for the past year. Looking at her, seeing how similar in appearance she was to his mother, he had suspected his father had wanted to have a tangible memory of his dead wife in some capacity.

When he'd received her missive, Bastien had commandeered the first ship he'd been able to secure and made passage to France, sending all sorts of petitions to heaven for him to get to his father's side before it was too late.

Yet when he'd arrived back in Paris and hurried to his father's house, it was to discover he had died only the day before.

Before he could put his plans into action and prove to his father that—

'It is difficult to believe he is gone,' Guerline said tearfully. 'Even though it has been three months.'

'I understand.'

'But he is here.' She pointed to her heart, and then her head. 'And here.' Then she pressed her forefinger to his chest. 'And here.'

'You made his last year more bearable, Guerline.'

She frowned. 'Did I?' she asked in a dubious tone. A faraway look came into her eyes. 'I feel as if he was the one to make the last few years of *my* life bearable.'

'Because he educated you?'

'He saved my life, Bastien. In more ways than one. Nursing him was my pleasure, my honour and my debt. There isn't anything I wouldn't have done for him.'

Guerline had referred to this 'debt' often since he'd returned home, but she hadn't yet revealed what it was.

They were silent as the memory of Philippe St Clare lingered around them. Bastien's gaze once more travelled around the study, seeing his father's presence imprinted everywhere. When he turned back to Guerline, he saw an odd expression on her face.

'What is it, cousin? Are you unwell?'

She opened her mouth as if to speak, and then shook her head as if she'd thought better of her words. 'It's nothing, Bastien. Tell me—have you and Mademoiselle Moreau formalised your betrothal yet?'

'*Non.* She released me from the contract this evening.'

Guerline's back stiffened. 'She released you?'

'*Oui.* She has no more desire for us to wed than I do.'

'But your father wanted your marriage more than anything.'

His nostrils flared. 'My marriage? Or my obedience, cousin?'

She said nothing and her shoulders drooped. 'I see...'

Feeling as if he'd struck her, he gathered his cousin into his arms. He kissed the top of her hair. 'No matter my feelings on the contract, I cannot thank you enough for caring so diligently for *mon père*.'

Guerline reached up and took his head between her hands and kissed his cheeks. 'I will go back home soon, but I pray it will not be long before I see you again, cousin.'

'I pray that as well.'

After Guerline had left, Bastien lingered a bit longer in the study before going upstairs to his bedchamber. Undressing himself didn't prove too difficult and he slid under the covers, brooding over the happenings of the evening. Lilas, lovely and sophisticated as she now was, wasn't going to hinder his original plan.

Why wasn't he comforted by that thought?

Bastien turned over in bed. He and his father had never reconciled the breach between them. For his first couple of years away he'd revelled in his newfound freedom. He'd thought his father would cut him off financially, but he hadn't. The man had clearly known of his whereabouts, as the bills he'd accumulated must have come to his father's notice at some point.

In the third year of his self-imposed exile the novelty of freedom had worn off. Many times he'd reached for quill and paper to write and ask to come back home. He'd left without permission, so it seemed only right he ask to return.

He'd never written that letter. Now he never would.

Bastien stared up at the darkened ceiling, his chest feeling as though it had been caved in. Should he have just given in to his father's wishes to marry Lilas? Would it have hurt?

It all came back to one thing.

Lilas was his father's choice—not his own. For that reason alone, he could not have gone through with the marriage.

Bastien sat up and kicked the sheets off, his naked body dark against the white material. No, that wasn't the only reason he couldn't go through with the marriage.

Thinking back to his earlier musings, he recognised that Lilas had awakened something else in him. A sense of connection with another person—someone who knew him as well as he knew himself. When they'd been alone, the pull of her, the draw of her mature beauty, had mingled with a childhood connection that was as powerful as an opiate.

Lilas's pain and anger at what she perceived as his abandonment of her only made the situation worse. If he had written that letter to his father and come home, he would have discovered sooner that her father had died and left her to live with strangers. Despite everything, he would have gone to her side.

Who had wiped her tears or held her close while she struggled with the grief of losing her only connection to the past? Who had reassured her or given her comfort as she was pressed into society?

Who had been her friend? A woman…or another man?

A faceless man with a white wig and rouge-painted smile danced before his eyes. He saw the interloper whispering into Lilas's ear. He could imagine her smiling coyly, saying to that man, *How wicked you are!*

A sharp pain made him wince, and he looked to see his nails had carved grooves into the base of his palm. Slowly he relaxed his fingers, feeling the blood rush through his hands again.

Bastien snorted and shook his head, willing his mind to cease this useless train of thought. None of it mattered now anyway.

This was what he had wanted to avoid. If he married Lilas there was a grave danger. Danger that she would make him feel emotions and sensations he wanted no part of. Just moments ago the thought, the very idea of another man being her friend, had sent a trickle of jealousy through him. Not enough to unnerve him or threaten his resolve, but its presence, its existence, meant he wasn't as far removed from his emotions as he'd like to be.

That simply would not do.

Bastien wanted marriage—not everlasting love. If Lilas had agreed to marriage he instinctively knew that their union would have ended up being something more.

Much more than what he wanted from a wife.

Despite his being so adamant, his heart remained heavy as he covered himself again and drifted off into a fitful sleep.

The next morning, when his valet dutifully brought the newspaper to him, Bastien perused its contents.

He came to an item of interest that stopped him in his tracks. His hands shook as he read, a fierce scowl dominating his features. Cursing, he stood up and threw the paper onto the floor.

'Monsieur le Duc, what is it?'

Snarling, he said, 'Prepare my carriage immediately.'

'What is wrong?'

He could barely get the words out through his gritted teeth. 'Mademoiselle Moreau has a lot of explaining to do.'

And she'd do it this very day!

'It is disappointing, but it can't be helped,' the Comtesse de la Baux said as she slathered creamy butter over airy bread.

Lilas poured a cup of hot chocolate now she'd finished telling her stepmother of the broken betrothal.

'Are you certain that this is the best course of action, Lilas?'

Lilas flicked her gaze over to where Pierre sat, looking at her with concern.

'Of course it is,' she assured him, all the while ignoring the clenching in the middle of her stomach.

Most of the night she'd tossed and turned in her canopied bed. Seeing Bastien again had evoked a painful memory of the last time they'd been together. The argument between him and his father. The way he'd rejected the notion of her as his wife. His dismissal of her friendship... It still hurt.

It was said that time healed all wounds.

Then why did her heart still ache?

'Don't let it bother you, Lilas.'

She glanced up and stared at her stepmother. The Comtesse's appearance bore an ageless quality. Dark, lustrous chestnut curls framed a face of unblemished skin. Although she was beautiful and gracious, something about her didn't sit quite right with Lilas.

The woman had treated her well since she'd come into her inheritance. Every day for the past four years her stepmother had gone out of her way to ensure her entrance into society. Private tutors, lessons in comportment, visits to the salons where intelligent conversation spanning all kinds of subjects took place… More than she could say.

It was due to her stepmother's constant urging that she had blossomed from an ash-smudged cinder girl into an heiress of some standing. But it was Lilas's own talent with her art that had made her soar in popularity. Her stepmother had had nothing to do with that besides providing a place for her to paint.

Yet in their entire time together Lilas had found it difficult to warm to her. It wasn't something she could articulate, but an instinctual knowledge that something was amiss.

There was a certain glitter in those blue eyes she couldn't account for. She did not know what it meant. In public, the Comtesse de la Baux presented a certain caring façade that disappeared the moment they were behind closed doors. She'd never been cruel or hurtful, exactly. Although there were times when Lilas sensed her stepmother barely tolerated her presence.

Lilas gave a mental shrug. Should she expect the woman to have the same affection for her a real mother would have? She should be grateful for the tepid kindnesses the woman had shown her after her father's death.

'Would you have preferred I married the Duc de Languedoc, Belle-Mère?'

'Louis desired your marriage to his dear friend's son. He is not here to feel the disappointment.'

How could the father she had never known hold sway over her life even from the grave? From what she'd learned from Pierre, Louis had been a doting father. Affectionate, stern when he needed to be, but devoted to his duties of fatherhood. He had treated Pierre as his own son, bestowing upon Pierre in his will a substantial portion of the unentailed part of the estate, to be inherited when he turned twenty-four—which Pierre had done three years ago.

If Louis hadn't perished in the carriage accident, and if her mother hadn't died in childbirth, what would her life have been like?

The daydream unfolded before her. Perhaps she'd be sitting across from Atalyia now, sharing confidences and dreams of the future. Louis would be gazing upon her mother's visage with the same look of adoration the previous Duc de Languedoc had acquired whenever he'd held a miniature of his dead wife.

Had that life been hers, rather than that of a servant girl, would she and Bastien have accepted a betrothal between their families as the obedient children of families of affluence? Would he have seen her as his ideal then?

Lilas gave a mental shake of her head. Why wallow in such fantasies? It did nothing but make her wistful about the unattainable. What she had now—this life that was rightfully hers—was because of her father.

If there was nothing true in this life except one thing, Lilas knew it was that she was meant to be a wielder of colour. Being a woman of status came with its troubles. Gossip could rip a reputation to pieces. She had learned to walk a fine line, being careful, ever so careful, to do nothing to bring dishonour to her name.

Trust was sparse.

Ever since Bastien had betrayed her, she'd learned never to allow anyone to get that close to her again.

Except last night when, despite everything within her that had told her to not fall for Bastien's eyes, she'd once again felt the magnetic draw of his personality. The connection that had always been a part of their curious friendship.

He'd interpreted her painting with such accuracy it

had shocked and upset her. In some ways, she *was* the rejected daughter of Adam. Thinking of her time in the orphanage and how powerless she'd felt, she knew she wouldn't be in a hurry to find herself in such circumstances again.

Sighing, Lilas glanced up to see her stepmother's blue eyes on her. Then she realised the Comtesse wasn't staring at her, but above her.

Turning, she felt her breath catch in her throat.

'Soeur Calme! I didn't know you were standing there!'

The nun made a gesture of apology, but she said nothing. In four years, Lilas had never once heard her make a sound. Not even the black habit flowing about her broke the cocoon of silence that enveloped her.

When Lilas had first arrived at Hôtel de la Baux, and had met the strange woman, Pierre had said she'd taken a vow of silence for the past twenty years. Nevertheless, she had a way of making herself understood.

'She is a strange creature,' Lilas had remarked when she'd learned of this. 'I can't imagine remaining silent for twenty years.'

'Perhaps she has nothing to say.' Pierre had shrugged. 'Few people do.'

'For twenty years?' Lilas had asked incredulously.

'Soeur Calme was my governess and she took care of me for many years,' the Comtesse de la Baux had responded. 'It is an honour for me to care for her now, in her later years.'

Lilas had refrained from mentioning that the relationship between the women seemed more like mistress and servant than a child with her respected former governess.

As it was, her stepmother ordered the nun to put out a dress for the day and then dismissed her. As the woman left, a furious knocking resounded through the room.

'Who on earth can be visiting us now?' the Comtesse asked. 'Are you expecting someone to call this morning?'

Lilas shook her head, listening to the faint sounds of a servant going to the door and answering it. Muffled noises, high and low, came together. A screech of some sort—a cry, perhaps? Then determined footsteps on the marble floors.

When the servant appeared in the room's doorway, his face wreathed in worry, Lilas's mouth fell open at the sight of the person who stood behind him.

Bastien!

The hair at the back of Lilas's neck stood erect. There was a primal force emanating from him. Something had greatly upset him, and it was clear that for some reason he thought she was the cause of it.

What had happened?

The simmering heat of Bastien's rage boiled under the surface of his skin as he stood there. He breathed evenly, trying to still the mad patter of his heart. He knew there were other people in the small breakfast room, but he only had eyes for Lilas.

'Monsieur le Duc,' said the Comtesse de la Baux as she stood, flustered. 'What an unexpected surprise.'

He had to bring his rage under control. It wasn't the Comtesse's or her son's fault that Lilas was so devious.

With a supreme effort, he tugged his eyes away from Lilas and said, as politely as he could, 'Madame la Comtesse.' He bowed. He turned to Pierre. 'Monsieur Damiani.'

His voice hardened when his gaze came to rest upon Lilas. 'Mademoiselle Moreau.'

Her eyes widened. He knew the ice in his voice could have frozen the Seine.

'*Bonjour*, Monsieur le Duc.'

She gave him a curtsy, and he saw a wrinkle in the centre of her forehead. He didn't return the greeting. So she wanted to pretend all was well? He was not so inclined. Childish games were for children, and he was a man.

'Madame la Comtesse,' he bit out in chilly tones, 'may I speak with Mademoiselle Moreau privately, please?'

Lilas's face scrunched further. He wanted to tell her to stop acting. Did she think he didn't know what she had done?

'That is highly irregular, *monsieur*.'

Oh, he knew it was irregular. He just didn't care. What he had to say to the traitorous Lilas was for her ears alone.

Her stepmother glanced at her, a silky eyebrow arched in enquiry. 'I take it this is something that cannot be spoken of in company?'

His mouth lifted in a travesty of a smile. 'Have I your permission? All I ask is for a quarter of an hour.'

'That's a long time, *monsieur*.'

A strained silence filled the room as the Comtesse de la Baux exchanged covert glances with Lilas. Were this a normal visit, he would have never interrupted their breakfast. But he wanted answers and he needed them now.

'A quarter of an hour and no more.' A pointed look of warning glared from the Comtesse's eyes before she and her son left.

Before the door could close, Lilas whirled on him. '*Monsieur*, whatever is the matter?'

The words he'd held back spilled forth from his mouth. 'This was your plan all along, wasn't it?'

She drew back at the venomous tone of his voice. 'What?'

Her violet eyes were wide with surprise, but he didn't believe it for one moment.

'Don't dare put on a pretence. You have used me and I want to know why!'

'I have no idea what you are referring to.'

He snorted. Without taking his eyes off her, he pulled out a rolled newspaper and spread it open before her.

She came forward, her face filled with confusion. She took the newspaper and browsed through the contents.

He watched intently, almost envisaging that he could read the newspaper along with her, even though he couldn't see it from his vantage point. So attuned to her was he, that he saw the moment her eyes latched on to the announcement of their engagement.

'This can't be right…' she breathed. The paper shook in her hand as if taken by a sudden storm. 'This can't be!'

'You planned this. Why?'

He almost choked on the words, his vocal cords tangling with each other. Beyond the anger was something that felt an awful lot like pain. Her act was so convincing he almost wanted to take back what he'd said. But no. He wouldn't fall for her lies. For whatever reason, Lilas was trying to control him just as his father had done.

He wouldn't stand for it—least of all from her!

Lilas set the paper aside. 'I didn't plan anything at all. This is just as much a shock to me as it is to you.'

He scoffed. 'Really? You aren't the one who has told the whole world that we are betrothed?'

'I— I—' she stuttered.

He'd never heard her stutter before. Which had to mean she was truly rattled. For an instant, the heat of his anger abated. Was it possible she didn't know anything about it? Was it the work of someone else?

But who? His servants were all loyal to him. Estienne wouldn't have done it. The Comte de Clareville would have cut off his tongue before he'd allow news of that sort to leave the House of St Clare.

There was no other explanation. She had done this!

An ache in his chest pierced him.

'Lost for words, are you? Far from agreeing to cancel the engagement, you've made all Paris aware of it.'

'Monsieur le Duc—'

'Is that why you didn't want to break the engagement while I was abroad?' His body bristled as he stepped towards her. 'You want to use my name to further your own ambitions? Is being the daughter of a *comte* not good enough for you? Now you want the world to know you are going to be a *duchesse*?'

'I did not do this.'

The stricken look in her face had dissipated, to be replaced slowly by a burning light in her eyes. Her lips thinned into a flat line. Was she upset that he had found her out? Good. He preferred Lilas this way. Headstrong. Volatile. Not timid and shocked as if he had hurt her. He hadn't done anything to warrant this subterfuge. She had!

'No one outside my family knew about our engagement,' he told her. 'It was up to you whether or not to go through with the contract. You've used me and I want to know why!'

'How dare you accuse me of this?'

'There's no one else who could have done it!'

She stomped towards him, her fists clenching and unclenching. 'I wish I were a man, so I could strike you down for that accusation.'

'If you were a man, we wouldn't be having this conversation at all.'

She came up to him, nearly toe to toe with him except for the voluminous skirt between them. Distractedly, he thought how lovely she looked in a rage.

'You said so yourself. There are no secrets between us.'

'And you intimated to me that that was no longer the case.'

'It's true. But why would I do this to us both?'

'Perhaps because of my title?' His brow arched into his hairline.

'Enough, Bastien!'

The sound of his name as well as her outraged voice cut through the words, sending a charged silence throughout the room. He stared down at her, seeing the slight stain of deep red along her cheekbones and flooding her throat. Her ragged breath sawed through the strained hush. Those eyes were hard as amethyst.

At last, with a voice rife with anger, she clipped out, 'You have known me all my life. When have I ever given you cause to doubt your trust in me? Tell me this instant!'

Lilas heard her words ricochet around the room, bouncing off the walls. She glared into his lion eyes, seeing their intensity, their predatory gleam. She didn't care how angry he was. She would not allow him to take it out on her. Particularly when she was innocent of any wrongdoing.

When the silence lingered, she asked again, 'When have I ever betrayed your trust?'

The tautness about his eyes eased in slow degrees, relaxing the hardened features of his face. 'You never have.' He inhaled sharply. 'Never.'

'Then why accuse me of something so heinous?'

He sent frustrated fingers through his hair. 'This has caused a significant disruption to my plans.'

Another mention of his plans. 'What are you talking about?'

'My father controlled every aspect of my life.'

His words came out hard and clipped. Although his eyes were fixed on her, she could tell he wasn't here with her but locked in the past.

'Do you know how often I fought against him? Mère was the only one who could keep us from striking each other.'

'I remember what you told me.'

'There was more to it than I revealed to you.'

Going over to the table, he invited her to sit with him. Looking down at her morning gown, she was glad it was decent, although it was more than improper that they were sitting like this. However, this didn't seem the time to mention it.

When she was seated he went on. 'I believed my father's obsession with needing control over everything stemmed from his banishment from Versailles.'

Lilas blinked. 'Your father was banished from Court?'

Bastien ceased staring down at her and shifted his gaze to the other side of the room. 'To be specific, the late King forbade my father entrance into Versailles because of his marriage to my mother. As to the reason—I daresay it had less to do with my mother's race as much as the mixing of noble and common blood. Or perhaps both. It's unclear, really. And although my father never stated it, I do believe he felt bereft of his right to walk those hallowed halls. Yet his love for my mother would not allow him to dwell on that loss. Some members of the elite ostracised him, while others didn't. But he certainly did fall out of favour with the Crown.'

His gaze drifted back to her, and she saw the colour of his eyes darkening to a deep amber. 'It will be my marriage that allows me to enter Versailles once more.'

'And the woman? Your ideal wife?'

'She will be in a position to bring the House of St Clare to the forefront. My rank helps, but being the Duc de Languedoc wasn't enough to save my father. I need a certain type of wife to help me regain the favour that was lost.'

'Why is it so important to you if it wasn't to your father?'

A jolt went through him, his eyes widening. 'What makes you think it wasn't?'

'He didn't try to gain the Crown's good graces during the time of his marriage, or even after your mother died. It must not have mattered to him that much.'

'It did,' he said with an emphatic nod.

Was he trying to convince himself? she wondered.

'He didn't speak of it, but I know it did.'

She wanted to stay angry with him. Her righteous fury still burned, licking at her flesh as if to eat it alive.

Yet how could she? His father must have thought that by controlling Bastien's actions his son's behaviour would speak volumes at Court more than anything else. Yet being under his father's thumb had only built resentment.

But she knew family honour was important, and having it was necessary. Hadn't the Comtesse de la Baux told her as much over the years?

She could hear her stepmother's voice in her mind. *'Honour is not only in the hands of men. It is a burden of women as well. You must never do anything to destroy our family's honour.'*

So Bastien wanted this woman, whoever she might be, to help him... That meant that he still did not consider her good enough to be that woman and help him regain favour with the Crown. Did it matter that she'd received the Queen's patronage? No. What mattered was she'd been a *fille des cendres*, and in his eyes she always would be.

Memories of his coming to her aid rushed through her brain. She couldn't ignore his past kindnesses. For that alone, she had to consider what he needed from her.

Backing away, Bastien spread his hands out. 'Mademoiselle Moreau, *je suis désolé*. I believe you when you say that you didn't announce our engagement in the paper.'

He didn't look apologetic. Bastien would never be the kind of man to cower before anyone. That was something she suspected his father had taught him, knowingly or not. But he had apologised. It wasn't enough, but it was a start.

The tension along her shoulders went away as she said, 'Very well, *monsieur*.'

The air in the room lifted. 'You can't begin to imagine my surprise when I saw it,' he said.

'No more than mine, *monsieur*. Surely you don't believe I have any desire to marry you?'

A cynical look came into his eyes. 'I find that hard to believe.'

'Why is that?'

'If you don't want to marry me, why didn't you rescind the contract four years ago? The power to dissolve our union rested in your hands. Why didn't you exert it?'

Her newfound sympathy was burned away by the anger sweeping through her at his words.

'How could I rescind the contract when I had no way to get in contact with you? Did you ever write to your father and tell him of your whereabouts?'

A stony expression came into his eyes. 'Whether or not I wrote to my father is beside the point. I'm sure he

knew of my whereabouts. You could have sought me out
if you had wished to do so.'

'If you didn't want to hear from your father, how could
I expect that you'd want to hear from me?'

The silence wailed between them, crying out for one of
them to break it. Bastien's face had tightened like granite.

Finally, she blew out a breath. 'I am unused to a life of
leisure. But neither am I interested in being a broodmare.'

'Is that why you don't want to be my wife?'

She glanced at him, frowning.

'I am not challenging you,' he said hurriedly. 'Just
curious.'

'Being an artist is what I have always longed and
hoped for. My work is highly sought-after now. I am not
interested in being your wife or anyone else's—vaunted
title and our fathers' wishes notwithstanding.'

'Is that really the reason?' he asked, in a quiet, almost
gentle voice.

His words lingered in the air. She wanted to tell him
that it was because he had betrayed her trust. He'd hurt
her badly that long-ago day. But from those broken frag-
ments she'd moved on, with her heart mended, and she
wouldn't risk it again.

'The reason doesn't matter. Not any more.'

'You believe I betrayed your trust,' he said, after a
long moment.

'And you believe I am not good enough for you.'

When had she ever been? Not even in the orphanage,
as a child, had anyone found her worthy enough to take
her under their wing. Once or twice some fortunate child
had been taken in by a desperate barren woman. But that
had been a rarity. Yes, she'd been rescued from the orphanage by Bastien's mother, and she was grateful for

that. But the life of a servant was hard, even at Château de Velay, and she'd often been lonely.

And now here she was, still alone and isolated. Still unworthy.

Bastien stared at her, saying nothing. What was he thinking? For all his talk about there being secrets between them now, he seemed to read her like a book. While she…

Was she so easy to read, then? Had she not learned anything from her stepmother about keeping her private feelings private?

She waited with bated breath to see what he would say to her accusation. Give her some hope that… That what? That she was wrong? When the idea of their betrothal being known to all of Paris must be an embarrassment to him.

His words from long ago echoed in her ear.

'When I marry, I need a highborn woman with an impeccable reputation. Not one who used to be a servant girl.'

When he opened his mouth, it was to say, 'We have a dilemma.'

She shrugged, wanting to get away from all this. From his presence. 'Perhaps not. Neither of us must confirm or deny this. We can simply let it die out, as it inevitably will.'

'You're very optimistic.'

'Tomorrow something else will grab society's interest, Monsieur le Duc. No one cares about our betrothal.'

Chapter Four

Bastien St Clare, Duc de Languedoc, and Mademoiselle Moreau are required to appear before Her Majesty the Queen of France.

The roar of blood pumping in Bastien's brain drowned out the world as he stared at the embossed wax of the broken seal of the Queen of France.

The heat drained from his body as he continued to read the contents. Along with the invitation, a personal message from the Queen was included, expressing her joy at their upcoming nuptials and saying that she would like to see them.

With nerveless fingers, he set the invitation on the table.

Dear God, he hadn't seen this coming at all.

Shakily he rose from behind the desk in his study, having gone there to go over the estate's papers. Although sunlight spilled from the window, he felt as if he were cloaked in darkness.

Yes, the Queen had given patronage to Lilas, but he'd had no idea she'd take an interest in anything more than that. The news of their engagement had spiralled out of control.

With a vague remembrance, he recalled joking that he'd receive an invitation from the Queen. And now he had!

While Bastien stood in the centre of the study, staring at nothing, a knock sounded at the door. Biting his lip, he inhaled a deep breath. He had no wish for company now.

Rolling his shoulders, he yelled, 'Come!'

'Cousin?'

He whirled around at the sound of Guerline's voice. 'What are you still doing here?' he asked. 'I thought you'd gone back home.'

She came further into the room, her eyes looking nervously upon his face. Goosebumps lifted along the strip of skin in the centre of his back. Why did he have a bad feeling about this?

'There's something I have to tell you first, cousin. But you look…odd. Are you unwell?'

Bastien pinched his nose. 'I have received an invitation from the Queen. She requires my presence with Mademoiselle Moreau at Versailles in a little over a fortnight.'

'Oh!' Guerline's voice rose with pleasure. 'How exciting.'

'Is it?' he asked hollowly.

'Of course, Bastien. The Queen must have heard about your impending marriage.'

He grunted. 'To put it mildly, Guerline.'

Neither he nor Lilas had fully appreciated the effect the announcement of their engagement would have on the populace of Paris. Overnight, invitations had poured in by the dozen for their presence at social events and private homes all over the city. In barely a week's time, everything had changed.

And now this.

'We have no wish to marry.'

Guerline shook her head. 'But it was your father's fervent desire.'

'Not mine.'

'Why must you be so stubborn? Mademoiselle Moreau is perfect for you. A blind priest could see that.'

'A blind priest doesn't have to get married.'

'Well, what are you going to do, then?'

Bastien folded his arms. 'I'm going to visit Mademoiselle Moreau. Then I'll know the answer to that question.'

'Wait, Bastien.'

He turned, wondering at the strange note in her voice along with the almost guilty expression on her face.

His forehead pleated and he slowly let his arms fall to his side. 'What is it, Guerline?'

She grimaced. 'If you were a blind priest, I'd ask you to bless me, for I have sinned.'

'Sinned? Guerline, please do speak plainly.'

A grunt escaped her lips. 'Bastien, I have a confession to make.'

Mademoiselle Moreau,
We are joyful to hear of your betrothal to the Duc de Languedoc. It pleases us to invite you to Versailles on the date as written on the accompanying invitation.
We look forward to your presence.

The personal message from the Queen had rocked Lilas to the core. How far she had come from her humble, wretched beginnings to receive such a thing! It spoke volumes about the change of her position in society. There were minor nobles who would give their eye-teeth for this.

She never had been presented at Court as she didn't meet the requirements for it, but a chance viewing of her work had garnered her the Queen's patronage regardless. Yet, for all that, Lilas almost wished she were a servant again. She glanced at the invitation once more. The summons requested hers *and* Bastien's presence.

Mon Dieu! This had little to do with the Queen's patronage and everything to do with her supposed engagement to Bastien.

She pushed the covers off the bed and got up. Esme, her maid, stuffed her into a dressing gown, and she sat at her dressing table.

'It's very exciting!' her maid commented. 'To gain an audience with Madame la Reine.'

'*Oui...*' Lilas drew the word out, her unseeing eyes fixed on the mirror before her.

'What must it be like to see her?'

'I've no idea.' Her heart thundered in her chest. 'Esme, will you help me?'

The maid gave an owlish blink. '*Mademoiselle?*'

She motioned for the woman to come and stand before her. Grabbing the maid's tiny hands, she clasped them in her own. 'I cannot do this alone and I will need you. You must help me look the best I possibly can. Even more.'

Esme bent and kissed her hands in a gracious manner. 'I will not fail you, *mademoiselle*. By the time I am done you will look lovelier than any woman there.'

Some of the tension drifted from her shoulders. 'Why are you always so kind to me, Esme?' she asked as the woman flittered around her.

'*Mademoiselle*, you have always been so kind to me,' was the maid's singular response.

Having been a servant, and knowing how dismissive those above could be, she found Esme's words a comfort to her.

'*Merci beaucoup*, Esme.'

Lilas dismissed the woman and sat alone. Around her, the silence screamed like a child. Her thoughts shrieked along with it.

With a harsh sigh, Lilas reached over a plethora of cosmetics and opened her ornate silver-gilded jewellery box. Scowling down at the contents, she shoved aside a pair of ruby earrings, flicked a pearl pendant into the corner and tossed aside an emerald ring until she found a tarnished silver key.

Rising and crossing over to the farthest corner of her bedchamber, she came to a standing rosewood armoire. Inserting the tiny key, she unlocked it and opened the doors. Kneeling on the floor before it, she pulled out the bottom drawer. There, lying in the centre of the otherwise empty drawer, was the silver *livre* Bastien had given her years ago.

How old she'd been, she couldn't recall. The other servants had been particularly cruel to her that day, and so she'd escaped. Hiding under the dangling fronds of a willow tree, she'd started drawing until she'd forgotten all else.

When she'd heard footsteps coming towards her fear had trailed through her and she'd jumped up to hide the parchment. Upon seeing Bastien, who even back then had had a presence about him, she'd relaxed.

He'd come to stand with her under the tree. Hooking

his hands on a low-hanging branch, he'd swayed back and forth above her. 'What are you doing?' he'd asked.

She'd stiffened. That was the day she'd become aware that although Bastien sometimes acted as an elder brother, he was still her master's son.

Fear had had her saying, 'Nothing, Monsieur le Marquis.'

His eyebrows had perched in his hairline, and he'd quipped, 'Such formality? What heinous crime have you committed?'

She'd shaken her head and stepped back. 'None, *monsieur*.'

The humour and amusement had left his face as he'd reached out and tilted her chin up. 'Lilas, don't be frightened. Have I ever given you cause to be fearful of me?'

Her shaking had subsided. *'Non.'*

His thumb had brushed her cheek. 'Whatever it is, I promise there won't be punishment of any sort. I swear.'

She'd ceased shaking altogether, and her shoulders had slumped.

He'd released her chin and held out his hand. Lilas had reached behind her and handed over what she'd been hiding.

At first, creases had formed in his brow as he'd stared at what he had obviously thought was a blank sheet of parchment. 'What do you think I am going to do?'

'You are my master's son.' Lilas had dug the tip of her left foot into the ground, head bowed. 'I took the paper without your permission.'

'Oui. I am your master's son.' Even then, he'd been comfortable in his nobility. 'But not right now.'

'I've drawn on it,' she'd said, and she'd shyly told him to turn it over.

She'd heard his breath catch. He'd taken in the accurate depiction of the meadows, with Château de Velay in the distance. Recreated with only ashes, a makeshift paintbrush and water.

Bastien had smiled at her. 'This is rather good.'

Her head had dipped. 'Do you think so?'

'I wouldn't lie to you, would I?'

He'd snapped his fingers in sudden inspiration. 'In fact, I shall give you this for it.' Bastien had reached into his pocket and placed a silver coin in the centre of her muddied palm. 'Your first paid commission.'

'My first patron,' she'd breathed, her eyes locked on the silver coin in her dirty hand.

The moment Bastien had discovered her work, everything had changed. He'd given her more than money. He'd bestowed focus upon her. The day Bastien had given her the *livre*, he had given her the means to rise above her station as a mere servant.

A gentle knock and Esme's clear voice broke in on her thoughts. '*Mademoiselle*, I have correspondence. May I come in?'

Lilas started. With careful manoeuvring, she replaced the coin directly into the centre of the drawer and slid it back into its slot carefully. Closing and locking the doors, she stood and went back to her dressing table, placing the key back into the jewellery box.

'Come in, Esme.'

The maid entered and handed a stack of letters to her. On the top, she saw an envelope with the symbol of the house of St Clare emblazoned on it. A slight tremble came over her fingers as she laid aside the other letters and opened his.

The note was a brief, pointed one:

Mademoiselle Moreau,
Expect me at three hours past midday. I shall like
us to visit Jardin des Tuileries.
B. St Clare

She set the missive down and looked at her reflection. A pensive expression met her eyes. They could no longer avoid being seen in public. She dismissed the high-handed tone of the note, knowing that behind it was the greater question.

What were they going to do?

One simply did not refuse to see Her Majesty, the Queen of France, unless one no longer had a desire to live.

'Esme, would you please tell the Comtesse de la Baux that the Duc de Languedoc will be coming later today? Also, I'd like to wear my navy-blue gown for when he arrives. We'll be going out.'

Later, while Esme drew a bath and Lilas prepared to receive Bastien, she pushed open the doors and went out onto the small balcony attached to her chamber. Above the faint sounds that Esme and one of the other maids made behind her, she heard the slight whistling of the wind. It played with the lace ruffles connected to the sleeve of her dressing gown.

Her stomach knotted as she stood there.

Was she going to be forced to marry Bastien? That couldn't happen. She'd worked hard for her life as an artist and she wouldn't give it up to simply be a wife. If that were her only goal in life, she could have married ages ago.

No, she'd maintain her independence. For to sacrifice it now would be to betray the young girl she'd once been, covered in soot and ash and praying for a family that never came.

* * *

When Hôtel de la Baux came into view, Bastien couldn't deny that some sort of lunacy had come over him.

Thinking back to when he'd last confronted Lilas, believing she had been the one to place the announcement in the paper, he was ashamed of his reaction. He'd behaved like an immature boy, accusing her without verifying if she had indeed let the paper know of their engagement. Why had he acted so out of character?

He wrestled for the answer before he realised the cause behind his actions.

He'd felt hurt.

For those few moments his heart had sunk to his feet at the idea of Lilas betraying his trust. He'd lashed out at her without thinking. When she had never given him any cause to disbelieve the fact that she'd never divulge his confidences.

He had to remember that Lilas wasn't his father.

Over the past week, the pressure had mounted. Lilas was already highly sought-after as an artist, as well as being popular in her own right due to her unusual rise in circumstances. For himself, as the new Duc, he'd had his own share of public fancy after returning home from aboard.

The novelty of their betrothal had torn through Paris like wildfire. Invitations for their attendance to one function or another had arrived at the house in rapid succession.

Now that the Queen was involved, they were more trapped than ever. One couldn't disappoint the Queen.

Lilas and he had to figure out what they were going to do about this, and quickly.

Bastien's eyes took in the structure in front of him.

Though less grand than his own residence, if only in size, Hôtel de la Baux nevertheless retained a charming exterior that drew the eye. Rays of sunshine flowed over its many chimneys and gabled roofs. Soft pink walls lined with long panes of glass brought a pleasant delicateness to the harsh stone.

'*Bonne après-midi*, Monsieur le Duc,' the manservant who opened the door greeted him, with an almost reverent bow. 'Mademoiselle Moreau is expecting you.'

The manservant stopped at the arched doorway of a salon, with vaulted ceilings and an enormous fireplace with an expansive mantel studded with curios. Lilas was seated on a dainty-looking settee. She rose from her seat and curtsied.

'*Bonjour*, Monsieur le Duc. It is good to see you again.'

Lilas's eyes lifted, and he found himself once again transfixed by her. She'd forgone wearing a wig and had instead dusted her own tresses, styled to emulate a naturally mussed hairstyle. Her blue gown afforded him a delightful view of her figure.

'*Bonjour*, Mademoiselle Moreau,' he stated formally, with a bow. 'I trust you are well?'

'I am,' she replied. 'Madame la Comtesse begs your pardon for her absence.' She gestured to the quiet maid by her side. 'My maid, Esme, will go with us as chaperone.'

'I am thankful that you are accompanying us, *mademoiselle*.'

The maid pinkened, her eyes filled with pleasure at his attention to her.

'Shall I send for refreshments before we leave?' asked Lilas.

Bastien declined politely. 'Shall we go?'

Moments later, he helped both women into the carriage and then called out to his driver. 'Jardin des Tuileries.'

The carriage rocked back and forth as it made its way eastward on Rue de St Dominique. Along the winding streets of the Quartier Faubourg Saint-Germain they passed the lofty, sprawling homes there, that preened like stone peacocks. Formal gardens surrounded them in emerald mosaics of design that drew everyone's admiration.

At the command of her mistress, Esme stayed in the carriage when they arrived—but not before Bastien had once again thanked her for her presence.

'I do believe you've gained an admirer, *monsieur*,' Lilas said with a hint of amusement as they strolled along the manicured paths of the Jardin des Tuileries, breathing in the intoxicating scent of pine. 'How wicked you are! Leave it to you to woo even the servants.'

'Did I do that with you?'

Lilas stumbled on the path and he darted his hand out and caught her. 'Are you all right?'

'I'm f-fine,' she stammered, yanking her arm from his grip as if he'd burned her.

He almost wanted to pursue the topic but, bearing in mind what he had to tell her, decided not to.

After several minutes of pleasant silence, Lilas remarked, 'It's hard to imagine that this was all abandoned and overgrown nearly twenty years ago.'

'Indeed. Perhaps nothing is abandoned for ever. Just forgotten until the right person appears and comes to look after it.'

Around them, others walked. The gardens were open to the public. But when they'd arrived he'd found a path less travelled, to afford them some privacy.

Cypress trees lined the way, like soldiers in uniform,

each providing a wide expanse of shade. Bursts of colour from the myriad flowers invited one's eyes to dwell upon the radiant soft petals. A piercing blue sky hung over the Palais des Tuileries, its enormous façade looming in the distance.

They turned a corner and found themselves in an even less populated area of the gardens. Here, box hedges formed a path to an extensive asymmetrical mosaic.

He glanced down at the woman by his side, seeing her brown berry mouth lifted in a tiny smile. 'Is there something to smile about?'

'I must come here and paint,' Lilas said. 'It's too beautiful not to do so. It would be a sacrilege.'

'We can't have you committing sacrilege, can we?'

And on the heel of that thought came another—one he wished he didn't have to tell her, but did.

'Mademoiselle Moreau, I have to tell you something.'

Lilas pulled her gaze from the loveliness around her, seeing a pensive expression on Bastien's face. 'What is it?'

Bastien cleared his throat in a purposeful manner. 'I should tell you that I have discovered who put the announcement in the newspaper.'

At this, Lilas straightened. She hadn't expected to hear this. 'Who was it?'

Was he embarrassed? From the rather sheepish look on his face, it appeared that he was. 'I am afraid the culprit exists on the St Clare divide.'

Her brow lifted. It took great willpower, but she refrained from saying, *I told you so.*

He grimaced. 'My father's former nurse is responsible.'

'Who is she? How? Why?'

'Excellent questions, Mademoiselle Moreau. It is my mother's niece and my cousin—Guerline DuValier.'

Lilas blinked, stunned by this news. 'I'd no idea you had a cousin other than the Vicomte de Vivarais.'

'My mother's side of the family chose to stay in Saint-Domingue, for reasons best known to themselves. But a letter from my father brought my cousin to France a year or so before his death. My father had grown weaker and he needed help.'

Her brow creased. 'I am pleased your father had someone to care for him. But I don't understand… Why would she announce our engagement in the papers?'

'My father told her to.'

Lilas shook her head. The explanation was almost too simple. 'Please explain.'

'For some reason Guerline feels she owes my father a great debt for educating her. When I returned home yesterday I received a full confession from her, detailing what she had done. Guerline told me that while she was caring for my father he'd made her promise to do whatever she could to force the engagement upon us, no matter what you or I said.'

'How did she know that we had decided to rescind the betrothal contract?'

A sheepish look came over him once more. 'I told her—never thinking she would give that information to the newspapers.'

'I see,' Lilas said slowly.

'It seemed she also made that promise to him on his deathbed.'

Lilas groaned. 'Are deathbed wishes so binding?'

'Indeed. Why shouldn't my father try to control me from beyond the grave? He is dead, and yet his will still holds sway.'

Bitterness filled his voice. She didn't blame Bastien. Even though he was dead, it did seem as if his father was trying to orchestrate things from beyond.

'We find ourselves in a bind, don't we, Mademoiselle Moreau?'

'We do? I thought it was simple. You and I will simply write a note to the Queen, telling her the truth. That we have decided to end our betrothal.'

Although they weren't touching, she could feel a new tension emanate from Bastien at her words.

'What is it?'

'Neither of us can do that.'

Lilas stopped walking. 'Why ever not?'

Bastien's eyes stared into hers, and then he let his lids drift down, obstructing her view of them.

'Remember what I told you about my father being banished from Versailles? There is more. My mother once said the King had hinted at a planned marriage between my father and a *princesse du sang*, tying the house of St Clare closer to the Crown.'

A deep sigh erupted from his chest.

'It came to naught because my father married my mother. A mixed-blood noble, while unusual, isn't all that rare. But a *duc* is something of an oddity. My father had to prove the longevity of his noble bloodline to four generations before the powers that be acknowledged my right to inherit my father's title.'

Lilas frowned. 'My stepmother's solicitor mentioned something along the same lines regarding my birthright as well.'

He reached forward and took her gloved hand in a sudden gesture. 'Mademoiselle Moreau, this opportunity presented to us by the Queen…we must take it.'

'You must be mad,' Lilas snapped. 'You have no more desire to marry me than I do you.'

'The Queen's invitation gives me a way to find favour with the Crown and strengthen my place in society once more. And just think of the advantages for you.'

Lilas couldn't believe what she was hearing. First she wasn't good enough to be his ideal bride. Now the Queen was involved she was suddenly perfect.

She almost snarled as she pulled herself away from his hold. 'I already have the Queen's patronage. My reputation has already begun to grow.'

His lion eyes ensnared her. 'Think of how much more this can do for you. Mademoiselle Moreau, haven't you received more requests for your services since the news of our betrothal was announced?'

She nodded. 'But—'

'Then you must see the benefits of this engagement. It may not be what either of us wants, but we can use this to our mutual advantage.'

The battle within her must have shown on her face, because Bastien took a step closer.

'We only have to pretend for a little while,' he said quietly. 'Once we have visited the Queen much of the furore will die down and we can quietly break the betrothal.'

There was an awful kind of sense in what he was saying. Along with the increasing number of those who'd sought her out to paint their portraits, her entrance into the more elite circles had certainly increased.

She pulled her gaze from him and stared out over the garden. The earnestness in Bastien's voice couldn't be ignored. And she knew how badly he wanted to gain his rightful place in society. He deserved that.

Hadn't he come to her defence during all those years when she had been a mere servant in his father's house?

Didn't she owe it to him to make his path as smooth as possible, as he had once done for her?

Lilas stared unseeingly around her. Though she hated the bind she found herself in, she knew that she would have to succumb to the dictates of society for now.

'Very well. I'll help you.'

The tension in Bastien's chest eased at Lilas's words. For a moment, he'd thought that she would refuse him. But she hadn't.

'*Merci*, Mademoiselle Moreau.'

She nodded, saying nothing as they continued their walk.

'We'll have to pretend to be a happy couple, you know.'

'I am aware of that,' Lilas stated. 'If we must look the part, we must act the part.'

'Have you received invitations for both of us?'

She slanted her gaze at him.

Heat crawled up his neck. 'That was a foolish question. I'll let you select which ones we should accept and then you can send a missive to me regarding the dates.'

'I shall.'

They came to a marble statue of two lovers entwined with each other, and Lilas paused and studied it with a keen eye.

'Don't you think it's extraordinary how a person can take a slab of marble or stone and hammer, shave and smooth it into something like this? I can feel their passion. His mastery…her surrender.'

'Interesting choice of words you use,' he said. 'Do you suppose men are always the masters and women their captives?'

Her eyes lifted from the statue, an amused gleam shining in them. He was glad to see that. It was better than the haunting melancholy which had been darkening her eyes.

'Well, men like to think so.'

Bastien let out a huff of laughter. 'You are correct. And yet all of history has shown a woman has more power in her little finger than the armed garrisons of entire countries possess.' His joviality ebbed away as a thought entered his mind. 'Tell me... Have you surrendered to a man's mastery?'

Lilas's chin lifted in defiance. 'You tell me... This woman you seek as your ideal wife... If she had taken lovers or had been married previously, would that matter to you?'

He blinked. 'To be frank, I hadn't thought of it.'

Bastien had thought little of his ideal woman lately. Between the estate, the mounting invitations and the other demands on his time lately, she had not crossed his mind.

He knew the right answer to give, but had to admit—at least to himself—that the thought of any man caressing Lilas in an intimate manner made his teeth grind together.

As she looked away to study the statue again, he glanced at her profile, seeing the strength outlined by the most perfect symmetry along with a delicate femininity. A vision of placing tender kisses along the long column of her neck entered his imagination. Tasting the sweetness of her skin and—

'So if I'd had dozens of lovers...' her rather tart voice interrupted his musings '...you'd want to know, so you could decide if I was still worthy of the St Clare name despite my promiscuity?'

This was one thing he could reassure her on. 'You would be worthy of it regardless.'

Her face slackened. 'I would?'

'A woman like you would grace any home you were in.'

'Clearly I am not graceful enough for *your* home.'

The dryness in her voice could have fuelled a fire.

Lilas spun away from him, leaving the statue of lovers and heading towards a path framed by giant bushes packed together, hiding them from the view of outsiders.

Bastien followed her, and was enveloped by the silence as he came upon an outdoor corridor. He caught up to her and took her arm, halting her steps. With a firm but gentle grip, he turned her around to face him. 'Mademoiselle Moreau…?'

'I haven't had any lovers,' she said in a low voice.

A shaft of triumph pierced his chest, but he remained calm. 'None whatsoever?' he asked with a casual tone.

Bastien found that hard to believe. Lilas had always been comely, even as a child. And her beauty had blossomed in the past four years.

'No man has taken any interest in you at all?'

'I wouldn't say that, exactly,' she remarked. 'I have garnered the attention of men before, but I never wanted any of them.'

'Not even a kiss?'

She shook her head, her eyes drifting over his face and down to his lips, where they lingered. 'Lovemaking isn't an expression of two becoming one so much as a transaction between two parties. Should I ever give myself to a man, I'd want to experience it as a true joining.'

They continued their trek down the path, but the air between them had changed. Undercurrents buffeted them like the waves of an ocean. He felt his own awareness of her innocence stir, found himself wanting to teach her all the ways it could be between a man and a woman.

But such actions would bind them irrevocably together, and he would fight with everything that was in him before he'd allow himself to fall victim to temptation. And yet, all he could focus on was the charged air between them, thick with things unsaid. And that certainly wouldn't do.

He stopped her again. 'Tell me what it is you want.'

Her startled eyes lifted to his, and then she ducked her head in a suddenly shy manner.

'What is it?' he pressed.

'I've been thinking of this arrangement between us, and of the…authenticity we must present to the world.'

'What of it?'

'If we are to do…this, then we need to act as lovers.'

His heart stopped.

'Not in that way,' Lilas said with consternation on her face. 'But…we must…' Her voice trailed off.

Bastien knew then. 'Do you want a kiss from me?'

The colour of Lilas's eyes changed. 'I do,' she breathed, ducking her head. 'Not because I actually want to, mind you.'

His brow wrinkled. 'What other reason is there to kiss?'

'I mean that I don't want a kiss just for the sake of it, but… Oh!' She huffed. 'All this talk of lovemaking, surrender and mastery… I am curious about those aspects of our false engagement, that is all. Shouldn't you be the one to show me?'

His heart thrashed against his ribcage. 'Is that the only reason?' His eyes drifted to her lips. They simply begged him to taste them.

Kissing her would be a mistake, a voice inside his head said. *Don't fall for her charms.*

For some reason, despite that sound advice, he couldn't take his gaze from her mouth, nor silence the thought that he had to be the one to give Lilas her first taste of passion.

'I don't want to make our circumstances more difficult than they are.'

'You were once my friend. Surely, as a friend, you can give me this experience.'

A friend. He lingered on that word. It was difficult to imagine a woman in such a way. Most were either mistresses or wives in his world. But Lilas had always been different. And she was right. He had been her friend, strange as it was. Couldn't he use this moment to prove something to them both? He wasn't in love with Lilas, nor she with him. If he did kiss her he would be doing them both a favour, that was all.

'Are you sure about this?'

Lilas raised her chin, bringing her lips directly in line with his own. 'I want you to.'

Lilas's wispy breathing filled the air between them as she stood poised for him to claim her mouth. Bastien sensed she was losing the spontaneity of the moment. He'd be lying to himself if he didn't admit he wanted the kiss, but he also wanted to give Lilas a chance to change her mind.

'Are you certain?'

She nodded, her lashes covering her eyes.

She was lovely and generous. Offering herself to him with such trust.

Using the tip of his finger, Bastien traced the outline of her lips. His head bent further, and he heard her breath lock in her throat. At the last moment he turned and nibbled the curve of her ear. She convulsed uncontrollably.

'Bastien…' she groaned.

Drawing back and tilting her chin upwards, Bastien trailed a finger down her throat and rested it at the base. 'Your pulse is pounding, Lilas,' he murmured.

'Please. Kiss me.'

He lowered his mouth to the trembling brown berry lips. He captured the sweet, moist taste of innocence. Felt her untutored responses quaking against his body. Her shyness charmed him…

Until her mouth opened and a soft moan escaped her.

Her fingers tangled with the hair at the back of his neck, sending jolts down the centre of his spine. His hand came to rest on her hips, and he drew her closer into his body, feeling her melt against him. Flicking his tongue forward, he tasted her sweetness, flavoured by hot chocolate, and the combination was evocative and heady.

Then, as quickly as it had started, it stopped, Lilas ripping her mouth from his.

He almost groaned at the loss, but bit back the sound. They stared at each other, and he saw his own shock mirrored in her face. Her hand shook as she reached up and touched her mouth, now swollen and red from his attentions. Those eyes darkened to a colour resembling twilight, just before night fell.

That wasn't supposed to happen.

Not just the kiss, but everything it had provoked inside him. He wasn't supposed to want to drag her back into his arms and sample her addictive taste again. He surely wasn't supposed to be thinking that he'd kill any other man who dared to place a kiss on those lips.

And certainly he wasn't supposed to be thinking that maybe being married to Lilas wouldn't be so terrible after all…

'Well…' She swallowed audibly.

Bastien wondered if she was having the same thoughts as he.

Pretending to be engaged had just got a lot more complicated.

Chapter Five

Lilas glanced once more at the ormolu clock on the wall. 'Half past six,' she murmured to herself. In half an hour, or thereabouts, Bastien would arrive to take her on their next outing. They'd been invited to the theatre to see a violin concerto performed by the popular mixed-blood violinist Joseph Bologne, Chevalier de Saint-Georges.

Though she was pleased for this opportunity to see another person like herself being favoured by the Queen's patronage, Lilas found herself unable to focus on the superb evening planned for her. She clasped and unclasped her hands several times, trying to still the jerkiness of her limbs. Her eyes fastened on the scrollwork surrounding the clock face. It depicted Ares, the god of war, slaying some contorted, foul-faced foe with his spear.

In the wild imaginations of her mind, instead of the god of war slaying his adversaries she saw Bastien. He wasn't destroying enemy hordes but herself, with his most effective weapon.

His kiss.

Lilas sighed and whirled around until she faced the large bay windows overlooking the grounds. If she hadn't kissed Bastien in the Jardin des Tuileries, maybe she wouldn't be feeling like this.

But could she forget that moment when he'd held her in his arms? When her ignorance of passion had shattered into a million broken pieces?

It would be easier trying to paint with her eyes closed.

When she had suggested he kiss her as a friend, she'd expected it to be a chaste meshing of lips. Perhaps a quick peck. Then he'd pressed his lips to hers.

Her eyes closed in joyful but horrible remembrance.

For the first time in her life she'd felt the desire for a man's total possession. She'd *wanted* to feel more of his lips upon her.

The memory still made her stomach quiver in response. It had been oh-so-brief, but within those few stolen moments she'd witnessed Bastien's mastery of her senses. And her own appalling but inevitable surrender.

Why had she been so forward with him? She must have stepped into a pit of madness.

No, that wasn't why she had done it.

It had been because deep down inside her she'd known she could trust Bastien with her first kiss. She'd told him it was because of their shared childhood, but that was only part of it. She'd always wanted Bastien to be the one to guide her into the wonders of love between a man and a woman. Only him and no one else. That was the reason she'd refused advances from the eager men of society. They weren't Bastien St Clare.

She'd now been granted her wish. And it was more than she'd ever dreamed it would be.

But she'd just made a mess of things by inviting his kiss. And not just that, but enjoying it far, far too much!

Was it that easy for a woman to forget herself, then? All her high-sounding ideas of physical joining and wanting her initiation into the act to be more than the loveless transaction that she'd seen in society now seemed a bit prideful. And things had become increasingly difficult. Now that she'd had a taste of his mouth it was impossible to escape the effects of his virility. Every day that they'd spent together since she'd found herself drawn to him, as if the force of his magnetism charged the room like streaks of lightning.

How could any woman alive feel an aversion to the Duc?

She pursed her lips. If she succumbed to his charm, she'd be tied to him for the rest of her life. She couldn't, *wouldn't* let that happen to her. She would not trade one form of servitude for another. This time not to a prestigious and well-respected household but to a single man. A man whom she had once trusted and who had betrayed her.

She finally had her freedom, and no one was going to take that from her.

Especially not Bastien St Clare.

Yet her emotions and wishes teased her resolve, shredding it like mincemeat, until she finally took out her frustrations in the only way she knew how.

By starting a painting of Bastien.

No one—not even Pierre, who tended to view her work with a critical eye—knew of it. This painting wasn't for anyone's eyes but her own.

The idea had come to her in the dark of night, as she'd tossed and turned restlessly in her bed. The thought of portraying her betrothed as Marc Antony had flared in her mind like a shooting star. Instantly she'd left her room and gone to the Salon Jaune, where she'd begun her initial sketches.

While she'd fumed at the injustice of being forced to

continue this subterfuge, at the outpouring of invitations for her presence due to the ever-widening spread of the news of their engagement, and her own mixed feelings about Bastien, an image of him as a Roman legionnaire had flashed in her mind.

Whenever she painted portraits she went with her first instinct. Bastien as a solider of bygone days would show his struggle at being his parents' son and his own person… She knew she had to portray him just like that.

As an artist, she was no stranger to the naked male form, but if she had to wager she'd guess Bastien would surpass all her previous subjects. From a purely aesthetic view, he was ideal. He had a powerful body, with muscular arms and legs that begged for definition on canvas in order to enhance all those physical attributes. Adorned in a Roman legionnaire's garb, he would send more than one feminine heart racing. More than that, Bastien would be a complex, challenging subject to capture on canvas.

But what she had already sketched didn't seem quite right. She could see the image in her mind, but something was missing…

Lilas pressed her hand against the window, feeling the coolness of the glass. She was starting to know more about him with each outing. And it was said an artist painted not just the subject, but the subject's soul. She splayed her hands out and stared down at her petite, dark brown fingers. Within her hands she held the power to capture Bastien's essence.

Sighing, Lilas pulled her gaze away from the window. Turning around, she almost screamed. 'Soeur Calme!' Her hand splayed against her chest. 'You startled me!'

The nun peeled herself away from the wall. She walked over to Lilas and put a hand on her arm, her grey eyes questioning.

'I'm fine, Soeur Calme. *Merci*.'

Soeur Calme nodded, and stepped away to gaze out of the window.

Lilas waited to see if the nun would break her silence. The pale face remained stoic.

When it seemed as if today would also go by without a word from the woman, Lilas went over to the fireplace and squatted down before it, seeing herself as a child, curled into a ball on the mat in front of the fire in the kitchen of Château de Velay.

So vivid was the memory it was almost a tangible thing. There were times when she almost missed the simplicity of her former life. Still, would she ever wish to go back to the way things were, having now experienced Bastien's kiss?

'Do get out of the ashes, Lilas, for goodness' sake.'

Lilas leapt to her feet and faced her stepmother, framed by the doorway.

Her stepmother's blue eyes drifted down. 'You're filthy.'

Lilas glanced down to see that the hem of her dress had a smudge of ash on it.

'It's only a small spot, Belle-Mère. You can hardly see it.'

The Comtesse de la Baux rolled her eyes and stepped forward, tugging the bell rope near the door. A tight smile creased her stepmother's face. 'That doesn't mean that you are to wallow in the ashes, Lilas. You're no longer a *fille des cendres*. You must always present a proper demeanour, *oui*?'

Lilas sighed. '*Oui*, Belle-Mère.'

Her stepmother's actions had become a bit erratic of late. When Lilas had revealed that, far from breaking the engagement, she and Bastien were going forward with it, her stepmother's mood had shifted.

Though she remained pleasant enough, a new coolness permeated her demeanour whenever she interacted with Lilas. They were much in each other's company, but a distance had always existed between them. Now, a chasm had grown. Lilas didn't know why. Had she offended the woman in some way?

The Comtesse de la Baux's eyes drifted to the silent nun behind her, who had turned and given a deep curtsy of respect. Her blue eyes remained brooding on the bent older woman's figure for long moments before she ordered, 'Leave us.'

The silent woman nodded and glided away, but not before showing deference to Lilas.

'Did she speak to you, Lilas?' her stepmother asked sharply.

'If she had, I suspect the earth would have shattered under our feet at the sound.'

The tension eased away from her stepmother's shoulders.

Esme appeared at the door. *'Madame la Comtesse?'*

'See to your mistress at once.' Her stepmother waved a careless hand in her direction. 'And do be quick. The Duc de Languedoc will arrive soon.'

Esme came forward, her eyes downcast as she knelt on the floor by Lilas's feet to clean the mark from her gown.

'Really, Belle-Mère, this is hardly necessary.'

'I don't want to see a speck,' ordered her stepmother, ignoring Lilas.

'Oui, Madame la Comtesse.'

Esme's eyes lifted to Lilas, and she gave her a reassuring smile before focusing on her task.

While the maid worked, her stepmother went around

the room, picking up items and setting them down again.
'I'm sure Louis would have been pleased to know you
and his dear friend's son are finally formalising your
betrothal.'

'I'm sure,' Lilas agreed, having no wish to reveal the
fact that the engagement was merely a farce.

'Isn't it interesting, however, that the Duc only wants
this now that you're in favour with the Queen?'

Lilas lifted a shoulder. 'It is something I have considered.' No point in lying about that.

'Ah, that's good, Lilas.' Her stepmother glided over to
where she stood. 'It makes his success sure, doesn't it?'

'Success?'

'His plan to use your status to gain favour with the
Crown again.'

Although Lilas knew he wanted this, hearing her stepmother say the words out loud unnerved her. It sounded
as if the only reason they'd agreed to this farce was for
his benefit.

But wasn't that the point? Also so Bastien could find
his ideal woman?

'He isn't using me,' she replied shakily.

'What on earth would you call it?' Her stepmother
laughed. 'Oh, dear... Don't let it bother you. Marriage,
after all, is only a transaction.'

That stung. 'Is it?'

'Surely you know that? He gets his family name re-
stored, a chaste, inexperienced wife in his bed, and a
broodmare to carry his heir.'

'That's not quite true,' she countered, feeling an odd
tremor taking hold of her limbs. 'Bastien...er...the Duc
de Languedoc and I have discussed this, and we will
both benefit from this association.'

'There is a small benefit to you, Lilas. You gain the

title of *duchesse*—an admirable status for a woman once only a maid.'

'I need a highborn lady, not a servant girl.'

Would she ever stop hearing those words? She'd come to terms with the limits of their pretend betrothal. No matter what her stepmother said, in the end, it wouldn't come to fruition. So why were her stepmother's words slicing into her soul with the sharp edge of an invisible knife?

'What is it, Lilas? You look a bit peaked.'

'It's nothing.' Glancing down at Esme, she saw the maid was still cleaning the spot on her hem. Should it really take that long?

'You can tell me what's bothering you, Lilas.'

'I assure you there's nothing the matter.'

Her stepmother gazed at her with intent blue eyes. 'There is. My words have offended you. Oh, dear.' She patted her cheek. 'I didn't mean to do that.' She reached forward and took Lilas's hands into her own. 'I do not say these things to offend or mislead you. I tell them to you because…'

Her voice trailed off and Lilas made a sound at the back of her throat. 'What is it? Why?'

Her stepmother's eyes held hers. 'I do not want you trapped in an unhappy marriage. Like I was.'

Lilas gasped. 'With my father?'

'Louis?' The woman shook her head. 'No! Heavens, we were very happy together. My first marriage—to Pierre's father.'

Her voice softened, but not with gentleness. With fear.

'My life with the Baron wasn't a pleasant one. I neither loved nor trusted him, though I tried my best. If we women must marry the men our parents choose, at the very least, we should respect the men we give our chastity to so we can live a life of harmony together. I never want what I experienced to fall onto your shoulders.'

In the entire time she'd lived with her, Lilas had never heard her stepmother being so open about her life. Even more, it seemed her stepmother wanted to protect her. 'I won't let that happen.'

'How?' A shrewd look suddenly replaced the pleading in her gaze.

Lilas almost told her that the engagement was fake, but stopped herself. It was enough that her stepmother was trying to help her consider all possibilities. Only a woman who cared about her would say something like this. Yet, the coolness between them continued.

'Belle-Mère, I—'

'Let us drop the matter,' her stepmother said in a brisk voice. A strained smile lifted the corners of her mouth. She let go of Lilas's hands and stepped back, leaving a peculiar chill between them. 'I only mentioned it because…'

'Mademoiselle Moreau, the Duc de Languedoc is waiting for you in the drawing room,' a manservant announced from the doorway.

'Please tell him I'll be with him momentarily.'

'It doesn't matter.' Her stepmother turned and ordered Esme to get their wraps. 'Shall we go?'

Two days later, Bastien lunged forward as his blunt épée struck Estienne's, issuing forth a bland, hollow echo around the clearing in the Forêt de Saint-Germain-en-Laye. Early dawn dew still dotted the tall oaks and beech trees while they danced in swift steps on the forest floor as they sparred.

Estienne's voice taunted him. 'Who are you trying to kill? Yourself?'

Bastien snarled and slashed downwards, but Estienne evaded the blunt sword before it made contact with his flesh. Sweat trailed in rivulets down Bastien's face. The warmth from the sunshine baked his skin. His wet shirt clung to his back as he stood there in the clearing.

Estienne and he sparred every morning at his home, but today he'd wanted to be away from the town house and had convinced Estienne to ride with him. Now Estienne stood across from him, breathing as hard as he was, with a quizzical expression on his face.

His grip on the hilt of the épée had a death-like tenacity to it. He could feel the edges of it making grooves along his palm. But he couldn't let go or else he'd fall prey to the whirling emotions within him.

'Are you finished?' he gasped out.

'I am, Bastien.' Estienne shrugged and set down his sword. 'It's not often I best you. Most times we come to a draw.' With a flick of his head, he nodded towards the welts swelling on Bastien's arms. 'You'll be bruised tomorrow.'

Bastien lifted his chin. 'I've time for another bout.'

Estienne shook his head. 'I have plans for the rest of the day, and I will not die by your hand before that happens.'

At Estienne's quip, he felt some of the tension ease away from his shoulders. With a sigh, he let the blunted épée fall to the soft grass a few feet away, and then sat on the still-wet dusty ground.

Estienne gripped his shoulder. 'Bastien, what is it? I've never seen you like this before.'

'I have known Mademoiselle Moreau since she was a child. But do you know, it's only now that I am really beginning to understand her?'

Estienne gave a scowl. 'I thought you said you and

she were going through with the betrothal.' Then a suspicious look entered his eyes. 'You *are* going to wed her, aren't you?'

'I am not.'

'Then you should break off the engagement.' Estienne's voice was heavy with reproach. 'It is not seemly to lead a woman along a path you have no intention of walking down with her.'

'It is something we have both agreed to.' Swiftly he told Estienne what he and Lilas had decided to do.

'I can understand you wanting to find your place in society again,' his cousin said. '*Sacré bleu!* Even my father would probably cease in his hatred of you should you be able to obtain such favour for our family once more.'

'One can only hope,' he muttered sarcastically.

'But really, Bastien. Why not go ahead with the marriage?'

Bastien pursed his lips. 'If I do, then my father will have won.'

'Won?'

He pulled away from his cousin. 'The only reason my father and the Comte de la Baux penned that marital contract was to keep me under my father's thumb.'

'I thought you said it was because they wanted to keep their families together.'

'I don't doubt that was part of the reason, Estienne. But he never wanted me to live my own life. Why do you think I left?'

'But he's gone now, Bastien. He can't dictate to you any longer.'

For Estienne, the answer would seem so simple. Bastien's father was dead, therefore there was no longer any reason to feel such a need to fight against his shadow.

Bastien rubbed his temple. His cousin couldn't see

that he wasn't just fighting his father, but himself as well. Ever since he'd kissed Lilas in the gardens he'd been plagued by a heightened awareness of her. Whenever he saw her, something hitched in his chest.

They were only pretending to be betrothed. He had to remember that. He must remember that!

Seeing the quizzical stare in his cousin's eye, he lifted a shoulder as he used a handkerchief to wipe the sweat from his brow. 'Can't he? Guerline's loyalty was such that she obeyed my father even after his death.'

Estienne frowned at him for a long moment. 'Tell me, Bastien. If you were to marry Mademoiselle Moreau, what would be the harm?'

Bastien balled the handkerchief in his hand. 'The truth?'

Estienne nodded.

'There wouldn't be any harm. I enjoyed her company as a child. Now, as a woman, she further intrigues me. That is all.'

He didn't tell Estienne any more. Such as the fact that her kiss had brought his dormant body to life. That after his father's death, and even before then, he'd experienced little desire for the bliss of female companionship. And yet for the past few nights Lilas had entered his dreams.

Her inexperience notwithstanding, Bastien knew he'd never have a cold marriage bed if he married Lilas. The fire within her violet eyes had leapt out to ensnare him. Visions of her Armagnac-hued body tangled in white silken sheets had followed him while he slept. Her thick hair loose and spread out on his pillow. Those violet eyes dark with desire, their depths igniting like flame. The way he'd make her cry out, the sighs and moans he'd capture with his mouth, the scratches her nails would inflict upon his back—

'Bastien?'

He jerked out of his thoughts and tugged at the loose collar of his shirt. 'I believe she would be a delightful companion in life.'

'Then why not make her yours? In the past four years you've not met a woman who comes close to invigorating you like Mademoiselle Moreau does, have you?'

Grudgingly, he shook his head.

'Then why not marry her? You'd have an advantage. You'd at least like your wife.'

That was what he was afraid of. Lilas was an easy woman to like, and such a thing could easily lead to the dangers of a deeper emotional connection—one he didn't even want to contemplate.

He pulled strands of grass from the earth, biting one. Estienne's words brought to mind something his father had said many years ago. That he and Carmen had also been friends. Hadn't Lilas used that same argument when she'd asked him to kiss her?

He found himself comparing Lilas to his mother and seeing similarities he wished weren't there. Perhaps it was in her upbringing, because her prior life as a servant made her so different. Now, among the elite, as they went from one function to another, she drew people to her with her unaffected personality. Though she maintained the calm façade of a lady, everyone sensed her genuineness. Where most people were content to keep to superficial trivialities, she wasn't.

Sometimes they argued vigorously about a subject, and he'd never felt so stimulated. She challenged him when she disagreed with him, and gracefully conceded when he made a point she couldn't refute.

He remembered seeing that same camaraderie in his parents.

It frightened him.

His father had loved his wife to the exclusion of all else. She had been everything to the man, and when she'd died his world had never again righted itself.

What if he did marry Lilas? What if he fell in love with her? Would he have the same reaction to her loss as his father had?

His ideal woman wouldn't affect his heart at all. She'd be a part of his life, of course. And over time they would grow to respect each other.

But Lilas would never settle for just a man's respect, he realised with some shock. She'd want his whole heart, because she would give him hers in return.

'What do you have to lose, Bastien?'

Without answering his cousin, he got up and dusted the seat of his breeches. 'Let's go. I have to visit my solicitor today.'

As they walked back to the carriage, Estienne's question gripped him. What did he have to gain if he went through with marriage to a woman who was rapidly becoming a constant presence in his mind? And what did he have to lose?

Everything, a bleak voice whispered. *Simply everything.*

The streets of Rue St Denis swelled with people from all stations of life. Peddlers touting their wares in loud, screeching voices to obtain a customer. Craftsmen and skill-smiths pounding or hammering at the towering buildings being constructed along the street. Merchants, shopkeepers, artisans, doctors and others of the *bourgeois* class wound their way up and down the street, searching for their next client or customer.

The sway of the carriage lulled Bastien. He wished he

were going to the de la Baux residence, but Lilas had a prior engagement to attend and they weren't engaged to meet until later this week. He wished he knew where she was. That way, he could see her and maybe talk to her.

He'd finished his business with his solicitor. Then, feeling restless for some reason, he'd given instruction for his man to drive around for a while.

As the curtains fluttered in the passing wind, he saw the Seine like a long thread, cutting through the city. When they turned down the prestigious street of Faubourg Rue Saint-Honoré their journey slowed down, as many carriages blocked their passage down the street. Glancing outside, he saw they had neared the famous shop Le Grand Mogol, owned by the woman who dressed the Queen herself: the Minister of Fashion, Mademoiselle Rose Bertin.

Anyone who was someone frequented her shop, to see the latest in fashion. The Queen's wardrobe boasted the most expensive gowns and extravagant hairstyles. In fact, a sort of fashion journal had come about in order for others to keep up with what the Queen wore.

Bastien sighed. Why had his man come this way? They could possibly be here for hours! Groaning, and about to direct his driver to turn down an alley, he spotted the de la Baux carriage.

His heart quickened. Was Lilas here?

Calling out to his man, he had the carriage stopped and flung open the door without any assistance. He hurried towards the boutique in hopes of seeing Lilas again.

'*Mademoiselle*, you look exquisite in my gown, *n'est-ce-pas*?'

Lilas nodded as she turned and surveyed herself in the long, ornate golden mirror. Mademoiselle Bertin had outdone herself in creating this gown. A brilliant golden colour that shimmered in the light, it highlighted the dark hue of her skin. It was shaped along the waist with a swathe of cream-coloured ribbons, the contrast adding an almost otherworldly look to her appearance.

She had ordered the gown some time ago. But Mademoiselle Bertin's schedule seemed to have opened up for her within the last few weeks and she had come for a final fitting.

'You are *magnifique*, Mademoiselle Bertin.'

The dressmaker gave a haughty sniff, but her light-coloured eyes gleamed as they looked over the gown. 'It is indeed a work of art itself, Mademoiselle Moreau. Very fitting for one who has been given patronage by Sa Majesté, Madame la Reine.'

Lilas felt as if she could rival the Queen herself.

Her cheeks burned at the traitorous thought. No, she could never do that. Although Mademoiselle Bertin had created a lovely gown for her, the woman would never give her best to anyone but the Queen.

What would Bastien think if he ever saw her in this gown?

It shouldn't matter what he thinks.

But it did. She wanted him to see her—really *see* her.

Several more invitations had arrived that morning. Almost greedily she'd taken them from Esme, wanting to accept all of them just so she could spend more time with him.

She'd gone mad. Truly mad.

'Are you displeased, *mademoiselle*?'

Only with myself.

She smiled, seeking to ease the concerned gaze of Mademoiselle Bertin. '*Non*, not at all. This gown is most beautiful.'

'*Bien, bien.* I shall have it delivered to you.'

With help from Esme and the shop assistant, the dress was carefully lifted from her person.

Dressed back in her own clothes, she made her way to the front of the boutique and allowed the young man who worked there to escort her to the carriage. He opened the door, and as he moved to assist her into the cab she heard her name.

'Mademoiselle Moreau.'

She felt Bastien's presence long before she saw him. He possessed an air about him that splintered in all directions. Her eyes searched the thick crowds on the street until her gaze landed on the shoulders of the Duc as he towered above all others and walked towards her in long strides that ate up the distance between them in but a few steps. People moved out his way even before he came upon them. He held so much command…

And what a figure he made! Tall, in a dark brown coat that stretched over his broad shoulders, he wore an old-fashioned tricorn hat that would have looked ridiculous on anyone else. Upon Bastien it sat atop his head and merely added to his magnetism.

As he neared her heart beat a feverish tattoo against her ribcage.

Then someone slammed into her from behind.

'Oh!'

She tried to keep her balance, but her arms flailed about before she fell to the ground. Before she could get her bearings, someone was yanking at her reticule. A robbery!

'Stop! Stop! Help me!' she cried out.

Her voice fell on deaf ears. There was so much noise on the street that her screams were drowned out. Even those who were close by were occupied with their own pursuits.

Lilas called out, 'Bastien! Bastien!'

Would he come to her rescue? Oh, how she needed him! But what if he hadn't seen her fall down? What if he couldn't get through the crowd?

Then you'll have to protect yourself, a grim voice in her mind told her.

Resolve hardened her face. A memory of one of the children from the orphanage trying to steal her meagre plate of food entered her mind. She'd fought off the girl with everything she had. She'd done it before; she'd do it again.

Lilas yanked hard on the strap of her reticule, sending whoever it was to the ground with her.

The assailant wore a mask with tiny slits that surely no one could see through. She had a brief impression of dark, cold eyes before she got more angry. How dared a vagabond try to steal from her?

She balled her fist and slammed it into the man's face. A shocked cry erupted from him and his grip on the strap slackened.

Around her, people seemed finally to realise there was some sort of altercation happening. People started to peer, trying to see what the commotion was.

The masked man rolled away, trying to get hold of her reticule once more. She fought against him, using every ounce of strength she had. Then she saw his hand move and a glint of metal flashed in the sunlight.

A knife!

The heat of anger drained away while a cold terror clasped her heart. He had a knife! Was he trying to kill her?

'Bastien! Bastien!'

Another commotion sounded behind her. She could hear the cries of people, but she didn't know what was happening. Suddenly Bastien appeared, tossing people aside as if they were nothing more than dolls. He launched himself at the attacker. They rolled on the ground, each trying to find purchase against the other.

Weakly, Lilas came to her feet, her heart slamming in her chest.

Back and forth the men went. Although Bastien had the greater size and strength, the attacker was nimbler. Hurriedly, she looked around on the ground. She had to help!

There! A fist-sized stone on the corner.

Swiftly she grabbed it and ran to where the men fought. She lifted it above her head, ready to strike the masked man, when he suddenly broke free of Bastien's hold.

'Stop that man!' she screamed.

The assailant shoved away the people who tried to block him, and before she knew it he'd disappeared.

Tossing the stone back onto the ground, she went over to help Bastien as he jumped to his feet. Though mussed and dusty from the fight, he looked none the worse for wear.

If anything, he looked murderously angry.

He grabbed her by the shoulders, one of his large hands lifting to caress her face. 'Lilas…Lilas, are you all right?'

She shook with reaction to what had happened. 'I'm all right. He tried to steal my reticule, but I wouldn't let him.'

'You little idiot!'

He shook her gently and then grabbed her close. She felt his lips touch her hair.

Before she could do anything about it, Bastien had lifted her into his arms, heavy dress and all.

'Bastien, please…put me down. People are staring at us.'

'Is that something new?' he asked.

She glanced up at his face, seeing a muscle leaping in his jaw. He emanated a palpable rage. Was it directed at her?

As he carried her through the crowd, and as the event began to play in her mind, she felt so foolish. Why had she risked her life over a reticule? If the man had stolen her reticule, so be it. She wasn't penniless.

Shame beat down on her like rain. No wonder Bastien was so furious with her.

'Where are you taking me?' she asked.

'Home.'

'But what about Esme?'

'Lilas, be quiet.'

His voice brooked no argument. She pressed her lips together and didn't say a word.

They came to his carriage. With Bastien's curt nod at the driver, the man scrambled down from the upper seat and opened the door. Bastien placed her inside with inordinate care and then walked away.

She wanted to call out to him, but shame kept her quiet. He was going to berate her for her foolishness, and she deserved it.

A short while later, the door to his carriage opened again, and Bastien came inside. He sat across from her. His golden eyes were hard like amber. The tension radiating from him scorched her soul. He said nothing, letting her sit and squirm under his gaze as if she were a child awaiting punishment.

She felt like one.

Swallowing, she said, 'Bastien, I—'

He grabbed her and pulled her forward into his arms. Without any warning, his lips devoured hers.

This was nothing like the kiss she'd shared with him in the gardens. His mouth moved over hers, deep and drugging, hard and gentle, punishing and soothing. She had nothing to hold on to but his coat, and her fingers knotted in the material. Flames engulfed her body as Bastien deepened his possession of her mouth.

Hoarsely he pleaded, 'Open your mouth, Lilas?'

She did as he asked—after all it was what she wanted as well—and his tongue delved inside. He licked at her softness, sipping at her. She tried to moan, to give some expression of her feelings, but he wouldn't let her.

Not that she cared.

She was drowning…drowning in a well of liquid fire.

At last Bastien ripped his lips away and rested his forehead on hers. Lilas felt boneless, as if he'd taken all the vitality from her body. If he let her go right now, she thought she'd fall into a heap of languid flesh on the carriage floor.

As it was, his arms tightened around her, and he buried his face in her mussed hair. The warmth of his breath tickled the shell of her ear as he spoke.

'I was so worried,' he gasped. 'I saw you fall to the ground, and I couldn't get to you soon enough.'

'I didn't know if you had seen me or heard me call out,' she whispered.

He pulled his head back and stared down at her. Taking his thumb, he pressed it against her sensitive mouth. 'Whoever he was, he is fortunate that nothing happened to you.'

'Is he?'

Bastien gave a slow nod, his eyes fixed on his thumb

as he massaged her lips in a way that made those feelings start to course through her again.

'Had he hurt you…' His voice trailed off.

With an effortless strength, he lifted her up and kissed her once more. This was different again, having none of the volatility of the first kiss. His mouth roved over hers in a slow, languorous way, as if he had all the time in the world to explore. She clung to him, not knowing how respond, only trusting him to take her where he wanted her to go.

He nibbled on her bottom lip, his teeth gentle, before moving from her mouth to the pulse pounding at the base of her neck. He pressed kisses to her collarbone, and she gasped when his tongue darted out and lapped at her skin.

She shuddered. 'Bastien…' she breathed.

'Do you like that?'

Lilas had no idea if she answered or not. Her body was racked with new feelings, and when he kissed her again her fingers clutched his head to hers.

When he pulled his lips away from hers, she moaned in protest.

'We have to leave. I must get you back home,' he told her.

'Bastien…'

Golden eyes flaring, he tweaked her nose and set her away from himself. 'Come on. I have sent your maid back home, and I know your stepmother and Monsieur le Baron will be waiting for you.'

Lilas felt as if the world had turned upside down.

Chapter Six

When they arrived back at her residence, Lilas peered out of the window to see her stepmother, Pierre, Esme and the other servants all waiting outside for her. The only one not there was Soeur Calme.

'Lilas, are you all right?' Pierre was the first to arrive at the door of the carriage as it opened. He glared up at Bastien. 'What the devil happened, Languedoc?'

'Less than what might have, Monsieur le Baron. And well you should remember that,' Bastien said in a gruff voice.

A look of silent communication passed between the two men. Lilas held her breath. A bit of her stepbrother's bluster went out of him and he pinched the bridge of his nose where his spectacles rested. *'Oui.'*

'*Mademoiselle*, I was so worried about you,' Esme added, her eyes bloodshot from crying.

'Now, back away, everyone. Let Lilas come out first,' the Comtesse de la Baux ordered, with a quick clap of her hands.

But Bastien alighted from the carriage first. He extended his hand, and Lilas took it as he helped her down.

Then, without saying a word to anyone, he lifted her in his arms.

'You can put me down, Bastien…er…Monsieur le Duc.' Though she had no doubt of Bastien's strength, she knew she was heavy with all the garments she wore.

'Lead the way, Madame la Comtesse,' he said, ignoring her.

The whole entourage followed him as they travelled up the path and into the house. He didn't let her go until they reached a small sitting room, made cosy and warm by a fire.

He set her down on a chaise, barely winded.

'Merci,' she said, with a dip of her head.

Esme flittered around her, anxious to ease her in any way she could. Lilas smiled. When she'd first entered society she'd tried her best to not utilise the services of a maid. Now she was glad for the comfort of her.

Pierre came and knelt before her, gripping her hands with his own. 'Lilas, what happened? Esme came running into the house, screaming that you'd been stabbed.'

Bastien walked over to the other side of the room, standing before the fire. She fixed her eyes on him while she spoke, as if she'd gain strength from his mere presence.

'Why would anyone want to hurt you, *mademoiselle*?' Esme asked, when she'd finished her tale.

'That is something I would very much like to know the answer to,' Bastien said from across the room.

Pierre looked furious, but there was more to his expression than that. Though the fire from the hearth was reflected in the glass of his spectacles, which somewhat obscured his gaze, she sensed that he was coming to some sort of conclusion.

Before she could question her stepbrother about this,

she heard the dulcet tones of her stepmother taking charge.

'Monsieur le Duc, I cannot thank you enough for coming to Lilas's rescue.' The Comtesse glided over to where he stood. 'I can't bear to think about what would have happened if you hadn't...'

'Let us be thankful that we do not have to think about it.' He came to where Lilas sat and looked down at her. As he did so, everyone disappeared from the room save themselves.

He crouched down, nearly at eye level with her. 'Are you sure you're all right, Mademoiselle Moreau?'

Was he talking about the attack, or about what had happened afterwards?

'I am, I assure you.'

His gaze roved over her face once more before he stood again. 'Very well.'

Despite the Comtesse's insistence that he stay, Bastien declined and left the residence.

For the rest of the evening, Lilas was cosseted almost to the point of suffocation. A bath was drawn in her chambers and Esme hovered about like a mother bird. Her stepmother wished to hear the story again, and it was late before Lilas had a chance to reflect on the happenings of the day.

Whenever she thought about the glint of the knife in her assailant's hands, she shivered. He might have stabbed her, and then where would she be? It was a miracle that Bastien hadn't been hurt. Who knew her day would end like this?

She turned in bed. Bastien had come to her rescue, and although the attacker had got away she wondered if that had been God's way of protecting the man from Bastien's retaliation! It was the first time she'd ever seen his strength displayed thus. He'd been magnificent.

And his kiss—!

Hours had passed and her lips still pulsed from his possession of them. He'd overtaken her—but she'd wanted that. What had she ever known of men and women except what she'd learned to capture in her art?

But now she knew what it was like to surrender to a man's mastery, to be utterly played like the strings of an instrument.

She closed her eyes and relived those wonderful moments in his arms.

A woman could be forgiven for submitting to that.

Submitting?

Her eyes opened. No, she couldn't allow submission. They were caught up in an attachment not of their own making. Bastien had no intention of making her his wife because she didn't fit his ideal. She had no intention of losing herself to him.

Sweet kisses or not, his rescue of her or not, she had to remain firm.

Lilas shuddered as a deep ache inside her heart pulsed.

A tiny voice in her head whispered a dream: What if he did care for her? Wouldn't his actions today have been even more amplified?

But she wasn't good enough for Bastien. And forcefully she told herself she didn't need to be. So long as she remembered this life was hers and hers alone, Bastien's feelings on her worthiness had no bearing on who she was.

She must remember that.

His kisses might overwhelm her, and his honour in protecting her might inspire her, but she mustn't forget that she would never be his choice of bride, and that as soon as possible they would break this engagement and go their separate ways.

Something wet trailed down her cheek. Confused, she put her finger to her face and drew it back to see a bead of moisture in the moonlight.

'Lilas?'

She jerked up in her bed, seeing her stepmother in the doorway. Dressed for bed herself, the woman came into the room.

'I did not mean to frighten you, Lilas. I just wanted to see how you were before I went to bed.'

'I am fine.'

The bed dipped as her stepmother sat next to her. 'I must admit, Lilas, I was quite upset and perturbed by what happened today. And, to be frank, I find something about the incident not...*right*.'

'Of course it wasn't right. I was attacked.'

Her body still quaked in reaction to the incident that now flashed through her mind, but she only had to think of Bastien for the nerves to dissipate.

He'd come to her rescue.

'That is true. But there's something else that bothers me.'

'Oh? What is it?'

Instead of speaking, the woman rose and went over to the doors before the balcony. A cloud chose that moment to shroud the moon, casting her stepmother's form in darkness. And in that accompanying darkness, shielding her from her sight, she heard her stepmother speak as if she were a disembodied entity.

'Don't you find it curious that the Duc de Languedoc was there to rescue you?'

Lilas shook her head. 'I don't. I was most thankful for his help.'

'I am grateful for that, too. But think of this, Lilas. He was there just in time to save you. Did you know he would be travelling those streets today?'

'Non...' Lilas said slowly.

'It all seems rather too…convenient, don't you think? The circumstances were too well-orchestrated, perhaps even staged?'

Pushing the covers off, Lilas stood from the bed and padded over to her stepmother. The moonlight pierced through cracks in the clouds, laying slices of light on the pale face that now took on an almost ghostly hue.

'Are you saying that you think the Duc de Languedoc planned this attack on me?'

'What else could it be?'

She thought about his passionate reaction to her escape, the way his lips had crushed her and soothed her at the same time. Those weren't the actions of a man who had tried to hurt her.

Were they?

'Why would he want to do that?' she asked.

'Do you know why men go to war, Lilas? It's not for love of King and country. It's for the glory. What man can resist accolades for his bravery, his prowess in dire circumstances?'

Lilas frowned. 'You're saying the Duc de Languedoc planned this attack for recognition?'

'My first husband thrived on attention,' said the Comtesse in an undertone. 'If the Baron entered the room and your attention wasn't instantly riveted to him he sulked for days. He was very much a boy.'

Her stepmother squeezed her hand and smiled in a gentle way.

'Think on it, Lilas. Before the week is out, news of this incident will have spread in the same manner as news of your betrothal did. People will talk about it, and the flames of gossip will continue to be fanned. He wants the Crown's favour. What better way than to ensure you and he remain on the tongues of the gossips?'

Her stepmother's logic made it hard for her to naysay her words as being fanciful. She didn't want to believe it, but that was proving difficult. Hadn't Bastien come at just the right moment to save her? And had he really been unable to fight off the assailant? Or had he simply let him go?

What to believe?

A wave of dizziness came over her and she swayed.

'Come now, Lilas. I've given you enough to consider, and you're still recovering from such a horrid day.'

Her stepmother wrapped her arms around her and led her back to the bed, where she tucked her in almost like a child. She even planted a cool kiss on Lilas's hot forehead and then walked away, shutting the door behind her.

Bastien's carriage plodded down the street under the darkened canopy of twilight.

After he'd left Lilas, he'd gone back to where the events had happened to see if he could question anyone. His questions had come back without answers. There wasn't much he could report to any authority.

Bastien seethed all the way home. Someone had tried to hurt Lilas. Why?

There had been plenty of other people in the crowded street who would have been perfect for a pickpocket's endeavour. But whoever it was he'd fought with, he'd singled out Lilas.

He brooded over it as the scenery passed by, but he might as well have been blind for all the attention he gave it.

His heart had plummeted to the ground when he'd seen Lilas being attacked. Without a care in the world he'd shoved people aside, trying his best to get to her as fast as possible.

Why? Why would someone attack her?

The question accompanied him all the way home.

When he went into his study he sat at the desk. The fear on Lilas's face had enraged him. Her eyes had been white and stark against her skin. She'd been trembling despite the fact she'd taken the assailant on.

The knife bothered him the most. Why would a pickpocket not use a knife simply to sever the strap of the reticule and make a clean escape?

Something about the incident didn't make sense.

Bastien rubbed his knee. It smarted from its contact with the assailant as they'd fought on the ground. Had he had his rapier, he could have done considerable damage to the man, and all his questions would have been answered.

Was that knife truly meant for Lilas?

The thought squeezed his heart with a cruel grip, nearly siphoning his breath.

It could never happen.

Bastien pushed away from the desk and walked over to a shelf of books.

His anger at her recklessness had been so great that the only thing he'd been able to do with all that pent-up energy was kiss her. He'd barely restrained himself, as relief and something more had surged through him. Her generous response and that desperate clinging had only fuelled his ardour.

If anything had happened to her…

Bastien swore and dug his fingers into his hair, scraping at his scalp.

The strength of his emotions surprised him. But surely he would have felt this way if any young woman had been attacked, wouldn't he?

Damn it, why didn't he have a ready answer to that? Or maybe he did have an answer and didn't want to articulate it. Things were getting beyond complicated.

Those kisses he'd shared with Lilas shouldn't have happened.

And yet they had.

The attack should have never happened.

But it had.

What did it all mean?

For the first time in a long while he wished his father were here. He'd have gone to him to see if the man could make sense of it.

A wave of sorrow cascaded over his senses. His father had always seemed to have the answer to everything—even Bastien's own direction in life. He'd resented that for so long. But now he wished he still had his father's confidence.

Or at the very least his counsel.

Her stepmother forbade Lilas to depart from her bedchamber the next day. Although Lilas told her she was quite recovered from the incident, the Comtesse refused to heed her wishes.

Esme—sweet Esme—catered to her every whim, and even some she didn't have.

'*Mademoiselle*, your bath is ready.'

She came back into the room from the balcony and undressed, and Esme helped her into the copper tub, the hot water fragrant with the scent of lavender and adorned with lilac petals. Closing her eyes, she leaned against the back of it and enjoyed the warmth, and the stinging sensation against her skin.

Esme washed her long, thick hair. Setting it on the side of the bath and then wrapping it in a towel, the maid went on to help her wash and then rinsed her.

Lilas put everything out of her mind as she submitted to Esme's gentle ministrations, then sat before the fire drying her hair. When it was time to dress, she sat at her dressing table. Glancing down, she saw a folded piece of paper.

'Esme, do you know who brought this to me?'

The maid looked over her shoulder. '*Non, mademoiselle*. I have not seen it till just this minute.'

Foreboding crept along Lilas's spine as she took the paper and opened it.

Faire attention.

A skitter went down her spine. *Beware.* Beware of what?

Looking at the handwriting, she didn't recognise whose it was.

'Esme, did anyone come in here while I was out on the balcony?'

The maid shook her head. '*Non, mademoiselle.*'

'Then how did this letter get here? Did you write it?'

Esme's eyes widened like saucers. 'I can't write, *mademoiselle.*'

'What about the other young girl who was with you?'

When the maid denied her literacy as well, Lilas frowned. How could someone have come up to her room without anyone noticing…?

What to do? Should she bring this to the attention of

her stepmother and stepbrother? But what would she say to them?

'*Mademoiselle?* Do you want me to finish dressing your hair?'

Lilas jumped at the sound of Esme's voice. She took in a deep breath and calmed her frantically beating heart. She'd been attacked yesterday, but she refused to let fear rule her life. If someone were trying to scare her, they would have to try harder.

'*Oui*, Esme.' Her violet eyes sparkled like gems of amethyst as she stared at her reflection. With each word she spoke, the flames of fury licked at her insides. 'Please. Finish. Dressing. My hair.'

News of the attack on Lilas, as well as Bastien's defence of her, rocked through Paris. Far from decreasing the interest in their engagement, it only fuelled it. For the past few days Bastien had been beset by visitors seeking to know the story first-hand, as well as bemoaning the state of criminal activity in the country.

Once the fervour died down somewhat, he ventured out to visit Lilas. Following a servant down the corridor to the Salon Jaune, as the man called it, he admitted to himself that he should have come sooner.

Her well-being had taken top priority in his thoughts. Had she sufficiently recovered? Did she have nightmares? Would she still be able to go before the Queen?

That last part didn't seem as important as the others. Frankly, if he could have postponed their appearance, he would have.

As they came closer to the room where Lilas was, the sound of tinkling laughter met his ears. Bastien paused in his stride, transfixed by the merry sound. He could stand and listen to her all day. Then a man's deeper laugh melded with her own. Like splintered glass, the spell was broken and he frowned.

He gestured to the servant to keep moving. As they drew closer to the door of the Salon Jaune, the laughter grew heartier. The man's voice grated on his ears. Dark thoughts rushed through his brain.

Why had he spent most of his time worrying about her, keeping his distance, only for her to attend to some… some…intruder? Had she any idea of the worry for her that had beset him? It had taken all his willpower not to take her entire household to Château de Velay, far away from the possibility of another attack.

The more he thought about who the devil was in there with her, the harder his feet stomped on the floor. He was barely cognizant of the rattle of various ornaments and curios on top of pieces of furniture as he passed.

Lilas gave another loud burst of laughter just as he came to the door, and his hands balled into fists.

'Who is in the Salon Jaune with Mademoiselle Moreau?' he demanded of the servant escorting him.

'It is Monsieur—'

When he heard 'Monsieur' he snapped.

'How long has he been here? Is this a social call? What are they talking about?' he railed.

The door to the Salon Jaune opened, and Lilas peered out. Dressed in the plain gown she wore for painting, she widened her violet eyes at him.

'*Monsieur le Duc?* Is it you making all that noise? Whatever is the matter?'

'Who is in there with you?' He wasted no time on pleasantries, seething behind his teeth.

'In here with me?'

'I know there's a man in there. Who is it?'

Lilas blinked for a moment. Then crinkles appeared

at the corners of her eyes and she pushed open the door further.

A manservant carrying a tray stood there. 'You may go now,' she said to the servant, although she fixed her eyes on Bastien.

The servant bowed, and with the briefest flicker of a glance at Bastien he left.

Bastien's face heated as he met Lilas's amused gaze.

'Whatever did you think we were doing?' she asked.

'I don't know,' he said stiffly. 'I heard you both laughing...you seem very friendly for mistress and servant.'

Another light laugh escaped her mouth. 'Perhaps you have forgotten my humble beginnings, *monsieur*, but I never have. Although Madame la Comtesse frowns upon my interest in the staff, I was chatting with Monsieur Laurent about his daughter. She has just begun to walk and he was sharing some amusing stories about her with me.'

If a hole had opened before him on the floor, Bastien would happily have stepped in it. Even more worrisome was the fact that he'd experienced his first real taste of jealousy. He'd never had such a connection with a woman before. Besides brief liaisons, nothing more than an assuaging of physical need had ever been necessary.

But this...? This possessiveness taking him by storm... This latent fear for her safety... That wasn't what he wanted to feel.

Only a few days left. After we meet with the Queen, then you can break the engagement and go back to your life.

'What are you doing here, *monsieur*?' she asked.

He cleared his throat. 'I wanted to see your well-being myself. Are you recovered sufficiently from your ordeal?'

Lilas groaned. 'More than that... I've been over-whelmed with so many others asking the very same thing I am tempted to write a column for the paper myself!'

He grinned. 'As bad as that?'

She lifted her hand and rubbed at her brow. 'Were you concerned that I would not be able to accompany you to see the Queen? I assure you, only death would prevent that.'

'I see.'

Bastien's gaze lingered on her hand. The sight of her paint-stained fingers sent a curious sensation down the middle of his back. What would it feel like to be clasped by those rainbow hands?

It was an evocative, mysterious thought.

'Is there anything else you want, *monsieur*?'

His back straightened. Was she trying to dismiss him? Well, that certainly wouldn't do.

Bastien ignored the voice that told him he had only planned to check on her well-being and then leave, keeping his exposure to this woman to the minimum. He nodded towards the easel behind her. 'What are you working on?'

A look of fright crossed her face. Spinning around, she darted over to the easel and fiddled with the canvas sheet she'd draped upon it. When relief slackened her features, his curiosity grew. What could she be hiding under the sheet?

'A piece that I wish to keep private,' she said as she glided back to him.

'*Bien, bien...* Then you have time to accompany me for an outing.'

Lilas blinked. 'An outing? I wasn't aware we had an engagement today.'

He gave a nonchalant shrug. 'Not officially.'

'Then why—?'

'I wish to have your company to myself today,' he answered softly, tossing all caution and thoughts of self-preservation to the wind.

Her lovely mouth parted and her sweet-smelling hot chocolate breath blew across his face. 'But why?'

'After the harrowing experience you had, I feel a certain sense of duty to look after you. Although we have no intention of seeing this engagement through, it would be strange if we were not seen together in public. The gossips do talk, you know. The last I heard, I'd come barrelling through the crowds to your rescue on a white horse.'

He expected her to laugh with him, but her eyes held uncertainty and wariness. It reminded him of that time in the *potager* four years ago, when distrust had first reared its ugly head between them.

Bastien bit back a groan. What could he have said for her to be gazing up into his face in that fashion? He didn't want her to say no. He needed her. He desired the anchored, homely feeling he wished he didn't need as he needed his next breath.

And it was in a breathless way that he asked, 'So, will you come?'

Lilas knew she should decline Bastien's invitation. Her stepmother's suspicions were starting to embed themselves in her mind. If he didn't want to go through with this engagement, then why did he want to go out in public with her again? Shouldn't it be the opposite?

She opened her mouth to tell him no, but was arrested by the look in his golden eyes. He'd never looked at her quite that way before. Earnest and a little vulnerable. Like a boy waiting for a treat.

In that instant she knew her stepmother was wrong.

Bastien wasn't spending time with her for what he could get from her. Not because of the engagement. Not because of public scrutiny.

But because he wanted her company.

A brisk wind blew as they walked across Pont Neuf. Others were doing the same, enjoying the activity and the weather. She'd brought Esme with her once more, and once again Bastien charmed her maid, making her eyes go wide with an almost child-like adoration. And Esme didn't pretend she was wanted when Bastien's driver stopped the carriage and they alighted.

As Bastien helped Lilas down, her eyes drifted over his physique. Her artist's mind, or perhaps her feminine one, took in the way his fawn-coloured coat rested on his powerful shoulders. He had no need of padding to enhance that muscular build as some other men did. His rather plain white waistcoat showed off the trimness of his hips and a flat stomach no corset needed to enhance.

How fortunate that he hadn't seen the painting she was working on! She had other commissions—more than enough to keep her busy—but her entire focus was on what she'd titled *The General*. She didn't want anyone to know…at least not yet. Not until she could figure out what was missing from the picture.

Her eyes drifted to his mouth. Like unwrapping a gift, she remembered the way his hard body had pressed against her softness. How those full lips had given her tastes of heaven. That masculine, woodsy scent she'd greedily inhaled and wanted to drench herself in.

'Mademoiselle Moreau?'

Bastien's voice jolted her out of her perusal. His knowing smile lifted the corner of his mouth. She expected him to tease her, but he merely asked if she was ready to go.

Pont Neuf—the New Bridge—although declining as a centre of activity which had once beat at the heart of Paris, still boasted a robust, lively air. A place of entertainment and crime, all Parisians were drawn to it. Although the Seine flowed under its arches in a rush of dark brown water, the sights along it kept one's interest away from its smell.

Jugglers tossed items into the air with seamless dexterity. Acrobats performed all sorts of feats for the wide-eyed attention of their spellbound audience. They even found a stall with a man professing that he possessed the ability to turn a group of old women young again for a modest price.

Lilas stood next to Bastien as they lingered and watched the performance of a troupe of musicians. The music was lively and happy, lifting one's spirits. One of the principal players, singing a lovely song about new love, came and sang before them, waggling his painted eyebrows with such exaggeration that she laughed. He planted an exaggerated kiss on her hand and presented her with a lilac bloom.

They wandered on after that. A few unsavoury characters eyed them, but one glance at Bastien's hand resting on the handle of his sword and they sought easier prey elsewhere.

Those brief encounters made her nervous. She swallowed the sudden lump that clogged her throat.

Something must have given away her nervousness, because Bastien glanced down sharply at her. '*Mademoiselle*, what is it?'

'It's nothing, *monsieur.*'

He stopped walking, a stern expression on his face. 'There are no secrets between us.'

A spurt of anger flared inside her. How dared he keep saying that when all they had between them were secrets?

'I beg to differ.'

His lion eyes glowed with indignation. 'Do you?'

She'd opened her mouth to retort when Bastien gripped her arm and drew her to one side of the bridge.

'What are you doing?'

'Lilas, let's pretend.'

She shook her head in confusion. 'We already are.'

'*Non, non.* Let's pretend just for a moment that you and I are not bound by that blasted contract. That the past four years haven't happened. That you are a servant girl in my father's house and I, your friend, am coming to visit you as I always have.'

'What are you saying?' His voice was low. Deep and hypnotic. She couldn't tear her eyes away from the intensity in his—as if he were willing her to heed his command, his wish.

'Pretend that we are back in the *potager* at Château de Velay and you are crying again. I come to you, ready to defend you in whatever way I can. What will you tell me?'

She could almost believe that she was back in that garden. Taking in a shuddering breath and letting it out again, she said, 'Some of those men that we pass...they frighten me.'

His brows drew together in the centre of his forehead. 'Did you recognise any of them? Did any of them look like the man who attacked you?'

She shook her head vigorously. 'It wasn't that. I just became afraid. Monsieur le Duc—'

He placed a finger on her mouth. 'Bastien,' he corrected softly. 'Remember, we are friends.'

The heat and weight of his finger rendered her motionless and breathless. She could barely speak.

'Bastien,' she croaked out, 'what if they had tried to accost you? What would you have done?'

His finger fell from her mouth and he took a step back, shock and some other powerful emotion contorting the planes of his face. 'You are worried about *me*, Lilas?'

'*Oui.*'

Heavy silence cocooned them in their own world, although the bridge still bustled with activity. She could almost believe they had become invisible, with only each other aware of their existence.

'*Merci*, Lilas.' The shock drifted away, replaced by the arrogance that was as much part of him as his nobility. 'But I couldn't possibly tell a *mademoiselle* like you what I would have done. Not for genteel ears as yours.' He stepped closer to her, blocking out the sky. 'I will say this. I have always defended you, Lilas. And I won't let anything happen to you.'

He lifted her gloved hand to his mouth, using his lips to smooth away the material of her glove until the skin of her wrist was exposed. With his eyes still locked on hers, he kissed her hand, and she felt the heat of his kiss clear to the soles of her feet.

That gleam appeared in his lion eyes as he whispered against the back of her wrist. '*Comprenezvous?*'

'*Oui*, I understand.'

The afternoon stretched out and they enjoyed themselves. They laughed, clapped and sang along as they toured the festivities on the bridge. They were often stopped by people who knew them through mutual circles of acquaintance. Bastien stood by her side, a solid tower who neither tried to take over any of the conversations she engaged in nor attempted to silence her.

Several times their eyes met, and her heart fluttered like butterfly wings. Bastien's eyes were golden like the sun, filled with light and warmth. Why couldn't it always be like this? Carefree, without anything hindering their view of the world. Just she and Bastien, enjoying each other's company. Lilas could almost believe the threat of marriage didn't exist. In that moment she was simply an artist enjoying her time with a *duc*.

After laughing at the antics of a mime act, she wondered aloud if they should find their way back to the carriage.

Bastien sighed, the sound drawn out and reluctant. 'You are correct. We should be getting back. As sweet and kind as your maid may be, I doubt she will appreciate us robbing her of her own free time.'

When they arrived back at the carriage, it was to see Esme and Bastien's driver with their heads together, both engrossed in conversation. Esme's pink cheeks rivalled the tulip glow of the setting sun.

'It seems almost a shame to interrupt them,' Lilas mused as Bastien's driver reached out and grabbed the maid's hand.

'Agreed.'

It was Esme who saw them first, and she jumped down from the driver's seat, making excuses which Lilas shushed. At her suggestion, the young woman rode with the driver, whose name she leaned was Jacques, thus giving herself some more time alone with Bastien.

As the carriage swayed, she went over the perfection of the day in her mind. Bastien had proved himself a wonderful companion, reminding her of the boy she'd once known. The boy she'd trusted without question.

Could she do that again? Open her heart to Bastien? Place her faith in him?

His quiet voice cut into her thoughts, low and silky. 'Are you thinking about the Queen's summons, Lilas?'

'*Non*. I was thinking of how perfect a day we've had.'

'So was I,' he said softly, his lion eyes gleaming in the relative darkness of the carriage. 'So was I...'

Chapter Seven

Mademoiselle Bertin's dress flowed around Lilas's figure like a cloud. The gold colour in the candlelight emphasised the combination of her complexion and her slenderness that needed no other enhancement. The tight-fitting sleeves stopped at the elbow and bloomed with dainty ruffles which made her arms appear most delicate and feminine. Her bosom nearly spilled out of the low neckline. She'd pinned a flower in the centre.

Esme had outdone herself as she'd prepared Lilas's hair. Her stepmother had wanted to hire the Queen's own hairdresser for the occasion, but Lilas preferred Esme's styling.

It had taken hours to get ready, but for once Lilas was thankful for the care that had gone into her appearance.

'My belly is in knots,' she said as she pursed her vermilion-stained lips. 'I have never been so nervous in my entire life.'

'Never, *mademoiselle*?' Esme quipped with the ease of a trusted servant. 'Not even when you had the exhibition almost a month ago?'

Was it really possible to have had her life change so drastically in such a short time?

Yes, it is, a voice in her ear reminded her. *You need only to look at your life to know that it's true.*

To think that Her Majesty wished for her and Bastien to meet in her private apartments at the little château her husband, His Majesty the King, had given her when he'd ascended the throne this time last year.

'Do you really suppose she has the walls covered in gold and diamonds?' asked her maid.

Lilas tilted her head as Esme made an adjustment to the two-feet-tall *pouf* balanced on her head. 'That seems a waste,' she scoffed. 'What use are gold and diamonds on a wall?'

Her maid pondered this, and then gave a quick nod. 'It does seem rather silly, *mademoiselle.*'

'There are many rumours about Her Majesty. Everything from the story that she spends the entire coffers of the country on one dress to the fact that she has twelve lovers at one time.'

Esme took a step back, her eyes shining as she looked over her mistress's appearance. Lilas scrutinised her reflection but could see nothing amiss. She was as perfect as she could be.

'Esme, you are truly the most skilled hairdresser in all of Paris.'

The maid blushed prettily under her mob-cap as she curtsied. *'Merci, mademoiselle.'*

The door opened behind her, and her stepmother entered. Her blue eyes assessed Lilas. As she waited for her to say something a wisp of sound caught her ears, and she saw Soeur Calme standing behind her mistress.

Although the nun remained silent, as usual, she managed to show her satisfaction. A smile graced the normally pinched face, giving her an illusion of beauty.

Still her stepmother said nothing. Finally, unable to

stand the silence, Lilas asked, 'Well, Belle-Mère. What do you think?'

When she met her stepmother's blue gaze, she could almost feel the iciness piercing her skin. 'The Duc de Languedoc will be here soon, Lilas.' She shifted her gaze to Esme. 'Go and make ready Mademoiselle Moreau's wrap.'

The maid left to do as ordered.

'Why aren't you saying anything? Will I do before the Queen or not?'

'You look very lovely, Lilas,' the woman said as she stepped further into the room. 'I only hope you don't arouse the Queen's jealousy.'

'You mustn't believe everything you've heard about the Queen, Belle-Mère.'

A shrewd look came into her stepmother's eye. 'You're only saying that because she's given you patronage.'

Lilas glanced once more at her exquisite appearance. Esme really had outdone herself. She would be sure to give her some sort of special recognition and privilege.

'That may be,' she agreed, with a downward bend of her head. 'But I would never bite the hand that feeds me. Especially not the Queen's.'

'I think the Duc will not be able to keep his eyes off you once he sees you.'

She could only hope so!

What would Bastien think when he saw her? She had dressed for him as well as for herself and the Queen.

Esme returned with her wrap, and her stepmother and Soeur Calme left. She held out a long silk cloak lined with white velvet and a muff made of the same.

She exited the room and began her descent. Her feet carefully took one step before the next, as she couldn't see the stairs. Thankfully, she had gone up and down these stairs hundreds of times over the last four years.

When she came to the landing that led to the second level of stairs she saw that Bastien stood there, waiting for her. Adorned in full Court dress, and a new white wig with curls tucked underneath, he wore a powder-blue waistcoat and breeches that hugged his trim frame with an almost womanly caress. For the occasion, he'd put the slightest hint of rouge on his cheeks, to bring definition to them.

His golden eyes locked on to her with such intensity she almost missed the last step and he helped her down.

'*Merci.*'

'I have never seen a more beautiful woman than you.' Awe filled his voice.

She blushed at the way he couldn't take his eyes off her. 'And you are very handsome, *monsieur*,' she said shyly.

What woman wouldn't be attracted to such masculine beauty? He would shame the statue of Michelangelo's *David*. And he was escorting her to the Queen!

She thought of their day on Pont Neuf, when they'd played a game of pretend. Tonight she was a princess, adorned in her finest, and Bastien her stalwart prince.

The night sky above them twinkled with stars, and as she peered out through the window of the carriage she couldn't believe she was there. An orphaned girl turned servant was now going to meet the Queen. She would bow before Her Majesty and stand before the rest of Court as a wielder of colour.

Even as joy rippled through her, it was followed by a hint of uncertainty. Her stepmother had trained her well, but would she do anything to embarrass herself or Bastien? Would she be able to stand before the unrelenting scrutiny of the Queen's Court as they assessed her? What about—?

'Don't worry about it.'

She pulled her unseeing gaze from the passing scenery. 'How did you know what I was thinking?'

He opened his mouth, but she said it before he could. 'There are no secrets between us.'

The carriage swayed back and forth as they made their way to the fabled court of Versailles. Butterflies took flight in her belly.

'Do you know what this reminds me of? The day Madame la Comtesse and Pierre brought me into society.' She laughed, seeing herself as she must have been. 'I could barely believe it. I'd no idea of the hardship that would come later.'

'What do you mean?'

Her mind travelled to the beginnings of her new life four years ago. 'There are so many rules… From how one dresses to where one sits, and even the proper behaviour of men and women. I had to learn all those things. And not everyone was kind or forgiving when I fumbled in my learning.'

'Is that what happened? Some were unkind to you?'

She gave a shaky laugh. 'It didn't matter about my station—whether I was a servant or a noble. All I could think was that I sat in a seat of nobility and had no right to be there.'

'And now?'

She lifted her shoulders. 'And now none of that matters. I wear the mantle of nobility well.'

Bastien's eyes roved over her again. 'That you do. Impeccably.'

Smiling, she glanced outside to see the towering, massive palace that was Château de Versailles.

Decorative fountains spewed out water in dazzling displays of artistry. The courtyards were manicured to perfection, with hedges cut and hewn within inches of precision.

From what she had heard and seen in illustrations, Versailles possessed the most exquisite, beautiful architecture. The Hall of Mirrors, where the King and Queen gave royal receptions and where nobles were received to see if they were invited to be part of Court, boasted mirrors from floor to ceiling.

The carriage turned towards the intimidating building and trepidation traipsed down her spine. Panic filled her. What did she know about being in the belly of a gilded beast like the Court at Versailles? If the people who lived under its roof could intimidate the Queen, how much more badly would *she* be intimidated?

'Mademoiselle Moreau?'

She jumped and looked at Bastien, who had an understanding smile on his face. 'Don't let this building or all those people inside make you afraid. You will go in there and discover something you won't have realised before.'

'And what is that?'

'You're better than most of them.'

There were people everywhere. The women were dressed in gowns with *poufs* as tall as three feet, bearing all sorts of headdresses depicting anything from a simple and elegant work of feathers and flowers to a battleship with sails and miniature sailors. And men dressed in high Court fashion with shiny white wigs danced attendance on the women.

She'd dreamed of this moment ever since she'd received the invitation. And of being here with Bastien by her side.

She smoothed the material of her gown and turned a

grateful eye on Bastien. Her breath caught as she realised he'd been staring at her the whole time. Did he see her apprehension? Her doubts?

Climbing out of the carriage, she waited while Bastien exited.

Turning to her, he asked, 'Are you ready?'

She shook her head. 'But that has never stopped me.'

The beauty of the palace glittered around them like the most majestic jewel of a crown. Bastien tried to keep his face impassive, so he didn't look as impressed as he felt. Everywhere his eyes landed was a feast for the senses. Luxury was a pauper compared to this ostentatious display.

Diamonds sparkled. Gold glinted. Marble shone like sunlight.

'How extraordinary!' Lilas exclaimed as they followed an attendant to where the Queen would be hosting them.

'Even during my Grand Tour I would have had difficulty finding something as spectacular as this.'

They passed by the Hall of Mirrors. The illustrations hadn't done it justice. It was as if the King had taken parts of heaven and stored them in his castle. It was almost overwhelming. It was night now, but in the daytime it must be filled with the glory of the divine. Darkness wouldn't be able to find a foothold there.

But perhaps that was the point.

'Do you see their faces?'

At Lilas's low murmur, Bastien pulled his gaze from the architecture and glanced around. A few of the palace's occupants were gathered about.

'What about them?' he asked. He looked around. They all looked very unimpressed with their surroundings. 'I wonder if it is because they are so used to this kind of glory that they no longer see it for what it is,' he mused.

'I could stay here all day and paint. There is so much to see.'

The attendant who led them was taking them by sparsely populated areas. However, it seemed the closer they came to where the Queen was, the more people became aware of them.

Bastien couldn't help but remark, 'They've all come to see the circus act.'

His resentment began to boil. When would it stop, this need for society to treat him as if he were different from them? Would he always be a source of curiosity?

More and more people followed them as they were led to the Queen. He could hear them whispering and talking about who they both were.

How important it was that they had both put their best clothing on? Lilas had taken his breath away when he'd seen her. And he was proud to have such a refined woman on his arm.

For a moment—just a moment—he felt the old weight of pressure on his shoulders. And then, for the first time, he did what his father had told him to do.

He ignored them all and concentrated on the woman by his side.

Lilas discreetly pressed her hand into his and squeezed it. That comforted him more than anything else.

When Lilas set her eyes on the Queen for the first time, she knew for certain that Madame Bertin only provided the very best for Her Majesty. Her own gown was a common rag compared to what the Queen wore.

Sitting in a high-backed chair, Her Majesty the Queen of France, Marie Antoinette, was adorned in the most beautiful gown Lilas had ever seen. The skirt was draped over extensive panniers—hooped undergarments that spread much further than hers, almost four feet on either side. The width provided everyone with the opportunity to see how well made her attire was.

The Queen was adorned with jewels and draped in a pea-coloured silk luxuriously textured with lace. She was topped with a three-foot powdered *pouf* bearing several peacock feathers, a large silk bow of a matching colour and a tiny bird's cage.

The woman looked like a goddess.

No wonder the rest of the world eyed her. Lilas had seen fashion plates of the Queen's gowns, but to see one in person was fabulous!

Lilas almost envied her—but then she looked at the Queen's face. The artist in her delved behind the white-painted face and vermillion-tinged lips. She looked past the pomp of her rich surroundings and saw...

A child.

Not a bad child, but one who didn't understand what her place was.

Lilas had heard rumours of how she had not been able to entice the King to her bed since they'd married when she was four and ten, only seven years ago. It was whispered that the Queen's Austrian mother berated her constantly for this inability.

One could not say that Her Majesty was a naturally beautiful woman. But she wasn't plain or hideous. And she'd been made to be beautiful.

There was something rather tragic about it, although Lilas didn't exactly know what that was.

She sent all other thoughts away as she moved with Bastien to stand before the Queen. With as perfect a motion as possible, she gave a deep curtsy while Bastien gave a formal bow.

A woman stood next to the Queen, obviously a servant of some closeness, and said, 'Vôtre Majesté, may I present the Duc de Languedoc, Bastien St Clare, and his betrothed, Mademoiselle Lilas Moreau.'

A hush settled over the room where everyone was gathered. One of the Queen's private apartments in the château, where only those most favoured were permitted entry.

A former servant girl…summoned before the Queen.

Yet this was where she was meant to be. What she'd always believed. It didn't matter about her past. She had truly become what she wanted. And no one could take it from her.

A deep sense of satisfaction settled over her as she stood and lifted her head to meet the frank gaze of the Queen.

'I am honoured that you have summoned us, Vôtre Majesté,' Bastien said, his deep voice seeming to reverberate around the room.

'I am glad to meet you, Monsieur le Duc.'

Her eyes came to rest on Lilas. 'You are a wonderful artist, Mademoiselle Moreau. I was so impressed with *Almost Eve*.'

'You are very kind, Madame la Reine.'

'Not at all.' The Queen laughed with a soft titter. 'False modesty will not get you anywhere here, Mademoiselle Moreau. You have a superb talent.'

'*Merci beaucoup*, Madame la Reine.'

The Queen's eyes drifted to Bastien, who had stood silent during this exchange. 'And you are the son of the last Duc de Languedoc. The King's father did not extend an invitation to Versailles to him because he had done something no one among us had.'

Thinking of all he had told her, Lilas wondered where the Queen was going with her words.

Bastien looked stunned. 'And may I ask, Vôtre Majesté, what was that?'

'He loved your mother.'

The simplicity of the statement made Lilas's heart lurch. She glanced over at Bastien, but he kept his face inscrutable.

The Queen motioned for Bastien to approach her. He sent a quick glance to Lilas before he did so, moving to stand just a few feet away.

'Madame la Reine…?'

'I hope by inviting you here I have in some way atoned for that gross error. You are welcome to stay at Versailles if you so wish, for you are the son of a noble house.'

Bastien stiffened, and Lilas fought to keep the tears from her eyes. It was an honour to be invited to Versailles and Bastien deserved it.

After a moment he said, 'You are most kind, Vôtre Majesté. I shall consider your offer.'

'As you should, *monsieur.*' She gave another curt nod. 'As you should… For once you are here you can never escape, as your father did.'

There was a note of warning in her voice. Not in a dark fashion, but in a way that said should Bastien accept her invitation to stay at Versailles he would be irrevocably drawn into Court life and all its vices.

The Queen's words had sent a surge of emotion through him, but Bastien masked it with a bow of acknowledgement. He'd done it. The House of St Clare had regained favour with the Crown.

So why, though he was pleased for this happy event, did he not feel quite the resounding sense of accomplishment he'd thought he would?

His father had claimed he'd never once pined for entrance into Versailles, although Bastien hadn't believed him.

'Should I live in a castle or eke out an existence in a hovel, as long as your mother is with me I am the happiest of men,' he had said.

Perhaps the old man had truly meant it after all.

When Lilas turned, Bastien could see that her eyes shone with pleasure. She looked as regal as the Queen herself…graceful and lovely. So far from the tearful cinder girl he'd held in his arms all those years ago.

A longing to share his triumph with her pervaded his being. So it was disappointing when he and Lilas were separated for dinner.

Everything about the meal was meant to engage all the senses. Roasted pheasant dressed in feathers, pâté stuffed inside a golden crust, and yet more delectable dishes, dressed and decorated to tempt the appetite. No less than ten courses were served, consisting of all sorts of food: cooked turtle served in its shell, clear soup and broth, new vegetables and airy and creamy desserts, along with other mouthwatering delicacies.

Bastien had been seated next to Fleur, the Duchesse de Villers-Cotterêts. Through their conversation, he learned she was a *princesse du sang*. A beautiful widow with pale skin and unpowdered black hair coiled about her head. Dressed impeccably in a gown of sky blue and white, she was a vision of loveliness.

'Is the turtle not to your liking?' she asked him now.

Bastien blinked from his unseeing stare and turned

to the woman by his side. 'It is, Madame la Duchesse. I was simply lost in my thoughts.'

'I can understand that, Monsieur le Duc. Madame la Reine has bestowed a great honour upon you.'

At her answer, he cocked his head to one side, sending unwanted thoughts away. 'How perceptive of you.'

'I am a very observant woman.' Her heavy-lidded eyes roamed over him. 'I make it a practice to be aware of... interesting people.'

Bastien saw encouragement in her eyes, but she wasn't as blatant as some women he'd met in the past. She simply looked as if she wanted to know more about him.

'Is that so?' he said.

'Who hasn't heard about the new Duc de Languedoc and his betrothed who was once his servant? An extraordinary story, to say the least.'

He glanced down the long table to see Lilas in conversation with another man, her face animated and bright. Forcing himself to not scowl, he took in the other man's features, seeing that he didn't lack in physical appeal. Bright skin. Robust physique. Alert eyes riveted on Lilas. Like himself, he wore a touch of rouge on his cheeks to add definition, and a white wig crowned his proud head.

'I see Mademoiselle Moreau has captured the eye of Saint-Georges.'

'Saint-Georges?' Why did that name sound so familiar?

'In full, Joseph Bologne, Chevalier de Saint-Georges.'

'I thought I recognised him. We enjoyed his violin concerto performance not too long ago.'

As if the man had heard his name—although that was impossible with the noise—he glanced up and met Bastien's eye. He gave a small, elegant nod, and Bastien returned it.

'Believe me, Saint-Georges and yourself are the kind of men many a woman would love to…' The woman stopped suggestively and then went on. 'He's a skilled violinist as well as a composer and a fencer. And a confidante of the Queen.'

From the way Lilas was gazing at the man, he could tell she was enamoured of him. Saint-Georges bent his head and said something, causing Lilas to grace the man with a genuine smile.

Perhaps because he had heard Lilas say the phrase so often, he was easily able to read her lips as she said to Saint-Georges, 'How wicked you are!'

Bastien pulled his eyes away. She'd often said that to him, and he'd felt as if the phrase was only meant for his ears. How dared she call another man wicked? *Bastien* was her wicked one!

You're mad…and you're starting to sound like Père.

Tonight, the thought didn't upset him as it usually did. He pulled his concentration from them and set himself to enjoy the company of the Duchesse de Villers-Cotterêts.

The meal went on for more than two hours before the Queen stood, signalling its end. During that time it occurred to Bastien that the Duchesse was exactly the sort of woman he'd been searching for to solidify his place in society. As a *princesse du sang*, she had the pedigree. As the widow of a man twenty years her senior, she had wealth equal to his own. As a woman, she wasn't a true beauty, but she had striking features which drew the eye.

She'd made it obvious that she found Bastien to her liking and held a genuine interest in him as a man, not simply as a *duc*. Despite that, her conversation tended towards gossip, and remarking on the other guests in cold, cutting ways. Never vulgar, however. She was a *duchesse* after all.

Perhaps for some other man Fleur would be a delightful companion. As for him, he knew she would bore him to tears before the ink had even dried on the marriage contract. A woman like her wouldn't challenge him or set his mind afire. When her eyes touched his, though they gleamed with interest, there wasn't a spark of flame in their depths.

She could never ignite him like Lilas did.

The admission almost made him start to sweat. It sounded far too much like his father's feelings for his mother. That overwhelming desire for her which had utterly consumed his sire.

Like an automaton, Bastien escorted the Duchesse when everyone followed the Queen as she went to another room that had been arranged for dancing. Lilas still stood with Saint-Georges, who gallantly kissed her hand, drawing laughter and teasing from the surrounding crowd, before joining a small ensemble of musicians and beginning to entertain them with lively music.

The pleased expression on Lilas's face only made Bastien angrier.

'Shall we join in the festivities, *monsieur*?' Fleur suggested.

Inhaling a deep breath, he forced a grin. 'It is a party after all, isn't it, *madame*?'

One that couldn't end soon enough for him.

Lilas searched fruitlessly for Bastien. Was he still with that stunningly beautiful woman who had kept his eyes focused on her the entire time during the meal?

When she'd looked at them together, Lilas had known immediately that Bastien had found the ideal woman he'd been searching for. From the top of her coiled head to the silver shoes, she met the description of what he wanted for his wife in every way.

That woman was perfect for Bastien.

It had taken all her strength to focus on Saint-Georges as he spoke with her, but then he'd drawn her out of her melancholy until she was truly enjoying herself, despite the pang in her heart.

When the dancing began, and a gentleman asked her to dance, she accepted, praying she'd remember all the steps she'd learned.

Soon, she thought nothing of it as the music became livelier and more energetic. Sweat moistened her face, but no more than anyone else, and she enjoyed herself. She danced for an hour before she stopped to catch her breath, ambling over to a secluded corner near the exit from the room.

She hid behind a large plant, trying to calm her breathing and soothe her disappointed heart. Her eyes flitted over the throng of people still dancing. After tonight, Bastien would come to her and formally ask her to break off their engagement, as that was what they'd agreed upon. Then she'd have to watch him and listen to the gossip as he and that woman...

'Mademoiselle Moreau?'

Her breath caught in her chest at the sound of Bastien's voice behind her.

She spun around. '*Monsieur?* What are you doing here?'

The moment the words were out of her mouth she wanted to take them back. What a silly question to ask!

He stepped closer to her. 'Do I really need to tell you?'

She shook her head, and at the same time the music began again. Without breaking eye contact, Bastien extended his hand and she took it. She couldn't do anything but take it. He led her out to the floor just as the music for a minuet started—a haunting tune with a violin that was undoubtedly being played by Saint-Georges.

Lilas was sure there were other people around her, but they all seemed to disappear from her sight.

Only she and Bastien remained.

He was a good dancer, moving with the masculine grace and precision the dance called for. His eyes were locked on hers, and no matter how far apart they were, she felt the pull of them like a magnet. Whenever they came back together their hands touched, and Bastien allowed his fingers to brush against the flesh of her arm, sending her nerve endings tingling with sensation.

It was so wicked of him, for just as she began to enjoy it, the dance called for him to move away. And then, when they came together once more, he'd do it again.

It was a strange sort of seduction that left her breathless and teetering on tenterhooks, waiting like some eager child for the next brushstroke of his finger, even as she knew it would torment her anew.

This was perhaps another game of pretend. In which she could forget that their engagement was only for show. That his ideal bride was waiting for him in the crowd. She could pretend that the look in Bastien's eyes meant he wanted her, Lilas, in every sense of the word. That she was more than good enough for him. That she was perfect…just as he was perfect for her.

When his hands touched her again, he stared at her intently, and awareness arced through her like lightning. His finger trailed down, caressing her inner wrist, and she forgot everything else as she shuddered at the sensation. Bastien's eyes shimmered like molten gold.

The dance came to an end, and Bastien looked as if

he wanted to eat her alive. Lilas wanted nothing more than to be devoured by her lion.

'Perhaps,' he said hoarsely, 'we should go to the—'

'Mademoiselle Moreau?'

Lilas jerked round and curtsied as the Queen came towards her, followed by her entourage.

'Madame la Reine.'

'Come…talk to me,' the Queen commanded, although she smiled in a gracious way, and Lilas did as she bade— although she peeked behind her for one last chance to see Bastien.

He'd just straightened from his bow when she saw his ideal woman come to him, laughing up into his face.

Lilas felt her heart drop.

Without a word, she followed the Queen, with a gaping wound in the centre of her chest.

'Tell me about yourself, Mademoiselle Moreau.'

Lilas didn't know if she could even speak. The sight of Bastien, staring so intently into that woman's face…

'What would you like to know?' she asked.

'Everything you can tell me. For instance, what about your mother and father? What do you know of them?'

She swallowed the lump in her throat. 'Very little, Madame la Reine. There is much mystery surrounding my birth.'

'Is there?' The Queen's eyes widened. 'Such as?'

'How did I end up at the orphanage? Who told my father I had died?'

'Fair…those are important questions. How long will you search for the answers?'

'I do not know, Madame la Reine. But I have taken the philosophy that I cannot change what I do not know.'

'Indeed.'

They were walking outside Versailles, along a secluded pathway hemmed in by conical trees all standing together like soldiers. A soft wind blew against them and Lilas lifted her head into the breeze.

'The wind feels fresh and invigorating here,' the Queen remarked. 'Heavenly scented by all the flowers in the garden. There are times when I come here to smell the flowers and remember...'

Her voice trailed off. Lilas wondered again at her sad expression. 'Remember what, Madame la Reine?'

'A simpler time,' was all she said.

Lilas suspected it had to do with her childhood.

'But I do remember a fairy story I once heard. Of a *fille des cendres* who found her prince.'

The Queen tilted her head slightly, and Lilas marvelled at the exceptional skill of her hairdresser for not a single item moved.

'You and the Duc de Languedoc remind me of it,' she said.

'Is that so?'

The Queen made an agreeable sound. 'Just like her, you have found your rightful place despite those powers that wish it otherwise. Despite the machinations of an evil stepmother.'

'My stepmother has been good to me.'

'Has she?' The Queen frowned. 'I seem to recall some rumours about her... She was married to a minor baron who had fallen on hard times, and he died in rather suspicious circumstances.'

'Rumours certainly seem to abound, don't they, Madame la Reine?'

A look of sardonic amusement came upon the Queen's face. 'That is true. You should hear what is said about me. Go on, Mademoiselle Moreau, tell me more about yourself.'

By the time they returned to the palace grounds the clock was striking midnight. Lilas let her eyes search the room for Bastien… And her heart plummeted when she saw him dancing once more with his ideal.

Lilas knew she'd found a friend in the Queen of France. Yet as the last gong of the clock sounded the magic of the evening dissipated, like dew under a hot sun. Though dressed in her finest, as she gazed at Bastien with his perfect bride she'd never felt more like a cinder girl.

As the carriage made its way from Versailles in the wee hours of the morning, a strained, stony silence filled the cab. Moonlight spilled through at intervals, revealing Lilas's averted profile, lined with tension.

'What is wrong?' Bastien asked, concerned.

Slowly, her head turned in his direction. 'Nothing is wrong, *monsieur.*'

Which meant the exact opposite.

'I want to know.'

'It has been a good evening…but rather taxing, wouldn't you say?'

Bastien almost believed it was mere tiredness that kept her so silent. But her voice held an odd high note, which proved she was holding back for some reason.

'Need I remind you, Mademoiselle Moreau, we do not allow secrets between us?'

'Perhaps it is you who needs reminding,' she said pointedly.

'What are you referring to?'

'Who was that woman you were with tonight?'

His brows met in the middle of his forehead. 'Woman? What woman?'

'The beautiful one with the dark hair.'

'That is the Duchesse de Villers-Cotterêts,' he replied. 'A widow who is also a *princesse du sang*. A cousin of the King several times removed, I believe.'

She turned her head away. 'She looked like your ideal. The kind of woman you need to help return yourself to good standing with society and the Crown.'

He shook his head at her perception. 'She did look like my ideal, didn't she?'

'You seemed very interested in each other.'

He shrugged. 'She was a delightful companion for the evening.' Remembering the kiss Saint-Georges had planted on Lilas's hand, he scowled. 'You seemed to find equal delight in *your* companion.'

'What are you talking about?'

'Saint-Georges.'

The tension eased from her, which only made him more annoyed.

'He is a fascinating man. Did you know he bested a fencing master when he was only seventeen years of age?'

'Impressive,' he said in a bland tone. Why did she sound so appreciative of the man's fencing prowess? 'Do remember you're *my* betrothed, Mademoiselle Moreau. And I expect you to act accordingly.'

'What does that mean?'

'He kissed your hand.'

The memory of it sent a hot thread of *something* through him.

'It wasn't a declaration, *monsieur*,' she said incredulously.

'Be sure that it was not,' he warned, all the while silently yelling at himself to be quiet.

'I would expect you to practise the same discretion with that *duchesse*,' she said.

'There is no need for your concern.'

Did she think he wanted the woman? Bastien paused as an incredible thought came to his mind.

'You're jealous.'

Lilas scoffed. 'Hardly. But I daresay the green-eyed monster sits upon *your* shoulders.'

Was he jealous about Saint-Georges? He couldn't be. That would mean he cared about Lilas in a way he'd always sworn he never would.

And he didn't.

End the engagement now, then. Call an end to this while you can.

That voice in his head was logical. Reasonable. And it sent a cold draught through his body. If he simply said the words now, they would begin the process of removing any need to spend time with her.

But the words clogged his throat. He couldn't get them out. Instead, he sniffed and said, 'Let us both remember we are in this situation until the betrothal ends.'

'I know that,' she snapped.

The rest of their carriage ride to Hôtel de la Baux was made in silence.

Chapter Eight

It wasn't right. It *still* wasn't right.

Lilas flung the paintbrush against the wall, seeing the paint splatter. She groaned and glared at the canvas, as if it were the problem and not her own underwhelming talent.

Bastien as *The General*. Why had she thought she could capture him in this light? What a foolish idea! What a ridiculous woman she was!

Her fingers clawed her hair and she pulled, certain that she'd left paint in her tresses, but she didn't care. Poor Esme would be beside herself, working to rid her mistress of the mess. But even the thought of inconveniencing Esme wasn't enough to stave off the melancholy she was experiencing. Staring at her unfinished work, Lilas sighed. What part of Bastien's essence was she failing to grasp?

Now she would never know.

That night at Versailles he had practically seduced her while they danced.

She wanted to talk to him about what happened. Had he simply been toying with her when he'd brushed and caressed her arms while they danced? Had it all been just a game to him? A way to pass the time?

No, that couldn't be it. He'd been as affected by those fleeting touches as she had. She was certain of it.

But now, after fulfilling the Queen's summons, their need for subterfuge was gone.

After his high-handedness in the carriage, she'd been tempted to open her mouth and crack the silence by announcing the beginning of the end of their association.

But she hadn't been able to bring herself to do it. No matter that she didn't completely trust him, and no matter that he had found his ideal wife that night, she still hadn't verbally ended their engagement, even though the contract gave her that right.

Let Bastien be the one to do it.

In the following days she'd waited with breath bated to receive a missive from him, stating that he wished to talk with her. Every day Esme brought her correspondence, which was overflowing, and she searched through it for the prophesied message.

It had yet to arrive, but she knew that it would arrive soon—it *must*, else she would go mad.

Indeed, her social engagements had grown more numerous, while demand for her work had reached heights she hadn't even dared dream about. Their upcoming nuptials appeared to remain the main topic of gossip, as all of Paris speculated who would be invited, the venue and the absorption of assets once they married.

Lilas went over to the window and pulled back the curtain, letting the sunshine flood in and light up the portrait. Going over to it, she scrutinised it, taking in every detail she had created.

What was missing?

She traced her finger over the images portrayed. Behind Bastien stood a crumbling tower, against an over-cast sky. Past the tower was a turbulent sea with a ship and distant figures of men upon it. Bastien stood with his legs apart, his hands on his hips, his eyes steady and gloomy, their golden light dampened from losses at war.

There he stood…a great man beaten down and alone. Alone?

Lilas jolted as she realised what was wrong.

No wonder she couldn't capture Bastien's essence in this painting. He would never suffer defeat by himself. He was meant to conquer. Bastien as Marc Antony stood alone, when he should be with his ideal. His Cleopatra. Fleur, the Duchesse de Villers-Cotterêts. They both knew that she was the one who'd fill all his requirements for the type of wife he wanted.

Lilas studied the painting again. After all, turmoil in life was never as difficult to navigate if you had some-one to share it with. And it was his ideal he needed by his side.

Despite the pang in her heart, she knew what she had to do.

She firmed her lips and reached for her sketchpad, determined to get the essence of Bastien, along with his ideal, exactly right.

Later, she returned to her room, exhausted from her painting session and somewhat dejected. To her critical eye, her new sketch of Bastien depicted him far better than before, now that she'd added his ideal bride.

Esme was there to remove her paint-stained clothes, but there wasn't enough time to rid her hands of all the coloured splotches. Bastien would be arriving soon, to take her to his uncle's house for the evening, and she'd already dallied at her painting for far too long. It would be a challenge to be ready by the time he came for her.

Through sheer will and Esme's fortitude she bathed and dressed in just enough time to have her hair styled into its *pouf.* When Esme had finally finished the arduous task Lilas thanked her, seeing the weariness about her maid's eyes.

'You are too good to me, Esme. While I am gone you must get some rest. I'll see to myself when I return.'

Stubbornly, the maid refused. 'I will see to you, *mademoiselle.*'

From the fierce expression in her eyes, Lilas knew she wouldn't be able to dissuade her. 'I thank you for being so diligent, Esme. Please get my wrap for me.'

Esme left, and Lilas looked down and saw her wrist was bare. Opening her jewellery box, she tugged at the little drawer inside it and froze.

Another note was folded there.

Her hands trembled as she looked at it. She'd not seen anything for the past few days, so she'd disregarded the first note she'd received. Now, here was a second one.

Swallowing to add some moisture to her throat, she picked up the note and opened it.

Ils essaieront de te faire du mal.

Her hands shook harder as she read the message again. *They will try to hurt you.* Who were 'they'? Who was trying to hurt her? Why?

Despite all the work that had gone into her appearance, she flopped down onto a dainty chair. The attack on her by the masked man had almost been forgotten, but now it rose to the surface of her mind once more, as if waving and cackling at her.

Why was someone trying to scare her? She'd done nothing to warrant this kind of attention.

The door opened without warning, and she glanced up to see Pierre in the doorway.

'Surely you're not going to keep the Duc de Languedoc waiting any longer, are you?'

Her stepbrother's brown eyes held amusement, but she couldn't bring herself to join in the jest.

'Pierre, look at this.' She held the note out.

Frowning, he came into her bedchamber and took it from her. Pushing his spectacles up his nose, he read the brief message and muttered a curse. 'Who gave this to you?'

She shook her head. 'I don't know. I found it among my jewellery. It's the second one I've received.'

Pierre gasped. 'The second one? Lilas, why didn't you speak of this earlier? Don't you know this could have something to do with the attack on you?'

Her face burned at his recriminations. 'Of course.'

'We must take it to the authorities.'

'I don't want that. Whoever this person is, I won't let them frighten me.'

'Then at the very least tell Languedoc. The man has an obligation to protect you as his betrothed. If I were him, I'd want to do all I could to ensure your safety.'

Pierre's words gave her pause. Should she tell Bastien? What would it mean if she did?

'You must, Lilas. It's wrong to keep him in the dark about this.'

A part of her knew Pierre was right. Bastien had spoken of his frustration about the lack of progress made by the authorities to discover the person who'd attacked her. As far as they were concerned, she should be happy she'd escaped with nothing stolen from her.

If she told him about this, he would go back to the authorities.

Perhaps it was because of her weariness, but although she knew Pierre was right, she was thinking of the image of Cleopatra she'd sketched to accompany her Marc Antony. That woman was the one who deserved Bastien's protection, not her.

What if tonight Bastien finally said the words to sever their betrothal? Did she want to add this to his load and force him to protect her when she would no longer be his responsibility? If he no longer wanted her in his life, who was she to delay her exit from it?

The ideal woman was within his grasp. She couldn't keep him from her much longer.

Ignoring the throb in the centre of her chest, she shook her head. 'I can't do that, Pierre.'

'Why not?'

'I just can't. And I want your promise that you will say nothing of this to the Duc.'

Pierre threw his hands in the air. 'This is madness, Lilas. He needs to know.'

'He doesn't. This is the second time I've received a note. If this person wants to harm me, wouldn't they have done it by now? Whoever they are, they want me frightened. And I refuse to allow fear to dictate my actions.'

'So you'll allow foolishness to take the reins instead?'

She glared at him. 'Promise me, Pierre. You'll say nothing of this to anyone. Not your mother, not the Duc de Languedoc—no one.'

'Lilas—!'

'Your word,' she demanded.

Pierre cursed again, and crumpled the note in his fist. 'Why are you so stubborn?'

'Pierre!'

'Fine. I won't say anything. This time,' he added.

When she opened her mouth to berate him, he held up his hand to stop her.

'I can't simply let this continue. Languedoc is your betrothed. If it happens again he must and will protect you.'

She struggled to hold in a scream of frustration.

'You must promise me that if you receive another note, you will tell me. Together, we will let the Duc de Languedoc know.'

She'd opened her mouth to argue this when Pierre interjected.

'Your word.'

Lilas seethed. How clever of Pierre to extract this from her. But she knew she would not have his cooperation at all if she didn't agree. Bastien wouldn't appreciate having to have her in his life longer than necessary, but Pierre didn't know that.

The image of Cleopatra flashed in her mind once more. She flinched, but there was only one thing she could do.

'Very well,' she agreed bleakly.

'"No one cares about our betrothal",' Bastien quoted sarcastically in the darkened interior of the carriage. 'Do you recall saying that?'

Lilas wanted to take her reticule and throw it at Bastien as they swayed back and forth on their way to his uncle's home.

She knew Esme should have come with her as chaperone, but she'd left the maid at home. It was irregular, and not what women in polite society did, but for once Lilas didn't care.

Bastien had said nothing about the absence of her maid, simply ordering the carriage forward. Maybe he understood that the rigid restrictions of society were grating on her.

'It has been well over a month since I made that erroneous statement. Must you throw it in my face?' she said in exasperation. 'How was I to know all of Paris would behave as if we were a circus act?'

'That is too generous a description,' Bastien said quietly.

She opened her mouth for a quick retort, but closed it without saying anything. What he had said was true.

'From what I can see, demand for your artistic skills has gone up yet again,' he went on.

'The demand is there—you are correct. But not for the right reasons.'

'You're being childish. Does it matter how you gain clientele as long as you do?'

'What could *you* know about it?' she spat.

'I seem to recall a time when you only had one patron.'

His eyes held her captive. She wanted to look away, but couldn't. 'I remember that time as well.' She sighed heavily, with a sense of inexplicable weariness. 'Why must we go to your uncle's home?'

'He insisted.' Then Bastien added wryly, 'Therefore it must be done.'

'I take it you don't like him very much?'

'You are correct. We loathe each other.'

'Then why are we going?'

'I'm not quite sure.' Bastien sounded as if he were mulling over his reasons. 'I've not seen him since Père's funeral. Whatever his reason for inviting me, he was most insistent that you accompany me. I am certain that it will be a small gathering—just us and my cousin. That's why you don't need a chaperone for tonight.'

'I see.'

They were silent after that for a little while. She tried to keep her eyes from straying to Bastien too often, but found it impossible. In the close confines of the carriage his presence swelled, crowding her in. Not suffocating her but overwhelming her.

She felt his melancholy and his unease. She remembered during an argument with his father years ago, before he'd left home, that he'd alluded to his uncle's vitriol about his heritage. What type of evening were they in for?

'We shall be there soon,' Bastien said unnecessarily.

She reached over the small space that divided them and touched his arm. Underneath the smooth material of his coat his muscle flexed. Retreating swiftly, as though burned, she settled back against the cushions of her seat.

Why had she touched him?

He needed it, a voice whispered in her head.

When Bastien pulled his gaze away from the passing scenery, she saw his golden eyes somehow pick up the faint light of the evening. '*Oui*, Mademoiselle Moreau?'

For a moment she was tongue-tied for no definable reason. Or at least for no reason she wasn't certain she wanted to explore.

'Everything will be fine,' she told him.

'I am thankful for your optimism. At least one of us has it.'

Peering out of the window, she could see they'd passed the Place des Vosges—the square that had once housed the elite, until their exodus to the Faubourg Saint-Germain Quartier. Those who occupied this space now were a few minor nobles and only one or two of the more powerful families.

As the carriage drew up to a modest home with Gothic influences and understated elegance, she gave it a critical perusal. Against the twilight sky a tall turret drew the eye, imposing and statuesque. Besides that, it was rather homely.

How odd... She knew how wealthy the House of St Clare was.

Although she said nothing as she was assisted out the carriage, something of her thoughts must have shown as Bastien said, 'My uncle squandered most of his wealth, whereas my father expanded his through various means, not solely relying on the rents and taxes of the land we own.'

'I see...' she murmured.

'As it is, this is now my uncle's only residence in Paris. Only his status as a St Clare keeps him from being thrown out on the streets.'

'But why should he dislike you for his own faults?'

Bastien walked with her up the narrow path that led to the large double doors. 'It's easier for him to blame someone else for his failures than to take responsibility for them. It doesn't help that his son, my cousin Estienne, likes me and, having accepted guidance in the past from my father, has made money of his own.'

'I'm glad one member of your family values you.'

Bastien nodded. 'You'll meet my cousin tonight.'

'So you do understand why your uncle loathes you so?'

'I may understand it, but I don't like it.'

'And yet you are here at his whim.'

He lifted a powerful shoulder in response and she understood that though the evening promised to be a trial for them, he would still endure it because he had a sense of obligation to his father's brother. Already she could see the tension settled on his shoulders. Bastien really had no desire to go to dinner with his uncle. But he would. He was the kind of man who handled difficult situations without hesitation.

'At least it will be a fairly brief engagement,' he said. 'An hour or two and then we can leave.'

Lilas decided then that she would do whatever she could to make this evening bearable for Bastien. Those lessons in womanly comportment and charm would come in useful tonight.

He had once stood up to those who'd made things unpleasant for her. In this way, she could finally return the favour.

'Sacré bleu!' Bastien cursed under his breath.

The foyer of his uncle's home teemed with guests. Women and men stood in clusters, chattering. They all turned as one as Lilas and he entered, giving out a cheer.

Estienne came up to him, his smile strained. 'I had no idea about this, Cousin,' he said in a low voice for Bastien's ears alone, as he clapped him on the shoulder in a congratulatory way. 'There wasn't time to send a message to warn you.'

'Why is he doing this?' Bastien hissed between his teeth.

There was no time for Estienne to respond as they heard his uncle's voice calling out, 'Welcome, welcome, Bastien!' The Comte de Clareville came towards the front of the crowd, smiling jovially. 'How do you like my little surprise for you and your exquisite betrothed?

Bastien fought to keep his mouth from falling open. Beside him, Lilas had stiffened in shock, though he knew she knew better than to let it show.

It wasn't so much the party that had taken him by surprise as much as his uncle's pleasant attitude. For as long as he'd been alive, the Comte had never greeted him with anything but disdain and contempt.

As his uncle neared, he saw the truth.

The man was furious—and desperate. A casual observer might be fooled into thinking the display of joviality was genuine. But Bastien knew better. Though his uncle's lips stretched wide, it was a travesty of a smile. The tightness around his eyes made it more than apparent.

What the devil had he done to offend his uncle this time?

'You are very kind, Monsieur le Comte…er… Oncle Olivier,' he corrected swiftly at the slight shake of the man's head. 'Such a wonderful surprise. I am…pleased.'

'I knew you would be.'

Bastien's nostrils flared, but a warning squeeze from both Estienne and Lilas, on either side of him, prevented him from saying anything else.

The Comte de Clareville turned to Lilas. 'Mademoiselle Moreau, it is an honour to welcome your arrival into our family.'

She gave an elegant curtsy to his uncle's stilted bow. 'Monsieur le Comte, it is my honour.'

'Please, call me Uncle, for you will soon be my niece.'

What was he doing? If it hadn't been for the people around them, Bastien would have taken the man to task. He himself had been forbidden to call him 'uncle' until tonight!

Lilas smiled in an agreeable way. *'Merci.'*

His uncle took them around and introduced them to his guests. Many of them Bastien and Lilas had met on more than one occasion, but there were others who were in his uncle's close circle who had always ridiculed him before, but were now apparently doting on him.

It seemed gaining the Queen's approval had done wonders for his suitability, according to his uncle's set.

Once the introductions had been made, dinner was called for. Unlike when they'd visited Versailles, they were seated as the guests of honour at either end of the long table, with his uncle on Bastien's right, and Estienne on Lilas's right.

It was a strange seating arrangement, but his uncle made much of it, causing a titter of amusement amongst the people there.

Throughout dinner, he was glad that Lilas was with him. Tonight she looked particularly lovely, in a dove-grey gown of surprising simplicity, devoid of any extravagant embellishment of jewellery, but what she wore was of excellent quality. Her *pouf* rose little more than a foot above her head, decorated with pearl combs and powdered. The contrast of her golden-brown skin against the gown was a delightful one, bringing attention to her queenly stature and poise.

His uncle's uncharacteristic attitude continued to grate, particularly since the man was cutting his eyes at him. Bastien longed for nothing more than to leave the curious scrutiny of the other guests and find out what was going on.

Having Lilas there was soothing.

The feeling both comforted and frightened him. He didn't want to feel that way around her even as he craved it. Throughout the seven-course meal he kept glancing at her, seeing the way she charmed those around her with her vivacity, her expressiveness, as well as that innate genuineness so lacking among the elite.

She was, quite simply, a delightful woman.

But he knew that soon she would be telling him that their engagement was at an end.

His fingers dug into his knee as he laughed appropriately with a man seated to his left. Every day he waited for a courier to bring official papers from her solicitor's office rescinding the marital contract. He'd tried to ignore the hitch in his chest as each day nothing of the sort had arrived. But it would inevitably come and he had to be ready for it.

After dinner, there was a natural drifting away to other activities. A group had gathered around the billiards table, while others hurried to an intellectual game of charades. Bastien and Lilas were drawn apart, pulled in different directions by the whims of his uncle's guests.

It seemed an eternity passed before he was able to excuse himself from the festivities, which looked as if they would go on for hours until the early morning.

He exited the room and went out into the small garden at the back of the house. Wandering along the short, winding path, he came to the centre of the garden, where a small fountain spewed out water. Only a compact space, it was pleasant, but lacked imagination. Bastien was glad of that, as there was nothing to distract him from his thoughts.

'Bastien.'

The skin between his shoulder blades tightened in response to his uncle's voice. Taking in a deep breath, he pivoted around. 'Why did you ask us to come here?'

There wasn't much light, but from his vantage point, he could see his uncle's contorted face. 'Why do you think? I had to give this party because people were beginning to talk. There wasn't any way I couldn't give my public acknowledgement of your betrothal.'

'I see.'

'Incidentally, I can't afford this—so the bills will be coming to you.'

Bastien's eyes bulged. He was so surprised he took a step back, as if struck in the chest. 'Are you mad? Why should I pay for an extravagance I didn't ask for?'

'Because you must. We can't let the name of St Clare be tarnished now that you have gained the Queen's favour for us once more.'

Bastien thought his head might catch on fire. 'I can't believe you'd think I'd even consider doing that.'

'You have no choice.'

From the mutinous look on the man's face, Bastien knew his uncle expected him to do as he demanded. He flexed his fingers and said, in a deliberate manner, 'Mademoiselle Moreau and I will take our leave.'

He'd moved to walk past his uncle when his arm was caught. 'Don't you dare walk away from me. You owe me.'

Yanking his arm away, he growled, 'I owe you nothing.'

'That's a lie. Philippe is no longer here to pay his debt to me so I will extract it from you.' His uncle snarled. 'Why do you think I've done this? When your father married that—that—'

Taking a step forward, until he almost touched noses with the man, Bastien whispered threateningly, 'Tread very carefully, *mon oncle*, with what you say about my mother.'

'Did your father tread carefully when he knew an advantageous marriage to a *princesse du sang* would have benefited me as well? He didn't tread carefully when he married your mother…spouting ridiculous ideas of everlasting love. No one of our rank marries for *love*, Bastien. We marry for social position. And your father ruined it for all of us.'

'Is that why you hate me so much?'

'That is enough, Monsieur le Comte.'

They both turned at the sound of Lilas's firm voice as she glided towards them. Her dove-grey gown shone almost white in the moonlight. Along with her powdered *pouf* and the glistening pearls around her neck she almost looked like an ethereal angel except for the hard glitter in her amethyst eyes. Instead, she appeared like a warrior angel.

'This has nothing to do with you, Mademoiselle Moreau,' the Comte said. 'I suggest you go back and entertain my guests while your future husband and I continue our *tête-à-tête*.'

'At least your pretence of fondness is over,' she remarked coolly as she advanced on them. 'As such, I will be just as blunt.'

'There's nothing you can say that I wish to hear.'

'*Bien*. Then you'll be silent.'

Bastien's mouth gaped open. 'Lilas...?'

'You are a horrid little man, Monsieur le Comte,' she continued, as if she hadn't heard Bastien.

Perhaps she hadn't. For himself, he could only stare in awe as she defended him.

'You hate my betrothed and you treat him poorly, and yet you still expect for him to pay your bills out of some familial obligation.' Her voice snapped like a whip.

'It's the least he can do after what I've suffered, thanks to my brother's actions. And you wouldn't know anything about that,' his uncle said snidely.

'I know more than you can ever understand. Have you ever felt the cold of night against your skin? Has your belly rumbled with the pain of want for food? You have no idea of real suffering, *monsieur*.'

'Do spare me this sad tale,' he mocked in a scathing tone.

'What about what Bastien has suffered at your hands?' Though his uncle stood a few inches taller than her, Lilas came up to him until she was right under his nose. 'I can remember him being bruised by the hateful words you spouted at him over the years. How you reviled his heritage. Insulted his beloved mother.'

The Comte de Clareville sniffed. 'Are you finished?'

Her head lifted higher. The image of her glittering eyes and proud demeanour burned in Bastien's mind and he knew he'd never forget it.

'I will be after I've said this. You will never speak to Bastien like that ever again. It is his decision if he chooses to settle your debts. But I will not tolerate any more mistreatment of him by you.'

'Oh?' A hard sneer marred the Comte's face.

Bastien's back muscles tensed like a coiled spring. He'd seen that expression many times over the years. It meant he was about to say something meant to cut her and tear her down. He'd suffer his uncle's callousness, but he wouldn't subject Lilas to it.

The Comte de Clareville leaned forward. 'What can you do to prevent me from speaking my mind? You're nothing more than a—'

Bastien's hands clamped on the Comte's arm and squeezed. 'Be silent, Oncle Olivier,' he said sternly. 'I will not be responsible for my actions if you insult my betrothed.'

His uncle tried to yank his arm away, but Bastien's fingers clenched harder.

'Let go of me!'

'Do you understand?'

'Fine. Let go!'

Bastien released the man and tugged on the edges of his waistcoat. Looking at Lilas, he held out his hand.

Sarcasm dripped from his voice as he said to his uncle, 'Though we appreciate your reluctant hospitality, we must take our leave.' He lifted a brow at his uncle's red, furious face. 'My carriage?'

'Why are you looking at me like that?'

Bastien blinked. He *had* been staring at her for some time as they travelled to her home.

'Am I offending you?' he asked quietly.

Slowly, she shook her head. 'It's disconcerting, that's all. You make me wonder if I've grown an extra appendage of some sort.'

His mouth lifted at her attempt at humour, but he couldn't find the wherewithal to join in with her teasing.

'You are truly remarkable, *mademoiselle*.'

She looked flustered at his words, her hands moving in a nervous way. '*Monsieur*…really…'

He continued as if she'd not spoken. 'The way you made him look like such a little man…I can't believe it.'

She had done something his father never had.

Defended him.

'*Monsieur*, you're still staring!'

'What of it?' Within his chest stirred something that felt like gratitude but was also…*more*.

'I don't understand why.'

On impulse, he moved and sat beside her in the carriage.

'What are you doing?'

The shafts of moonlight that entered the narrow windows landed on her face. He ignored her questions to reach out and gently caress the side of her cheek, brightened by pearly light.

'I have never had anyone do for me what you did tonight.'

Lilas's head bent in sudden shyness. 'I didn't do much except try to—'

'No, Lilas,' he argued, dropping formality for a moment. 'You have no idea what you've done. When I left home, my last interaction with my uncle was fraught with anger. We almost came to blows.'

'Did you?' Her expression showed him her concern.

'Estienne had to pull us apart and remind us of our familial bond. My uncle said horrible things to me. Such as—'

She lifted her finger and placed it on his mouth. 'Shh…' she whispered. 'Don't repeat his vileness. It serves no purpose.'

He took her hand in his. 'That's true.'

'Hearing his words tonight caused me to reflect on my own past. You were blessed to have the love of your parents, but I didn't. No one protected me until you did. Your uncle will never truly understand what it means to have nothing. He will never grasp what it means to make a life of your own and fight to keep it. But I do. And I believe you do, too. I couldn't let him continue to hurt you like that.'

Although her hand was gloved, he felt her words and her touch go straight through him. '*Bien sûr!* You of all people would understand.'

She'd been subjected to that for years, he knew. He'd come to her aid when she was growing up in his household, and now she'd come to his. Not out of any sense of obligation, but because she'd wanted to. How could he not be moved by such a show of support? A woman's fury unleashed but restrained.

The journey continued in a haze as he tried to suppress the burgeoning feelings coursing through him.

Slowly, he lifted her hand and peeled off her glove.

'What are you doing?'

She tried to tug her hand away, but he tightened his grip around her wrist. In the meagre light of the carriage, he saw numerous dark patches on the back of her hand and fingers.

'What are these?'

'Please…' From the tone of her voice, she seemed more embarrassed than anything.

Using his thumb, he rubbed the back of her hand gently, feeling the warmth and softness of her skin. He heard her breath hitch in her throat and did his best to hide his smile.

'Tell me,' he ordered.

'It's paint. I didn't have the opportunity to clean my hands as I wanted to. You weren't supposed to see them.'

Unable to look away from those slender, paint-splotched fingers, he lifted her hand to his mouth and planted a kiss. The scent of lavender once again titillated his nostrils and he inhaled deeply, holding the scent of her in his lungs. The tremor that went through her made him smile.

'You are a generous woman. Perhaps you always were, and I've only just become aware of it. Regardless, I've told you that you're never to hide your secrets from me.'

'I haven't, *monsieur*.'

This time when she tugged her fingers, he let her go.

'It's just the first time you have noticed it for yourself.'

'Is that a reprimand for my lack of perspicacity?'

She shook her head as she slid her glove back on. 'It is simply an observation. Sometimes what we are searching for is right in front of us. And it's been there all the time.'

He sensed she was talking about something other than what she'd done for him tonight. But what that was, he couldn't tell.

'For defending me to my uncle—*merci beaucoup.*'

The air in the carriage shifted, becoming laden with something that was both dark and light. His awareness of her as a woman superseded everything else. No one had ever come to his defence as she had. He had been taught to simply stand firm when ridicule and insult came his way. His father had dismissed his uncle's poisonous words and insults without ever showing that he cared about what his own family or the rest of society thought of him.

Lilas...sweet Lilas.

Gratitude and something else warred within his body, transforming into another emotion entirely.

'Lilas, I want to kiss you.'

Chapter Nine

The silence screamed between them. Bastien hadn't planned on saying that out loud, but he had, and he wasn't going to take it back.

Lilas gasped, her sweet breath blowing across his heated skin. 'Bastien, we mustn't.'

'I know, but I want you.'

This close, he could see her breathing escalate. Her *pouf* was still intact, although leaning somewhat to the side because of her position. The pulse at the base of her neck thumped rapidly. A smouldering fire stirred under his skin. The sweet mounds of her breasts rose and fell rapidly. Moisture dotted the palms clamped in his hands.

Her violet gaze drifted downward and lingered on his mouth. Perhaps she wasn't aware of the signs. Perhaps she didn't even recognise it in herself. Fortunately, he was experienced in the tell-tale symptoms of desire.

His own eyes fell to her lips. Plump and luscious, they captivated him. He'd tasted them twice before, and each time he'd been ravenous for more.

'You look very delectable, Lilas,' he murmured.

Her eyes widened. 'How wicked you are,' she breathed.

The phrase only heated his blood more. 'There are many wicked things I wish to do to you at this moment,' he said bluntly.

'Bastien!'

'But a kiss will do for now.'

She licked her lips, and he bent his head and followed the damp trail with his own tongue. She jolted in his arms as if she been caught on fire.

Bastien tasted the freshness, the plumpness of those brown berry lips, and his mind whirled in pleasure. Was it because it had been so long since he'd last kissed her? Or was it because it was Lilas, herself, he was savouring?

Regardless of the reason, he wanted to stay here in this moment, capturing the taste of her innocence and feeling her untutored responses quaking against his body.

Her eyes fluttered closed, and she sighed in an age-old sign of capitulation. And now he was there, drowning in the softness of her essence. Her mouth trembled with uncertainty against his. Her nervousness evoked a tenderness in him he hadn't felt before.

He drew back. 'Open your mouth, *ma arc-en-ciel*. I want to taste all of you.'

My rainbow. The endearment slid off his tongue with an ease that surprised him. He remembered imagining how it would feel to be clasped by her rainbow hands, wondering what it would be like to have those talented fingers adding colour to his world.

Now he knew.

How shyly she obeyed, her quivering against him increasing. She parted her lips and he delved inside to sip all her sweetness. He longed to savour every inch of her mouth. The taste of her could bring a man to his knees.

He tugged her gloves off her rainbow hands again and they rose to wrap around his neck. His arm tightened around her when she started to kiss him back. Now she wasn't so unsure, but eager. Little moans escaped her as the kiss grew in intensity. He loved that sound. It skittered across his back like the soft pads of a cat's paw.

She nipped at his mouth and the blood rushed through his veins. He could feel himself about to lose all his restraint. Her hand slid up into his hair. With her nails, she scraped gently at his scalp, her fingers digging through the mass of his long, thick, fine-stranded hair.

He growled, and let his hands start to caress her body, skimming over her slim waist, feeling the heat of her skin burning his palms through the fine material of her gown.

Then she suddenly pulled her sweet mouth away and halted.

The silence hung in the air, heavy with an undercurrent of unspoken emotions. Their breathing was laboured. His heartbeat pulsed erratically. He felt indelibly imprinted with Lilas in his mind.

'I don't think we should—'

'Lilas, look at me.'

'There's nothing—'

Bastien gripped her upper arms gently. 'You're not going to ignore this thing between us, Lilas. You are not going to pretend indifference to me now.'

Her eyes were still downcast, their long curling lashes like arcs of darkness lying across her cheekbones.

'Do you want me to stop?'

Bastien prayed she'd say no, because it was difficult to pull away from the ocean of feeling he was drowning in. But he would if she wanted him to.

'Tell me to stop and I will.'

Years of moral upbringing warred with the thickening blood in her veins. How hard it was to resist something that felt this good. That sent her senses soaring up into the night sky.

Bastien traced the outline of her ear.

'Please…' she begged, using her lashes to veil the burgeoning desire surely visible in her eyes.

She remembered when he'd kissed her before…how her body had responded to him. She wanted to feel that again.

His finger trailed down from the corner of her mouth to her chin, leaving a wake of fire along its path. Nerve endings singed from the passage of that skilled finger. He lifted her chin until she had no choice but to look deep into his molten gaze.

'Please what, *ma arc-en-ciel*?' he murmured. His voice had deepened.

She trembled, saying nothing out loud. The way he kept calling her his rainbow…

Please kiss me, take me, make me yours—

He breathed against her ear. 'You, *ma arc-en-ciel*, will try to fight this desire with every breath in your body, even though you and I both know I will be gentle with you.'

'Oh, Bastien!' she breathed, shivering as his words washed over her. They were so wicked, the things he was saying, but she couldn't stop him even if she wanted to.

And she didn't want him to.

He leaned forward, nipping her ear with his teeth with enough sharpness to make her jump, but then laving it with his warm tongue. 'What is it, Lilas?'

'You're making me…itch.'

Her face burned as he gave a low chuckle that made that itch get worse. His arms went around her and drew her into the strong clasp of his body.

'Do you know why, *ma arc-en-ciel*?'

She shook her head, her body shaking as if she were caught in a freezing storm of ice. But instead of ice, heat raced over her, taking hold of her limbs.

The passing lantern light danced in his eyes, brightening them to gold once more before shadowing them in darkness. 'Will you let me show you?' he asked. 'I promise I will not do anything you don't want me to.'

Lilas let her lids drift shut, lest she see the triumph in his gaze. 'Please…'

The next moment his mouth had captured hers again. Instead of the drugging, urgent kisses they'd shared earlier, this was a slower exploration of her mouth. He kept his touch light and soft, almost chaste.

It made the itching within her worsen. She pressed forward, wanting the hardness of his mouth against her. Wanting to be swept away on the tide of pleasure that had overwhelmed her before.

Infuriatingly, he didn't let her control the kiss. He cupped her head and plundered her mouth in soft, soft kisses. Each time she wanted more. Then she became aware that Bastien was trembling. His whole body shook from head to toe, as if caught up in a mighty storm. Yet his mouth continued to be gentle and coaxing.

She pulled her mouth away to see, in another brief flash of light, his beaded brow. 'Bastien, won't you kiss me like you did before? You're making the itch worse.'

A hard laugh came from his throat. 'I'm trying to be something approaching a gentleman, Lilas. But I find I am having to restrain myself. I've never felt this way before. I have to be careful I don't devour you.'

Lilas felt a sense of power grip her. Some wanton imp inside her came to life. Reaching up, she wrapped her arms around his head and brought his mouth firmly back down to hers.

Something broke in Bastien—she sensed it. He gripped her harder and began to devour her as he'd said. His lips tugged and gently nipped at her, sending all sorts of sensations through her. He pressed her mouth open and delved inside, sending her eyes rolling into the back of her head at the pleasure.

'Lilas…' he growled as he stopped and touched her forehead with his own. His laboured breathing filled the carriage. 'I can't. Sweet, sweet one. You're going to make me go mad.'

'Is that so?'

She revelled once more in her power and clutched him closer, letting the waves of pleasure take them where they would. His mouth moved down to the base of her throat, where he suckled at the pounding pulse he found there. His unsteady hands reached for her bodice and snatched it down with one swift tug.

She gasped and he instantly stilled.

'Will you let me?' His question came out raggedly.

'Let you do what?' she breathed, not sure what he meant.

'I want to taste you, Lilas. But I promise I won't do anything you don't want me to.'

Her nipples met the cool air of the interior of the carriage, hardening into pebbles. She closed her eyes. '*Oui*, Bastien…'

When his mouth closed over one nipple, she bucked under him. Lightning arced through her, and she cried out. Never in all her life had she expected to feel something like this. Bastien's warm, moist mouth suckled at her breast. With each stroke of his tongue, her back arched. That itch grew ten times worse as a feeling of tension stretched inside her like a tightrope.

Her hands moved restlessly over him, trying to find

an anchor in the maelstrom of emotions rocking through her. It wasn't until her fingers dug into his hair and pulled that Bastien stopped.

'Oh!' she wailed. 'Why did you stop?'

He swallowed audibly. 'I thought that was what you wanted. You pulled my hair.'

She blinked. 'I didn't know. I just…I just—'

'Don't be afraid. I'm here.'

She clutched his shoulders. 'I—I—'

'Do you want me to stop, Lilas?'

She couldn't even speak. Her fingers dug once more into his hair.

'Tear out every strand if you want, Lilas,' he said darkly.

Pressing herself closer, she eagerly rode the waves of pleasure that grew in intensity as Bastien bent his head to her breasts once again and the ecstasy devoured her as if it had never stopped.

His mouth moved to the other peak, which was desperate for his attention, while his fingers skilfully rolled the one he'd just left. She hissed.

When he pressed her breasts together and drew both turgid peaks into his mouth, the tightrope inside her finally snapped. She screamed as waves crashed over her, clinging on to Bastien as if her life depended on it.

Spent, she collapsed back onto the seat, her limbs hanging limply at her sides. Boneless… She felt boneless. If she had to move, she would only fall into a puddle on the carriage floor.

When some semblance of sense came back to her, she turned her heavy head to see Bastien looking down at her with masculine satisfaction, his eyes glowing but his face hard with tension.

'You looked beautiful, dying in my arms.'

'It felt a lot like dying,' she breathed in wonder.

'It's not called *la petite mort* without reason.'

As her heart slowed down, she saw a strange look cross Bastien's face as he stared at her. She couldn't quite identify what it was. Then he moved suddenly, and a protest erupted from her mouth.

'What is it, Bastien?' she asked when he remained silent. 'Is something wrong?'

His eyes blazed with heat.

She wanted him to go further, to continue.

Then, with an anguished sound, he buried his face in the warm hollow between her breasts, murmuring against her flesh but doing nothing more.

She squeezed his shoulders. 'Bastien?'

'Don't speak,' he said in a tortured way. 'And for pity's sake, cease that delightful wriggling.'

'How can I? You make me itch.'

Bastien laughed, and groaned, and burrowed deeper. His arms came around her waist and tightened, nearly stealing her breath away. She tried to move, to get more comfortable, but his hold tightened further, in warning, and she stayed still.

Then, after what seemed like an interminable amount of time, he took in a deep breath and lifted his head from her breasts. 'The scent of you is enough to drive a man insane,' he said gruffly. 'You make me feel crazed.'

He had taken her to a fever pitch—was he now stopping? 'I am not hindering you.'

'I know,' he said in a mournful tone. 'I am hindering myself. God help me.'

His fingers shook as he traced her mounds again, but went no further. He reluctantly drew away from her and rubbed his hands over his face.

Heat flooded her face as she sat up, seeing the way

her chest was exposed so blatantly. With shaking fingers, she did the best she could to cover herself up again.

The carriage had pulled up in front of the house. Then Bastien opened his mouth and said the very last thing she expected to hear.

'We're getting married, Lilas.'

Lilas stared at Bastien. 'What did you say?' Her voice sounded hoarse to her own ears.

'You heard me. We're getting married.'

She could see the servants loitering about in the doorway, ready for her to exit the carriage and make her way up the path. At any other time she'd have hurried out of the carriage, cognizant of the lateness of the hour and those who wished to go to their warm beds. However, her feet had become rooted to the floor, unable to be move, so great was her shock.

'Surely you can understand that after what just happened?'

His voice held a note of practicality. They might have been discussing the weather for all anyone knew. How could he be so calm about it? What she had experienced in his arms was still sending dwindling ripples of sensation inside her. It had rocked her entire world, sending the earth crashing beneath her.

Lilas had held on to her chastity, intending to give it to a man she could love. Or, if love did not come into their relationship, she wanted at the very least to be able to respect the man she would eventually give herself to.

She'd always avoided being in situations that might cause her to forget that vow.

Until tonight.

Now, as she stared at the darkened face of the only man who had ever touched her, she wanted to kick herself. He'd shown his desire for her, and though she'd had no experience with men in that way, she was certain he'd not received his own rapture during that interlude. And he didn't seem bothered by it.

'No,' she said slowly. 'I don't see why we need to get married just because of that.'

An odd grunt sounded from Bastien, but since she couldn't see his face she had no idea what it meant.

'Even you must be able to see that it's necessary for us to wed, Lilas.'

'Weren't you the one who declared we would end this engagement once we'd visited the Queen?' The bitterness that accompanied the words turned her mouth downward.

'That is no longer an option.'

'It is no reason to—'

'Surely you realise the wisdom behind going through with marriage now? For both of us. We'll solidify our positions in society. You as an artist, and me as a noble-man who has regained the favour of the Crown. We can make it a marriage of convenience,' he interjected. He leaned forward, the light from the moon slashing across his face. It looked inscrutable. 'We can marry and then, when the time is right, seek the proper channels for an annulment.'

'An annulment?' she whispered. 'Is such a thing even possible?'

'We will make it happen…despite any opposition. I know I encouraged you tonight, Lilas,' Bastien continued in that damnably calm voice, 'but I truly believe a marriage on these terms is the only way forward for us.'

She shook her head. 'I can't do that.'

'It's late,' he said, as if she hadn't spoken. 'Go inside and we'll discuss this tomorrow.'

'It is tomorrow,' she said stupidly. He had her so rattled.

'So it is. *Non.*' He placed a finger on her mouth when she started to say that she didn't need another moment to make her decision. 'Get some rest and we will talk soon, Lilas. I promise.'

Esme was there to assist Lilas out of her clothes. If she noted their rumpled state, or the way the *pouf* she'd spent over an hour dressing was askew, she said nothing.

Half an hour later, Lilas thanked her maid and sent her to bed.

She went over what had happened in the carriage. Bastien's proposal…!

How could she agree to that?

She turned over on her side, settling her head against her hands. Now tiredness was starting to seep over her. Perhaps it was sheer exhaustion that made her reconsider what he'd suggested about a marriage of convenience.

The expectations of Paris society had mounted to a fever pitch after that night in Versailles. She wouldn't be surprised if invitations from across the world came to her doorstep.

If they were to have a marriage of convenience, it would solve a problem. No long engagement…no more pressure from society. And then, after an agreed-upon time, they could annul it and go back to their lives. She as a painter and he to his ideal wife.

Lilas bit her bottom lip. Could she live, even temporarily, within the confines of such a marriage? Maybe if she hadn't experienced that ecstasy in his arms, or felt his own response, she'd feel more confident about doing so. There was definitely something to be said for blissful ignorance.

He knew exactly what to do with her…tuning her pleasure like he would an instrument. Even now, her face heated at the memory of her wantonness. Never to experience that again would be a tragedy.

Yet she still didn't trust Bastien. Her stepmother's words entered her mind. Was Bastien only doing this because now that he had royal favour again he could continue to use her?

Thinking back to his proposal of a marriage of convenience, she sat up and hugged her knees. Again, her stepmother's words sounded a warning.

The thought of a marriage without love was distasteful to her. As a young girl in the orphanage, before she'd even discovered the truth of her ancestry, she'd dreamed of a husband to love and a family to cherish. And during her time as a servant she'd captured glimpses of the previous Duc de Languedoc and his wife, seeing their obvious affection for each other and secretly wanting the same for herself.

So how could she let herself agree to a marriage in name only?

But Bastien was right about one thing. They could not avoid marrying now. Societal pressure being what it was, there was a certain expectation of them which simply could not be ignored.

Thinking of his mouth upon her, she closed her eyes. Nothing had prepared her for such ecstasy. Her body felt branded by everything he'd done to her. Knowing there was more to learn was enough to make her limbs weak.

How could she suppress the desire he'd evoked? If she and Bastien agreed to a marriage of convenience, and later an annulment, did she really want another man to touch her as Bastien had?

She shuddered. The idea of another man's caresses repulsed her.

But how could she want more from Bastien when he

didn't care for her? How could she trust him not to hurt her or betray her again?

No, it was better this way. As Bastien had said, they would each benefit from a marriage of convenience. He would withhold his mastery and she wouldn't surrender to it. Nor would she risk becoming a broodmare. She'd have the name of St Clare without any of the responsibility of being a real wife.

Sleep began to drag her eyelids down. When she met Bastien tomorrow she would...

Something moved outside on the balcony.

The tiredness vanished in an instant as she jerked awake. 'Who's there?'

Alarm raced through her as she waited. The curtains shifted, and then parted. She sat up in bed, her mouth open, ready to scream, when she saw the outline of a familiar black habit appear.

'Soeur Calme?'

The nun came forward.

Lilas swallowed several times before she croaked out. 'Why are you in my room?'

Soeur Calme halted, her eyes apologetic and entreating. She bent and patted Lilas on the arm in a reassuring way.

Lilas patted the silent woman back. 'What are you doing here, Soeur Calme?' she repeated.

To Lilas's utter shock, the nun sat on the bed. In the darkness, it was hard to see, but she could just make out her pale, pinched face. The woman leaned forward, beckoning Lilas to do the same. More from surprise than obedience, Lilas did as she asked.

The nun's mouth opened and closed. Lilas felt a cold sensation take over her body. Was Seour Calme trying to speak to her? But why? For what purpose? An intense look of concentration came over the nun's face. Once more, her mouth opened. This time, Lilas felt a soft wisp of air land on her cheeks.

Seour Calme was talking!

'I don't understand what you're trying to say,' Lilas said, gripping the nun's hand. 'But I will wait until I do.'

Squeezing her hand back, Seour Calme pressed her fingers against her Adam's apple. Then, with a visible look of determination stamped on her features, she opened her mouth. Lilas leaned forward eagerly, waiting with bated breath to hear what her first words would be.

In a wispy breath, she said, 'Kill you…'

Lilas started. All the heat drained from her body.

'Kill me?' She backed away from the nun. 'You want to kill me?'

There was nothing more frightening than a breathless nun threatening to murder her.

Vigorously, Soeur Calme shook her head. *'Non…'* It was little more than a hush of air.

For a moment, Lilas was confused. Then her mouth dropped open as she realised the nun was referring to her mystery enemy. 'Who is it?'

'Must be careful…' the nun gasped.

Lilas wanted to ignore what the nun had said, but couldn't. Soeur Calme had broken her vow of silence to warn her. For that alone Lilas had to take the nun's word. It was something she had to confirm, at the very least.

'Who wants to kill me?' she pressed.

Without warning, the nun rose from the bed and glided to the door. Lilas shoved the covers away, trying to stop her. 'Soeur Calme—wait!'

But the door was opened and shut in less than a minute.

Lilas sat back, her mind churning over what the nun had revealed.

Could she trust what the older woman had said?

How could she not?

She thought back to the attack. For a while, she had pretended that nothing had really happened. That it had been a one-time incident. Surely a pickpocket wouldn't have tried to kill her?

She lay down again. If what Soeur Calme said was true, then the only question that remained was, who was it that wanted her dead?

The pungent, odorous scent of the Seine, the lifeblood of Paris, wafted to Bastien's nose. The river rushed under the five arches of Pont Royal, muddy and dank. Despite this, it still provided a sense of tranquillity. Travelling down the river, he saw barges dipping low into the water, weighted with cargo. More barges further down the embankment were being dismantled after their last trip down the river, readied to be sold as wood.

Movement along his peripheral vision revealed a group of poor naked children, laughing and playing in the water, their pale bodies glistening in the sun.

'Probably the first time those children have bathed all year,' Lilas remarked as she smiled and waved back at one enthusiastic child.

'Indeed.'

Further down, a woman dressed in tattered clothing dipped her washing in the water.

Bastien said nothing for a moment as he gazed down the length of the bridge, catching a glimpse of the Pavillon de Flore, an extension of the royal residence of the Palais du Louvre. It looked lonely standing there.

A church bell rang out in the distance and the little

children jumped and danced, singing 'Frère Jacques' with wild abandon. Lilas laughed at their antics and called down, encouraging them. Another woman of society would have ignored them, finding them distasteful, but that wasn't Lilas.

And that was making things even more difficult for him.

Before his father's death, he'd lived like a monk for over a year, experiencing no pleasure in the company of women, nor indeed having any desire for it. At the time, he'd thought little of it. His father and mother had both admonished him to restrict his passions as a young man, and he'd never been the type to overindulge.

But even his experience with his first woman paled in comparison to what he'd shared last night with Lilas. The moment their lips had touched, he'd known his world had shifted.

He should have realised one taste of her wouldn't be enough. Long after he'd left and taken his frustrated body to his bedchamber, he'd remembered the delicate, innocent flavour of her mouth and her skin and wanted more.

Was it merely because it had been some time since he'd indulged in the pleasures of the bedchamber? Or was it something else?

Her response had been all he could have wanted and more, proving that if he were to make their marriage real, neither would regret their physical coming together.

When he'd mentioned a marriage of convenience, he'd thought the answer to their problems had come to him. Many couples had such arrangements—they wouldn't be doing anything that others had not.

An inner voice mocked him. Had any man ever had a wife as lovely and desirable as Lilas Moreau and not taken her to his bed? When she'd writhed under him in her pleasure, it had been the most beautiful sight he'd ever seen.

But it was a sight he had to deny himself.

Last night in the carriage, his desire had flared dangerously out of control. Bastien longed to blame his self-enforced celibacy for his reaction, but he knew that wasn't it.

It was Lilas herself that made him wild.

He thought back to his parents once more, recalling an event as a young boy, when he'd found them locked in a passionate embrace. As a child, he'd had no idea what they were doing. They'd simply looked odd to him. Yet his father's words echoed through time. 'Only you, my dear Carmen. Only you.'

Those words had been spoken to Bastien's mother with such devotion…with a kind of desperation bordering on obsession. At least to his mind.

And, irrational as it was, Bastien knew he didn't want any woman in his arms but Lilas.

Such a dangerous thought! Was he turning into his father? No, that couldn't be. He wouldn't fall in love with Lilas. He couldn't let emotion override all else in his mind.

And desire? taunted the little voice in his head.

Thinking of his sleepless night, tortured by visions of Lilas, he nonetheless tried to put it in perspective. Desire was what made mankind grow in number. It was a physical entity and nothing more. So it could be resisted.

Unwanted, the image of that night in the carriage rose in his mind yet again. How quickly he had slipped into madness! And he hadn't done nearly what he could have done to her to bring her pleasure.

Yet he'd found himself fighting for restraint.

That didn't matter, he told himself stubbornly. Any

man, after a long bout of celibacy, would have reacted the same way.

The thought gave him a modicum of comfort. He inhaled softly. He *could* control his desire for Lilas.

A bird overhead cried out, and to his fanciful mind it sounded as if it were laughing at him.

Ridding himself of the odd thought, he turned to Lilas. 'Are you going to marry me?'

'I am. But there are some stipulations I wish to place upon our arrangement.'

'Such as?'

'I agree with you that it should be a marriage of convenience. I have no wish to have it consummated in any way.'

'I see.'

'Should your masculine urges surpass your ability to control them, I suggest you hire the services of a mistress.'

Her eyes were defiant, daring him to disagree with her terms. Could he, though? After last night, it was difficult not to want her in every way possible.

'Perhaps your ideal would consider being your mistress?'

For a moment he had no idea who she was referring to. Then he remembered the Duchesse de Villers-Cotterêts and heaved a sigh. 'Though I enjoyed talking with her, she isn't the woman I want.'

Something flashed in her gaze, but he had no time to identify what it was as her lids drifted down, veiling her expression.

Remember, you can control desire, Bastien. Not love. And you mustn't fall in love with your wife. Ever.

An ironic smile twisted his lips. 'I'm certain most men would fall at your feet for such an opportunity.'

'I am not marrying most men, *monsieur*. Just you.'

The idea had merit. If they kept to a marriage of convenience, then he would be able to live his life as he saw fit. His father wasn't there to restrain his actions. He needed to focus on maintaining his family's position in society.

The memory of Lilas falling apart in his arms would dissipate over time. Bastien could barely recall the faces of the other women he'd had brief liaisons with. Not that he'd had many…

'Very well, *mademoiselle*. I agree to your terms.'

Thinking of it sometime later, Bastien applauded Lilas's stipulations. He didn't want to become more attached to her than he needed to be. He had to be careful that this marriage worked on a social level only. He would not become like his father and let emotion gain a foothold in his heart.

Chapter Ten

'You are *très belle, mademoiselle*! *Très belle!*'

Lilas's smile was strained, while Esme's eyes glimmered with unshed tears as she stood back and assessed her mistress.

Even to her own critical eye Lilas knew she'd never looked better. The lavender dress was a work of art. Supported on panniers that spread the skirt of the gown outward nearly three feet from her hips, it flowed down her figure in a cascade of intricately threaded brocade. A myriad of tiny diamonds embedded in the shimmering cloth caught the light every time she moved. The golden underskirts contrasted with them in a complimentary way, giving a warmth to the gown that enhanced the brown tones of her skin.

Esme had shown her skilled talents as she styled her *pouf* to rise above her head nearly three feet. Within its powdered depths, flowers of all sorts nestled. Daffodils, roses and lilacs, in an arrangement of soft colours that blended subtly with the rest of her attire. Her mouth was painted with vermilion and her cheeks dusted with rouge, and she presented to the world the very image of bridal aristocratic pride.

Never had Lilas looked as beautiful as she did now.

Never had she felt more depressed.

She was marrying a man who did not love her.

The door to her chambers opened and Pierre stepped in. He was dressed in a stately blue waistcoat, snug breeches, long white stockings and silver shoes with golden buckles. His wig gleamed in the light. His admiring gaze swept over her.

'Lilas, you are exquisite.'

She smiled at his kind words, because she knew he meant them. 'Where are your spectacles?' she asked.

'I have them, but I knew that I would be blinded by your loveliness so I took them off.'

She laughed at his foolery, but was thankful for his levity.

'I know that your father would have been so happy to see you on this day. It is my honour to stand by your side in his stead.'

Her heart clenched at his words. 'Do you think he would have liked me?'

Pierre came forward and took her hand in his. His eyes were earnest as he said, 'When he thought you were dead, he loved you. Knowing that you were alive, he adored you.'

Pierre kissed her hand and told her that he would meet her downstairs when they all left to go to the chapel.

'Where is Belle-Mère?'

'She is getting ready. Although it is your wedding, I'm sure my mother will somehow make it her moment.'

She smiled, as she was expected to, but inwardly she wondered at Pierre's words.

Her stepmother had been acting rather strangely as the wedding day drew closer. Once she'd found her sitting still in the drawing room, wringing her hands. When

Lilas had walked into the room and asked what the matter was, the Comtesse had dismissed her concerns as fanciful. But as preparations continued, Lilas had been forced to send more examples of odd occurrences to the back of her mind.

At least after today she would not have to be privy to her stepmother's private life any more. Her art and being Bastien's *duchesse* would fill her days.

'We need to leave soon. It would be rather awkward if the groom showed up on time and not the bride.'

Pierre left, and Esme continued to fawn over her appearance. Lilas stared unseeingly at her reflection.

Never had the loss of her parents been so apparent. What would they have thought about her meteoric rise as an artist, being so sought-after in this fashion? Would they have been proud of her?

More than that, what would they have thought of this marriage of convenience? From what the former Duc de Languedoc had shared about her parents, it seemed they'd truly cared for each other. Her marrying for convenience seemed a travesty, but what other choice did she have? Her parents had been fortunate to love each other. Would they have been disappointed in her settling for less, even though she was marrying the man her father had wanted her to?

'What is wrong, *mademoiselle*? Are you not happy?'

Lilas pulled her mind from her melancholy thoughts. 'I am fine, Esme.' At the worried look on her maid's face, Lilas reached out and grabbed the other woman's hand. 'Truly I am fine. One cannot help but be nervous on a day as important as this.'

Placated by those words, Esme continued to work on her appearance while Lilas's thoughts delved into all that was wrong with this day.

Well before anyone would get up and bother her, Lilas had gone to look at her painting of Bastien once more. She still hadn't finished it, but would have it sent over, fully concealed, to her new home. The servants would be under strict orders not to unwrap it.

That day in the kitchen garden four years ago, Bastien had told her that he wanted a portrait of him and his wife on their wedding day. She'd had no idea then that *she* would be his wife. Was the portrait she had created still valid now she was to be his wife, rather than his ideal? She didn't know.

The past month and a half had been filled with activity. Lilas would have preferred the traditional route towards her wedding. Being confined to her home, then just a ceremony and a lavish dinner. But her stepmother had wanted an ostentatious display to match her and Bastien's popularity. And it had seemed wrong to deprive Paris of the opportunity to see them wed with the Queen's approval.

So the chapel had been selected, the invitations sent to three hundred guests, who had all accepted. And additional staff had been hired for the event.

Esme hummed above her head as she put the finishing touches on her *pouf.* The door to her bedchamber opened, and her stepmother stepped in, looking elegant in a peach-coloured gown that highlighted her slim figure and clear skin and made her blue eyes look even colder.

'Are you done with your mistress?' she asked Esme.

Esme came down off the small ladder she'd used while she styled Lilas's hair and backed away. '*Oui*, Madame la Comtesse.'

'We don't want to keep your bridegroom waiting. It isn't proper.'

'I am ready, Belle-Mère.'

Her stepmother came forward and looked her over. Under that flinty blue-eyed gaze Lilas felt as if she were being dissected, much as a man of science might do to some sort of specimen.

'You look radiant, Lilas.'

The way her stepmother said it, Lilas wondered if she really meant it.

'*Merci.*'

Not for the first time, she was glad that after today she wouldn't be subjected to her stepmother's presence for long periods of time any more. When the ceremony was over, and the papers signed, she would be Lilas St Clare, Duchesse de Languedoc.

How unfortunate that after four years she felt no closer to the woman than when they'd first met. She would miss Pierre's company far more than her stepmother's.

Feeling horrible for that treacherous thought, she stood carefully and went over to where her stepmother stood. 'Belle-Mère, I want to thank you for all you have done for me these past four years.'

'There is no need for that Lilas,' said her stepmother breezily. 'You are Louis's daughter, not mine.'

Esme gasped, clearly seeing the way the words cut. Lilas was glad for it, because the sound covered up her own sharp intake of breath. Why was her stepmother being so cruel? What had she done to deserve such rancour?

Something of her confusion must have shown on her face, because her stepmother sighed and rubbed at her temples.

'Forgive me, Lilas. Although weddings are joyous occasions, they are still rather time-consuming. So much needs to be done.'

'I understand, Belle-Mère.'

'You don't,' the woman retorted. 'Not really.'

'What do you mean?'

Her stepmother levelled her gaze at her for a long moment, her eyes sparking in an odd way, before she ordered Esme out of the room and shut the door behind her.

'Lilas, listen to me… It is not only the wedding preparations that have put me in this rather sour mood on what should be the happiest day of your life. It's the fact that I do not trust the Duc de Languedoc.'

'Because he was there during the attack?'

'More than that, Lilas.' Her stepmother gripped her hands. 'Look into my eyes. Are you sure you want to do this? Are you sure he won't hurt you?'

Lilas frowned, unhappy with the direction her thoughts were taking now that her stepmother had planted the seeds of doubt. Bastien wouldn't hurt her—not in a physical sense. Goodness only knew that if he were going to do so, he'd had more than enough opportunity already.

Emotionally, it was an entirely different thing. This marriage wasn't all that she'd hoped for, but it would allow her to keep her heart intact and pursue her artistic endeavours. If some part of her wished for more, then only she would know about it.

'He won't hurt me. I'm sure of it.'

The Comtesse de la Baux stepped back. 'I hope for your sake that you're right.'

Her stepmother's words haunted her as they travelled the short distance to the chapel where the wedding was to take place. Lilas stared at her clasped hands. She couldn't suppress the thought that maybe…just maybe…her stepmother had an insight and intuition about Bastien that she didn't.

Soon she arrived at the chapel, seeing some of the

city's poorer citizens standing outside, waiting for a glimpse of her as she exited the carriage. Though her heart was thudding heavily in her chest, she took the time to let the bystanders look their fill.

She could remember how the people of the city had acted when the Queen had married years ago, with a guest list of five thousand and onlookers numbering two hundred thousand. She couldn't compete with that sort of extravagance.

By the time they'd climbed the stairs and entered the chapel the music had begun to play. Her stepmother handed her a bouquet of orange blossoms, symbolising her virginity, then Lilas took in a deep breath and began the long trek down the aisle towards her future.

Was that a look of fright in Lilas's eyes?

Bastien fixed his gaze on his soon-to-be bride as she came down the aisle. She looked lovely. A perfect foil to his own elegance. His solid white wig was new, and expensive, his white gold-threaded coat and waistcoat gleamed, and his shoes shone, their buckles glinting in the light.

Looking at her, seeing that hint of fear, he wondered if she was regretting the decision for them to wed. He had to admit that part of himself wanted to feel that regret.

All these years away, and despite his every effort, he was doing exactly as his father had told him to do.

Marrying Lilas Moreau.

That goaded him in more ways than one. He had spent so much of his life trying to get out of his father's clutches, and here he was, right back in them. What did that make him? Was he so easily controlled?

Estienne's words haunted him as he waited for Lilas

to complete her march towards him. *'Would it be so ter-rible if you were to marry her?'*

No, it wouldn't be terrible if he married her.

Today, he felt the loss of his father more than he ever had. What he wouldn't give for a moment of his time, his presence. While he'd dressed for the wedding at his home his heart had throbbed anew. Regrets and recriminations had hurled themselves upon his head.

Why had he gone away? Why hadn't he tried to heal the rift between them before it was too late?

Why hadn't he apologised? To keep his pride? What good was pride when you couldn't say hello or goodbye to your loved ones any more?

The only thing he had to cling to was the fact that marrying Lilas was his idea, not his father's.

For one thing, during this past month of wedding prep-aration he had come to admire anew everything about his future bride. More and more, he knew that being with Lilas was the right thing.

Not because his father had decreed it.

But because he knew it was the right thing for himself.

Being in her company and knowing she would soon be his was something that had quietly rested at the back of his mind, giving him peace. There was a rightness to their union that had nothing to do with their fathers' wishes.

He frowned as his eyes drifted from Lilas's lovely form to the Comtesse de la Baux. The woman was stand-ing off to one side, in her place, but her eyes were fixed on him. Though her rather intent stare made him some-what uneasy, he ignored her.

When Lilas approached, she gazed up at him. Her eyes looked into his own, questioning, hoping, begging.

At the distinct clearing of the throat from the priest,

they both faced him and then knelt on the floor, before the crucifix that hung above them, taking this first step into marriage.

Bastien surveyed the guests who were enjoying their repast at Hôtel de Languedoc. His uncle stood nearby, greeting people, but they'd kept their distance from each other. Ever since that night of the dinner, he'd made a vow only to interact with the man when it was necessary.

Looking over the room, he saw Lilas holding court with a few women. In her wedding finery she appeared more radiant and resplendent than any other woman there.

Without warning, the Duchesse de Villers-Cotterêts appeared before him, as if she'd stepped out of air.

'I hoped I would have an opportunity to speak with you, Monsieur le Duc.'

Her clear eyes held his with a steady regard.

'Did you?'

'I am going to speak bluntly. I sensed you were attracted to me when we met at Versailles. Was that not true?'

Bastien blinked. That was a highly inappropriate question to ask a man on his wedding day! 'I am not sure I understand what you mean.'

'Don't pretend you didn't find me desirable.'

Bastien mentally shook his head. So he'd been wrong. The Duchesse wasn't the woman of calm and sense he'd thought her. Thank goodness he had never even considered her to be his ideal.

'I did not find you desirable, Madame la Duchesse. Perhaps you should remember how important this day is to me and my bride and cease this vulgar conversation immediately.'

Her face turned a deep shade of scarlet.

'I can assure you I have no interest in any other woman but my wife. Not now, nor in the future.' He leaned forward. 'I think I've made myself perfectly clear, don't you?'

The woman looked as if she wanted to run far away. 'E-Every happiness, Monsieur le Duc.'

She curtsied and bowed, before skittering away like a mouse. As she did so, he pulled his eyes away from her and they slammed straight into Lilas's furious gaze.

Lilas had kept polite company with her many guests, but the hour was growing late. The food had been excellent, but she'd barely been able to eat a bite. Now, she took a small sip from the drink someone had given to her.

Soon the Comte de Clareville, taking the place of Bastien's father, would lead her and Bastien to the wedding chamber above stairs, where they would consummate their marriage.

At least, that was what everyone thought.

What a farce it would be to lie in her marriage bed alone, instead of in Bastien's arms. Although it was what she'd said she wanted, she couldn't suppress the disappointment she felt. Memories of what they'd shared in the carriage had often sifted through her fitful sleep, leaving her desirous of something she could never have.

It didn't help that she'd caught him having a conversation with the Duchesse de Villers-Cotterêts and seen the way they were so intent on each other. Lilas hadn't wanted the woman at her wedding, but due to her status and position in society it wouldn't have been proper not to have extended her an invitation.

The Duchesse was dressed well, rivalling most of the

women who'd also attended in their best finery. Lilas had felt her nostrils flare at the sight of their heads together.

She'd given Bastien leave to find a mistress since she would not share his bed. Why should it upset her to see that he was in all likelihood doing so? As long as he was discreet…

Such an idea left a sour taste in her mouth.

The Duchesse had bowed to him in a graceful manner and glided away quickly, her face flushed, with Bastien staring intently after the woman.

Lilas had longed to scratch the woman's face.

Just then, Bastien glanced at her, and their gazes held across the room. She couldn't read his expression. His lion eyes were hypnotic.

Had he and the Duchesse already planned to meet? Surely Bastien would at least give her the pretence of a wedding night before seeking another woman's bed… wouldn't he?

'Are you all right? You look a little peaked.'

She turned at the sound of her stepmother's voice from behind her. 'I'm fine.'

'Are you worried about performing your duty tonight, Lilas?' asked her stepmother, her blue eyes staring searchingly into her own. 'Or is it something else?'

When her stepmother had taken her aside and told her what she should expect on her wedding night, Lilas hadn't had the heart to tell her that some things she had discovered on her own. Not to mention the fact that what she'd shared in the carriage with Bastien that day still teased her mind, although she'd tried her hardest not to dwell on it.

'I'm fine, Belle-Mère.' She took another sip of the punch in her hand. 'I've been wondering when we should leave—to begin that part of our wedding, if you will.'

'Are you so eager, then?'

Lilas lifted her shoulder. Had she and her stepmother had a different sort of relationship she might have shared some of her inner thoughts with her. As it was, she thought it prudent to go along with the idea of maidenly nerves. 'I want it to be over with as soon as possible.'

'Well, finish your drink. While you do that, I will go and fetch the priest so he can bless the bedchamber.'

Her stepmother walked away and Lilas stared out at the large gathering that still hadn't dissipated. Somewhere among the crowd was Bastien.

Her vision became blurry. She blinked her eyes, but nothing happened to change it. In fact, it was growing worse. Not only that, but a heaviness suddenly came over her limbs, weighing her down. She could barely take one step in front of the other.

This couldn't be happening. Not on her wedding day.

'Lilas!'

She heard her stepmother's voice from far off, growing fainter. Then her legs went out from under her and she fell, smacking her head on the edge of a table before collapsing onto the floor.

When Bastien heard the Comtesse de la Baux's cry he was talking to Pierre. Their conversation stopped in mid-sentence, and he turned to see the older woman kneeling by Lilas's prone body on the floor. His heart pounded as he raced across the room, wondering what had happened to his wife.

He fell to his knees beside her, wrapping his arms about her waist and drawing her close. Her head lolled to one side and her eyes fluttered, as if she were trying to decide if she were going to wake up or stay asleep.

'Lilas? Lilas!'

He firmly slapped her cheeks—not to hurt her but to rouse her to full wakefulness. All the while he asked questions of the Comtesse de la Baux. The way his heart was slamming in his chest, it threatened to find its way outside the cavity. What could have happened—and why?

'Mère, what has happened to Lilas?' Pierre's voice rang loud in the room, causing all activity to quieten as the onlookers followed the source of that anguished cry.

'I was talking to her, to see if she was ready to go to the marriage chamber, and then she swayed and fell to the ground.'

Bastien listened to what she said, but there was something nagging at the back of his mind. He could not take the time to focus on it now, though. What was important was seeing how Lilas was.

Her wedding gown, though beautiful, was now a hindrance, due to its sheer size and width. The panniers had lifted off her hips, sending her dress askew and revealing her undergarments. Somehow in the fall she'd lost one of her shoes, so a stockinged foot peeked out forlornly from underneath the vast quantity of material.

Swiftly, he pulled her dress down as best he could, to preserve her modesty. 'Madame la Comtesse, can you have one of the servants bring a damp cloth?'

It was thrust into his hand seconds later, and he used it to tenderly wipe Lilas's face.

'*Madame*, would you please be so kind as to tell our guests to leave?'

How he wished they had stuck to tradition and had a small, intimate ceremony, because now news of this incident would spread throughout Paris within an hour.

'I will see to it.'

When she had left, he looked at Pierre. They did not

converse very often, but when they did he found the man to be an amiable one, who truly saw Lilas as his sister.

'She's fainted, but whatever has affected her doesn't appear to have poisoned her.'

'This isn't good,' Pierre said, his face darkening. 'Everyone who was invited was hand-picked by us. So that means that someone here has put something in Lilas's drink to render her asleep. Who among us would have done that?'

The muscle alone his jawline ticked. The attack by that masked man and now this!

Pierre leaned forward. '*Monsieur*, there is something else you should know, if you do not already.'

'And what is that?'

'Lilas told me of two incidents in which she has been warned of being in danger. Twice a note was delivered mysteriously to her chambers. She told me this in confidence, but if she did not tell you, I feel it is prudent for you to know now.'

Bastien thought flames might engulf his head. Not only had she been attacked, but someone close to her was warning her that she would come to harm!

He gently caressed her face, his fingers trembling against her skin. '*Ma arc-en-ciel,*' he whispered, 'Didn't I tell you there should be no secrets between us?'

Was her distrust of him so great that she felt he could not protect her? The idea wounded him like the stab of a sword.

He knew what he had to do. 'I am not going to let her stay here, where anyone can get to her. We are going to Château de Velay.'

An approving expression appeared in Pierre's eyes. 'Under the circumstances, I cannot disagree with you.

It is going to take you a few days to get there. Are you going to be all right?'

Bastien looked at him.

Pierre grunted. 'I can see I ask a foolish question.'

Chapter Eleven

Lilas wandered towards the willow tree, seeing its dangling fronds swaying in the breeze. It was the same one that sheltered her all those years ago. The one that had marked the most significant moment of her life, when Bastien had bought her drawing for one silver *livre*.

As she pushed aside the branches to hide under its massive shade she hoped to find solace and the answers she needed for the great questions in her life.

Coming back to Château de Velay had filled her with mixed emotions. She hadn't expected to miss the country estate of her childhood all that much. But walking about the grounds now brought back so many things she had forgotten.

Or rather, things she'd pushed to the back of her mind once she'd discovered her identity as the daughter of Louis Moreau.

She'd done everything she could not to think of her childhood. Now circumstances were forcing her to think about the past. Or rather, reconsider the past. Whoever had put the sleeping draught in her punch had done so as a threat. They could have so easily poisoned her, but that clearly hadn't been the point.

Whoever it was had used the incident to warn her off.

That was the conclusion Bastien and Pierre had come to when she'd awakened with a throbbing headache, a sore temple and her wedding day finery ruined.

Thankfully, she had not had to suffer too much humiliation, as Bastien had got them out of Paris within two days. It had taken nearly a week to travel to Château de Velay, but he had secured guards to protect the carriage, travelling via well-trodden roads and doing whatever was necessary to ensure their comfort and safety.

The question remained: Why? Why was someone trying to warn her off? To hurt her?

Lilas picked up a blade of grass and wrapped its length around a finger. What threat did she pose? To whom?

Esme had smothered her with care, while her stepmother had refused to let her do much of anything. At first, her stepmother and Pierre had decided to stay in Paris after her disastrous wedding, but Bastien had extended them an invitation to stay at Château de Velay. He had known that for Pierre at the very least, concern for her wouldn't abate with distance.

At first, she had been thankful for their presence. Then, as she'd remained confined to her bed for several days, treated as a porcelain doll, she'd found herself going mad with the dullness.

When that treatment had threatened to go into a second week of her being shielded from the world, she'd fought tooth and nail to regain her independence. On the one hand, she'd appreciated everyone's concern for her well-being. But if they'd continued to treat her like that then whoever it was that wanted to do her harm would succeed in curtailing her life anyway.

Sighing, she tossed the blade of grass away from her

and leaned against the trunk of the tree. Her life had altered since the day of their wedding in other ways too.

Her chambers were adjacent to Bastien's, but she'd never seen inside them, and nor had Bastien utilised the connecting door. They had agreed to this arrangement, but Bastien had created an emotional distance between them too.

He was polite, and cordial, seeing to her every need. If she'd been a guest in his home she would have found his behaviour impeccable as a host. But she wasn't his guest. She was his wife. And though it was a marriage of convenience, Lilas hadn't expected to lose the one thing that had always sustained her from her earliest days, when she'd been a cinder girl in his father's home. His friendship.

Her stepmother's words still haunted her. On her wedding day, the woman had asked if she believed Bastien wouldn't hurt her. How foolish of her to answer as she had!

Now, despite her assertion that he wouldn't hurt her, all she could feel was a physical ache in her chest at his continued distance.

To be fair, she knew he was spending much of his time trying to find out who it had been that had put the sleeping draught in her punch. Though she admired him for dedicating his time to this endeavour, it also frustrated her.

'Lilas?'

She lifted her head to see Bastien walking towards her. Although the heavy curtain of willow branches hung between them, whenever the wind blew she was able to see his form.

Even from far way she was aware of him. He'd taken on a less formal appearance here, in darker-toned breeches and waistcoat with plain shoes. The wind whipped at his hair, which was pulled back into a *queue*, sending long wavy strands of it about his face. Despite his relaxed exterior, he nonetheless bore the commanding air she always associated with him.

Two days had passed since the last time they'd met. Although they were secluded in the country, he had business to attend to, along with trying to discover the villain who'd tainted her drink.

The only thought running through her mind as he approached was that her stepmother had been right. He only wanted the approval of society, and he had already obtained that from the Queen. Now that he'd received that, what good was she to him?

Her mind travelled back to those passionate moments in the carriage. How could a man who had given her a taste of heaven behave so coldly to her now? Had it all been an act? Had he ever really cared about her at all? Desired her? Wanted her?

'Are you well, Lilas?'

She gave a slight nod. 'I am.'

He stepped through the branches, coming to stand next to her. Those golden eyes looked searchingly into her own. What was he thinking about? Some estate business? Was he considering her in any way?

'Why are you sitting alone under here?'

She averted her gaze, staring down at the material of her gown. 'I wanted the quiet of the meadow to soothe my thoughts.'

'In what way?'

How could she tell Bastien he was the source of her mental chaos?

Instead, she equivocated. 'Does it matter?'

'To me, yes,' he said bluntly.

She sighed. 'I do not know who is trying to hurt me and for what purpose. I do not believe I have given anyone cause to hate me. So why?'

Bastien cleared his throat. 'Pierre and I are still looking into the matter, although we now think it might have something to do with the inheritance from your father.'

She frowned. 'But I don't inherit anything directly. My firstborn son does. There is nobody else to inherit.'

'I'm aware of that, but it is the only thing we could think of—even though we don't really understand why. I brought you to Château de Velay to protect you, but also to make sure that if someone is trying to hurt you, for whatever reason, then we will be able to find out who is doing it.'

'Do you think it's someone within our household?'

'I don't know, but if anyone tries again we'll be ready for them.'

'Very well.'

They sat under the willow tree in silence for a little longer. When it became difficult just to sit there, Lilas blurted out, 'Bastien, what's happened between us?'

His expression closed. 'What do you mean?'

'You've created a distance between us.'

Although he didn't move, she could feel his withdrawal from her.

'I haven't been cold to you, Lilas.'

'Bastien, we've barely seen each other since we got here. When we do, you act so very politely to me.'

'That doesn't seem criminal, Lilas.'

Her blood heated up. Was he toying with her? Dismissing her concern about the chasm that had appeared between them?

'Perhaps it isn't criminal, but it's certainly cruel.'

'In what way?'

Lilas pushed against the trunk of the tree to raise herself off the ground. Bastien immediately stood to help her, but she rebuffed his assistance, too angry to accept his help.

'When we agreed to this arrangement I did not think you would be the sort of man to use a woman for his own gain. Perhaps I am not your ideal, but I have at least been your friend.'

The edges of his lips tightened. 'My ideal?' he repeated.

It was as if flames scorched her head. 'You sought your ideal to give you what you wanted, but she couldn't do for you what I could. Now that you have found favour with society again I am of no use to you any more, am I? You only married me because it's what all of Paris, including the Queen, expected of you.'

A muscle leapt along the side of his jaw. 'Is that what you think?'

'What else could it be, Bastien? How often have you told me there are no secrets between us?'

The fronds of the trees swayed behind them as the wind blew. A fine tension took hold of her limbs. Although he didn't move, she sensed Bastien's personality looming over her. His next words sent the breath shuddering out of her chest.

'Why didn't you tell me about the warning notes?'

Lilas's mouth opened and closed several times before she spoke. She appeared lost for words, and Bastien indulged in a perverse sense of satisfaction at her discomfiture.

When she finally spoke, she said, 'Pierre told you?'

That wasn't what he wanted—no, *needed* to hear. 'Is that all you have to say?'

There she stood, looking almost like a young girl in a lavender gown less formal than some of her other attire. Fitted to her waist, trimmed with white material and belted with a white sash. A large, brimmed hat topped her unpowdered tresses, and the hairstyle gave her an almost natural appearance, although he knew her maid had likely spent a considerable amount of time to bring about that effect.

Fresh-faced and innocent as she appeared, it was hard to keep his voice even and unaffected when he wanted to take her by the arms and shake her for her duplicity.

'Is that why you've been so distant towards me ever since we got here?' she asked.

Bastien inhaled. That was part of the reason. The other part had to do with fighting the feelings that threatened to overwhelm him with their intensity.

'No secrets between us, Lilas. Yet you kept them from me.'

Hypocrite, a voice in his head whispered.

He didn't try to argue with himself because it was true. He was a hypocrite. She might have kept her secrets, but he had his own.

Every day since their wedding Bastien had fought an uphill battle to keep himself from becoming like his father. Being held captive by an overwhelming love that imprisoned his heart wasn't what he wanted. Such feelings had utterly destroyed his father. He had to avoid that state of emotion at all costs.

But it was so hard when Lilas lived under his roof. Initially they'd been separated by their social status. She a cinder girl and a maid in his home—he the son of a *duc*. Now they were joined for ever in holy matrimony...

No, not for ever, he corrected. Just until they could seek an annulment at the appropriate time.

'Why did you keep them from me, Lilas?'

She turned away from what she must have seen was the accusation in his gaze. 'I did not mean to hurt you, Bastien. I just thought it was better that you did not know.'

'Do you not trust me to protect you?'

The idea that she found him lacking in any way stung. Hadn't all those years of championing her when she'd been bullied by the other servants been proof of his ability to take care of her? Though four years had separated them after she'd gone to live with her family, did she really think that fundamental part of him had vanished?

A startled look came into her eyes at his question. Her voice shook. 'Of course I do. I swear to you, Bastien.'

Something uncoiled in his chest, and the underlying tension that had clenched all his muscles eased away. It wasn't until it had gone that he realised the thought that she didn't trust him had bothered him more than he'd thought. But the look in her face showed that she really did believe he could take care of her.

It was reminiscent of the look she'd used to have as a young girl.

'If I had known about the notes I could have done more to help you.'

'I didn't want you to know because at the time I didn't want you to feel obligated to me, when we were both certain our betrothal would be broken. I knew your search for your ideal must continue.'

'My ideal…?' he repeated.

Her head was turned away, and he took a moment to linger on her profile. He had to admit it, if only to himself: he was starting to believe his 'ideal' had rainbow-coloured hands, eyes like gemstones, and an inner fire and flare strong enough to burn the world if she so desired.

He hadn't even begun to forget that night in the carriage. There were times when the memory would take hold of his senses and the sound of her cries of pleasure, the feel of that frantic grip in his hair and the taste of her in his mouth would eat away at him until he could hardly sleep.

But now that she was his wife—his to do with as he longed to—he had to control that desire more fiercely than ever before.

Lilas didn't make it easy. And not merely because of the desire she aroused in him. Château de Velay had carried his mother's memory for a long time. Now Lilas was slowly making her own presence supersede that of his mother.

Her change in circumstances had caused her to view the staff at the château in a different light. It was with some satisfaction that he recalled her first meeting with them—including Madame Fournier, who'd tried to hide. Lilas had calmly changed their duties, assigning them based on what each person was physically able to do, rather than what the status of the servant dictated.

There had been many a downcast face on those who had been cruel to her before, now terrified that she would make their lives difficult and wreak her revenge upon them. But she had risen above it beautifully, as he'd known she would.

In a rare moment of camaraderie, Lilas had admitted to Bastien, when he'd asked her, that the thought of revenge had been in her mind for a few moments. But she had told him there was enough vengeance and harm in the world. She had no wish to add to it.

'Being their mistress is all the justice I need.'

And what was more important than her management of his home were the little things about her that he'd noticed.

She adored hot chocolate and had it prepared every morning along with a sweet of some kind.

No matter what service any of the servants performed, she thanked them often, treating them as people.

He'd set aside a room for her to do her painting and she spent hours in it, creating her works of art, completely engrossed.

How she could handle the pungent smells of the various oils he'd no idea. Once, he'd sought to go in there, but she'd barked at him furiously and forbidden him to enter her space.

When his mother had fallen ill, her good works with various charities had ceased. Recently Lilas had taken up his mother's endeavours once more, going once a week to the orphanage with drawing implements and paper, giving the poor mites lessons along with food, clothing and some sweets.

Though Lilas couldn't know it, believing him to be keeping his distance from her, he was, on the contrary, very much aware of her movements.

Lastly, he knew what time she rested at night—hearing through their connecting door her maid getting her ready and then the rustling of the canopy bed as she shifted to make herself comfortable.

All those things made it more difficult to keep his heart from softening towards her. Bastien had used her duplicity with the notes to keep her at a distance, much as she had accused him of doing, but it was also to protect himself from…

What? Falling in love with her?

No, he would never fall in love with Lilas. He couldn't. That would be a mistake of monumental proportions.

'Bastien?'

He took in a sharp breath, unaware that he'd been

staring at her for some time. Her nostrils were flaring like a horse.

'I take it you were thinking of her again just now? That woman? The Duchesse?'

His eyes widened. If he didn't know any better, he would think she was jealous. That couldn't be it, though.

'I *was* thinking of a woman, as it happens, but not the one you mean. I was thinking of my mother.'

At that, the ire in her face disappeared. 'Oh.'

He hid a smile at her crestfallen expression. If she was jealous, then he would revel in it. She'd caused him more trouble than he wanted.

A strange urge made him say, 'There is something I want to show you, Lilas.'

'What is it?'

'It is a painting of my mother I think you would like. In a way, you remind me of her.'

Her chin dipped. 'That's very kind of you to say, Bastien,' she said shyly, clearly pleased by his words.

His heart thudded when she looked up from beneath her lashes, those violet eyes of hers holding him captive.

If she reminded him of his mother, then was he his father after all, despite his every effort?

Was he in danger of losing his heart to this woman just like his father had lost it to his mother?

Lilas couldn't tear her eyes away from the painting.

'Your description did not do it justice, Bastien.'

Lilas inched closer to the magnificent portrait of the former Duchesse de Languedoc, Carmen St Clare.

By anyone's standards, she'd been a beautiful woman. Golden and svelte, with a slimness unenhanced by undergarments. In the portrait she was dressed in an unusual gown of blood-red, pinched along the skirt and dotted with dozens of rubies. The ruffles of the sleeves were a dark gold, and a handkerchief was tied around her neck. Her hair was black as ink, with a blood-red flower resting above her ears. Not only did she have striking features, but there was also a fire in her eyes the artist had captured expertly.

'It is… There aren't any words…'

'I agree.'

Bastien drew closer to her. Lilas's breath caught as she felt her husband's nearness. It was the closest he'd come to her since their wedding day. As subtly as she could, she inhaled, to take in his wonderful masculine scent.

Shuddering, she forced herself to focus back on the painting and searched for the signature of the artist. She frowned when she didn't see one. 'Do you know who painted it?'

'That, *mon arc en ciel*, is a closely guarded secret. Père would never reveal that information. I asked him many times, but he refused to tell me.'

'I don't understand. Look at how magnificent it is! Why wouldn't someone want to claim ownership of that perfection? I could live to be a thousand years old and never attain that sort of technique.'

'You are a wonderful artist, Lilas. Let us not forget that.'

They both studied the portrait again, then she jolted as, without warning, she heard Bastien speak again.

'I remember the day I came in here and saw Père weeping at the foot of this painting. When he glanced at me his eyes were red, filled with tears of anguish. "The other half of myself is gone," he told me that day.'

He swallowed audibly, a melancholy air emanating from him. Lilas held herself still, afraid to do anything that would stop him from talking. He hadn't been this forthcoming since their wedding day. Now she relished his words.

'I knew what my parents had was rare, but the idea of his love for my mother holding him captive in such a way felt like a cautionary tale. I wanted no part of it.'

She licked her dry lips. Careful to not disturb the haunting stillness between them, she kept her voice low, almost a whisper. 'Why?'

'Her death caused him to become a broken man. You may not remember it, Lilas, and it was kept from the household, but he didn't emerge from his chambers for almost two weeks. He refused company of any sort. My father never got over her death, Lilas. He was a shell of a person.'

She touched his arm before she could consider the action, trying to infuse the connection with her sympathy. Underneath the material of his sleeve, his muscles tensed. Would he push her away?

With his eyes locked onto the painting, he clamped his hand over hers, flooding her skin with warmth.

Her shoulders sagged. He hadn't rejected her.

'It didn't matter to him that I had also lost my mother,' Bastien continued. 'The kindest woman I ever knew. That perhaps I needed him to care about my sorrow as well as his own. Most of his life he controlled my actions. But when I needed his comfort there was none to be found for me. The only one to give me comfort was you.'

Lilas lifted her eyes to his profile, but he wasn't looking at her.

'You are the only woman in my life to treat me as a friend, to defend me, besides her.'

'Bastien, I—'

'Don't say anything Lilas. Let me speak.'

He must have seen her nod, though he made no acknowledgement of it. His fingers tightened on her hand.

'I've seen what love did to my father. It ruined him. Because of love, he lost his standing with the crown. It was I who regained it. Why should any man give his heart to a woman only to suffer such pain?'

He was afraid. Bastien was afraid to open his heart to love.

Lilas thought the floor would crack under her feet. How had she never guessed this? He had kept this vulnerable part of himself so well hidden. No wonder he wanted a woman like the Duchesse de Villers-Cotterêts. As his ideal wife, she wouldn't be prone to unwanted emotions or swept away by passion.

An ideal woman indeed!

Lilas firmed her lips. She could not let him continue to think in his fashion.

'And what of you, Bastien? Did you love your father despite his need to assert his dominance over you?'

He was silent for a long moment. 'I did. It crushed me that I was not here for his death. Thankfully, Guerline was at his side.'

'Do you regret loving your father? Would you rather you'd hated him?'

Bastien spun in her direction, keeping her hand in his. 'I don't regret loving him.'

'At least you can grieve, and it shows your great capacity for emotion. I do not have the luxury of that. I never knew my parents so I can't experience the same feelings as you. I have dreamed of them at times, wondering what my life would have been like had I been a part of their family. I mourn them, but not as a daughter should.'

She sighed.

'Do not fault your father for his pain, Bastien. It was

his pain to bear and not yours. It is my belief he'd rather have had the pain of losing his wife than never having had her in his life at all.' She looked into his eyes. 'Do you understand now? It's an honour to grieve, for it means those who have gone were deeply loved.'

His other hand reached up and cupped the side of her face. Tenderness softened his eyes to orbs of honey. Her heart leapt in her throat. She couldn't look away. Slowly, very slowly, he bent his head. She had the idea he was giving her time to pull away, to stop his kiss. But she didn't move. Instead, her eyes fluttered closed as his mouth neared.

His lips were cool against her own. She thought he would deepen the contact. Yet his mouth was gentle, so very gentle against her own. As if he were afraid of bruising her, hurting her. The hesitancy of it made it more poignant, for she knew he was sharing something with her he never had before.

His pain. His anguish. His own perceived weakness.

She remained still under his kiss, desperate to let him know that she accepted all of it.

When he drew back, his eyes were bright. 'Sweet Lilas,' he murmured. 'Sweet, sweet Lilas…'

Later that night, long after Esme had retired and Lilas had ceased to hear Bastien moving about his chambers, she rose from her canopied bed and glided over to the corner where the easel she'd hidden there lay flat. Swiftly, she set it up, and stared at the painting before her.

His kiss this afternoon…it had made hope beat inside her like never before. Wretched, dreadful hope.

The portrait was finally finished. She had repainted his Cleopatra, but she wondered now if that had been a mistake. Especially when she considered the way he'd spoken to her today, revealing his innermost thoughts in a way that he'd never done before.

Once she gave this painting to him—if she ever did—would he guess at the one secret she had never revealed? That she wanted him in a far deeper way than he could have ever imagined?

Lilas's words about love and loss still haunted Bastien two nights later.

He pushed aside the covers and sat up in bed. Though he'd tried to act as if nothing had changed, he knew it had. Lilas's words had crawled into his skull and buried themselves deep into his brain. Somehow she had made sense of his father's pain and communicated it to him in a way he finally understood.

He regretted he'd never had the chance to apologise to his father. Never had the chance to see him again. But he could still grieve for the man whom, despite it all, he had loved.

A weight fell off his shoulders with the admission, and instead of regrets he was bombarded by sweet memories of his sire. Images and things he hadn't considered in some time, so focused on what he had done wrong. Now he could recall the good times they'd shared, the happy moments, and even the more mundane parts of life that made up being a family.

Lilas had given him that.

Bastien's eyes drifted in the dark to the connecting door between them. He could hear her moving about in the room, although it was late into the night. What could she be doing at this hour?

Don't open the door, a voice whispered. *Protect yourself.*

He wanted to heed that wise counsel. His thoughts

were not safely ensconced in this room. They were leading him down the uncharted path that led to the room behind that door.

Where his wife slept.

Or not, as was the case right now.

Since the first moment he'd kissed her his defences against her had started crumbling. He had learned to forgive his father for being eaten up with grief, but that still didn't mean he had to feel the same thing himself.

Bastien had told himself that every single time his eyes landed on the form of his wife—which seemed to have happened a lot in the past two days. He should have found something to take him away for a few days—long enough to conquer that burgeoning *thing* inside him. That *thing* making his breath lodge in his throat whenever he saw her. That *thing* that made him want to seek out her presence for no other reason than wanting to be with her. That *thing* which made him long to relive those moments in the carriage when she'd given herself to him so sweetly.

That *thing* he was doing his best not to acknowledge or admit existed.

But ignoring it wasn't making that *thing* go away.

Instead, as each hour passed tonight, it clawed at his insides, making it impossible for him to get any rest. He hated being in her presence, but equally he longed to stay there. When she laughed, the sound teased his ears in a pleasant way. Her amethyst eyes sparkled like the gems they resembled, and when their gazes, met for whatever reason, he felt as if he were drowning.

That *thing*, whatever it was, would not leave him alone.

And it wasn't helping that he could still hear Lilas

moving about in her room. The narrow door separated them. She was so very close and yet so far away.

No, she's not far away at all, a hateful little voice taunted. *She's just there.*

He listened intently to her movements, feeling like a lunatic beset with an obsession. He couldn't stop himself from following the sound of her footsteps as she came closer to where the adjoining wall was and then moved away again.

What was she doing?

Then he heard a thud, and a small cry.

That was enough to have him shoving a robe over his long nightshirt and going over to the door.

His hand lingered on the doorknob.

Don't go in there. Don't do it. She hasn't made another sound, so she must be all right.

But what if she was lying on the floor, hurt?

The argument went back and forth.

As if he needed another reason, his mind called up the image of her on their wedding day, unconscious and wounded. The memory sent a chill through his body. He didn't want to see her like that ever again.

He would just check on her briefly, to see she was all right.

Opening the door, he stepped in. There was enough candlelight to illuminate her where she stood, but not too brightly. Lilas whirled around. The flickering light of the candle danced on her face, showing her eyes wide and shocked in her face.

'Bastien, what are you doing in here?'

Chapter Twelve

Bastien tried to give her some logical explanation for why he was standing there in the doorway, staring at her like some crazed fool.

Nothing came to mind. How could it when he was seeing Lilas in a way he'd never seen her before. His mind was crowded with images of Lilas over the years—the starved orphan, the efficient servant, the lady of status, a favourite of the Queen, his bride. Yet he had never seen her like this.

She was dressed in a lavender dressing gown, the open lace sleeves flowing over her delicate rainbow hands like a pair of bird's wings. Her hair was plaited into a long braid and lying on one shoulder. He'd seen her dressed in many a capacity, but never like this.

He found this version of her the most arresting of all.

'Bastien, why are you in my chambers?' she asked.

Finally he cleared his mind for long enough to answer her question. 'I heard you make a noise and wanted to see to your welfare.'

Her brow lifted. 'I'm fine—as you can see.'

He could see that quite clearly. 'What happened?'

'Nothing of importance, Bastien.'

Bastien shifted his gaze to behind her. 'What is that?'

'What is what?'

'You're hiding something. I can tell.'

He could almost see a bone-chilling fear cascading over Lilas's body. Her eyes were wide, almost bulging. He could hear the faint sound of her breathing seesawing through her teeth. Even the pulse at the base of her neck pounded.

She looked terrified.

'What is it you don't want me to see, Lilas?'

Her voice trembled as she said, 'It's something I don't want anyone to see.'

'Why not?' His brow furrowed in deep grooves. From what he could see, it was a painting. 'Isn't art to be enjoyed by the viewer?'

'That…' She took in a deep breath. 'That depends on who the viewer is.'

Staring at her, seeing the way she was acting, he was reminded of when they were young and she had been terrified to show him her first drawing. She was acting the same way now.

The painting must be extremely personal to her.

'Lilas, you know I don't like there to be any secrets between us.'

'We're allowed to keep some.'

He shook his head. 'Not us. I want to see your talent, Lilas. I promise I won't ridicule it in any way.'

Bastien's curiosity was further piqued when Lilas's expression changed, as if she were considering his request. What could the painting be? Could it be a portrait for the Queen, perhaps?

'The painting is for you,' she said, shocking him into stillness.

'Is it, now?'

She nodded slowly, but the fear on her face increased. 'Do you remember when you said that I should paint a portrait of you and your wife as a wedding gift?'

'I do.'

'This is that painting. Although of course I did not know what the circumstances would be at the time.'

'What do you mean?'

She came closer to him, her long dressing gown fluttering around her. As always, when he looked at Lilas, she stirred every part of his senses. Tonight, her effect was more potent than ever before.

Perhaps it was his own desire for her clamouring for release.

Or, worse, that *thing* beating at him again.

Any man would go insane with this woman to tempt him.

'When I started this painting I thought you were going to marry the Duchesse de Villers-Cotterêts. She was your ideal.'

Bastien shook his head. 'I told you she wasn't. Are you going to let me see it?'

It would be incredibly awkward to have a painting of himself and the Duchesse de Villers-Cotterêts as his wedding portrait. There would be a lot of explaining to do!

Lilas rolled her shoulders and lifted her chin, before stepping away for him to see.

Marc Antony and Cleopatra.

He saw himself, of course, looking rather stoic for a Roman general. She'd shortened his black hair, giving it a decidedly soldier-like appearance. Dressed him as a general of the era. He could almost think he was looking at an ancestor of his from long ago.

As for Cleopatra…

'She's you.'

Standing by Marc Antony's side was Lilas, portrayed as the Egyptian Queen, standing in front of a crumbling tower with a turbulent sea and an overcast, dreary sky behind them. His sandaled foot hovered over the head of a blue-eyed asp, its inevitable end captured in glorious detail.

He came further into the room, coming to stand by her side as he studied the painting with admiration. How well she'd painted it, giving the work such a sense of reality he could almost hear the waves crashing against the shore.

Slowly he reached out and barely let his finger touch the surface, following the line of Cleopatra's form.

'Do you like it?' she asked.

He heard the breathlessness in her voice.

'I do.'

He couldn't tear his eyes away from it. But though he wasn't looking at her, he sensed it when Lilas shook her head.

This was what he had been trying to avoid…to ignore. The sight of them together. For there was something so very right about seeing himself with Lilas. Though she'd depicted them as a historical couple, the bond her Marc Antony and Cleopatra revealed was reflected in their own bond now.

He let his finger fall away and turned to face her. That *thing* gripped him hard and mercilessly, making him throw everything to the winds. Bastien had fought this battle for too long, against a force too strong to defeat.

It's not too late. Leave now.

It was far too late. And from the look in Lilas's eyes as she stood there, she also knew it was too late—for both of them.

Without another word, he reached out and dragged

her into his arms. He clamped his mouth down on her brown berry lips, groaning at the taste of her he'd missed so badly. He kissed her as if his life depended on it. Perhaps it did.

'Lilas, *ma arc-en-ciel*,' he breathed into her mouth, holding her head gently but firmly between his hands.

He parted her mouth and delved his tongue into its depths, like a deprived man in the desert who had just come upon an oasis. These long weeks of patience and restraint were finally coming to an end.

Lilas moaned, and her fingers dug into his shoulder, the nails marking his skin. The pain only enhanced his own pleasure as he drew away from the delights of her mouth.

'Please don't stop,' she begged.

'There's no chance of that,' he promised her, knowing there wasn't a power on earth that could rip his arms from her now.

Their bodies connected, interlocking with each other from their mouths all the way down to their hips.

Like a flame to dry wood, his desire for his wife burned fiercely. He longed for a deeper discovery of her, and let his tongue mesh with her tentative one, making them dance with each other to see what sensations would come.

A shiver went down his spine as her hands clutched at his neck and her fingers spread across his jawbone. His body tensed and his hands did their own exploration, feeling her smooth curves covered by the gown, singed by the heat emanating from her.

Further down he dragged her hips against his until she gasped, feeling the evidence of what she was doing to him. Her brown cheeks reddened. He murmured soft words to her, not quite cognizant of what he was saying, going more by instinct than anything else.

Soon, he lifted her into his arms and carried her to the bed. Gently, he lay her down. With dexterous fingers he unplaited her hair and spread it out on the pillow. Drawing back, he studied the dark angel before him. He was so used to seeing her with powdered hair or wigs, confined in ornate dresses and gowns, that to see her like this was a study all its own.

'Bastien, you're staring,' Lilas said, her voice high and breathless.

'So I am,' he said. 'I've never seen you like this before.'

'Like what?'

'Free. Released of everything that confines you.'

'Well, you are the only man I've ever wanted to give myself to, Bastien.'

'I'm honoured.'

And he meant that. He had dreamed of this moment for so long, and now it was here, more beautiful than anything he could imagine.

She lay prostrate, like a sacrifice on an altar, offering herself. A hesitant smile lifted her swollen mouth and then she raised her arms, as if beckoning him to fall into the well of pleasure of which she was the source.

How could he resist?

His fingers trembled as he undressed her, taking his time as much as his lack of restraint would allow. But couldn't a man be forgiven for being a tad impatient to caress such silken Armagnac skin? Could any man ignore the high, slightly sloped mounds of her breasts, topped with pouting black peaks, that drew his mouth to them like magnets?

Bastien tried his best to fight back the wildness that

clawed at his insides when his wife writhed beneath him, digging her hands into his hair. His teeth gritted as she twisted her limbs about his body, sighing and gasping and sending him out of his mind, breaking him into a million pieces.

In the end, he took her down a path of pleasure which she eagerly followed. Entering her with what little control he had left, he waited until she was ready and then began that relentless climb, surging forward with her until they both reached the top, dying and being reborn in each other's arms…

Lilas forced her eyes to open the next morning, although she craved more time to sleep. Her night had been a long one.

She replayed Bastien's lovemaking. The feelings and sensations that had racked her body had nearly catapulted her into the sky. The things he had done to her! And with every stroke of his fingers, every kiss upon her flesh, every surge into her body, he had told her that he loved her.

No, he hadn't said it, but his lovemaking made the actual words unimportant.

'Mademoiselle?'

She jerked around, seeing Esme at the door, a delicate flush on her maid's face. Her own face warmed. It was apparent from the destruction of the bedchamber what had gone on in this room.

Well, she was now a married woman—truly and unequivocally.

Glancing around the room, she searched for her husband, but he wasn't there. Why had he left her chambers? Had he an early-morning appointment or business matter to attend to? Even if he did, after what had happened last night she had hoped to wake up in his arms in much the same way as she had fallen into an exhausted sleep in them.

'Esme, can you draw a bath for me?'

She was glad for her maid's silence as she did what she asked. Getting out of bed, she winced at the various aches and pains from her husband's attentions. She loved every single one.

Her lack of knowledge hadn't stopped Lilas from basking in the feel of his skin against her palms. She'd revelled in the fact that her touch could send him groaning and make him lose his control. Rather than being a submissive recipient of his loving, she'd been an active participant in it.

When the early hours of the morning had come and gone he'd finally rested his head on the mounds of her breasts, sensitised by his rapacious desire for them, and fallen asleep, but even in that she had been content.

Now, sitting down at her dressing table, she took in her dishevelled appearance. Did every married woman look like this in the morning—as if she had thoroughly been made love to for several hours?

He'd made her feel so…so *delicious*. As if she were a sweet and he were the one craving her.

What she'd shared with Bastien had been worth the wait.

Lilas held her hands up, seeing the paint splotches she'd forgotten once again to get rid of the day before. Throughout the torrid night Bastien had responded to their touch repeatedly, whispering sweet words about being caressed by her rainbow hands. Several times he'd shuddered violently when she touched him.

Her eyes drifted to the painting.

When he had come to her chambers a part of her had

wanted to send him away. She'd known if he'd remained in that doorway for more than a few seconds, she'd want him to stay the entire night.

She had intended on showing him the painting at some later date, but it hadn't been until he'd seen the work of art that he'd capitulated to the bond between them.

He must have recognised what she'd been trying to say in those colours and brushstrokes on the canvas.

That she loved him.

Though she hadn't said it to him last night, surely he would know her feelings from the nature of her passionate response, how she'd so freely given Bastien every part of her being as he'd taken her again and again?

By the time she had bathed, dressed and sat for Esme to do her hair, the late-morning sun had come up.

There was a knock at the door, and she admitted entry.

The Comtesse de la Baux came into the room. 'I wanted to know if—'

Her stepmother stopped whatever she had been going to say, her eyes roving over Lilas.

'I see,' she said after a moment.

Lilas's face burned with embarrassment. She didn't want to pretend she had no idea what her stepmother was referring to. Knowledge of her entrance into womanhood must show on her face in some fashion.

'How can you tell?' she asked.

'You look…awakened.'

That was the perfect way to explain how she felt. But instead of dwelling on that, she asked, 'Is there something you need?'

Her stepmother stared at her for a moment. 'I want to talk to you. Alone.'

'Esme is completely trustworthy.'

'I understand, but there are things I need to tell you and I want no one else to hear.'

In the past, her stepmother would have ordered her maid away, but that had changed. Lilas was mistress of Château de Velay and the staff all obeyed her.

With a nod from Lilas, the maid curtsied and left, shutting the door behind her.

'Lilas, I do not believe it was wise of you to make your marriage one in truth. If you had kept Bastien as a husband in name only, you could have had the marriage annulled before anything untoward happened. Now that is impossible.'

'I have nothing to fear from Bastien. He would never hurt me.'

'Are you so certain, Lilas?' An odd light appeared in her stepmother's blue eyes. 'Men— especially men like your husband—can use their prowess to seduce you and then their hands to destroy you.'

'Bastien would never do that to me.'

Would he?

The older woman shrugged. 'I wash my hands of this, then.'

Her stepmother then changed the subject, talking about a ball they had been invited to this evening. A country affair, but no less fashionable for that.

Despite her every effort not to be affected by her stepmother's words, throughout the day Lilas could not help but ponder them.

What if this was all some sort of ploy by Bastien to secure his standing in France?

Could a man who had shared such great intimacy with her be so devious?

Why couldn't she answer that question with an unequivocal no?

Throughout the day, Lilas expected to see Bastien. From what she'd learned from the servants he was about the grounds somewhere, but never once did she see him.

Surely he wasn't trying to avoid her?

Lilas dismissed the thought. No, he wouldn't do that to her—not after last night.

Even so, the lingering doubts clung like burrs…

When evening came, and she'd gone to her bedchamber to ready herself for the ball, she still hadn't set eyes on Bastien. She tried to keep her traitorous thoughts at bay. He wasn't avoiding her. He was simply busy.

Padding over to the balcony doors, she reached out her hand to unlock them when she saw the key was still in the keyhole. Had Esme forgotten to lock them? It wasn't like her to do that. Shrugging, Lilas pushed open the doors and walked out onto the balcony.

The fresh cool breeze of the coming twilight chilled her skin and she shivered in a delicious manner. Goosebumps appeared on her upper shoulders under the thin dressing gown, and she rubbed at them vigorously. Going over to the railing, she gazed at the grounds. The cool caress of the wind helped to soothe her overheated skin and dampen down the ache which had taken hold in the core of her.

Her bedchamber overlooked the gardens at the back of the house. The paths and hedges formed a maze in which one might easily get lost if one chose to. Perhaps she and Bastien could walk in the gardens tomorrow.

She'd already explored them by herself, because his duties had kept him so busy, and she'd found a tucked-away pavilion in an area reminiscent of a Chinese garden. It had a small pond studded with lily pads where tiny frogs hopped back and forth croaking, and it was secluded from the rest of the house.

Leaning on the balcony rail, she stared out over the darkening landscape, thinking about that spot. Maybe she and Bastien could go there tomorrow. Maybe he'd sit next to her on the bench that sat a little way back from the pavilion that overlooked the pond. Maybe he would gather her close to him and press a kiss to her mouth.

She shuddered and licked her lips. What was happening to her? He was making her wanton. But did it matter so long as this wantonness was only with him?

She straightened up and rested her hands again on the wrought-iron rail in front of her.

She heard a distinct crack before the rail gave way under her hands.

She screamed and jumped back as the railing fell from the balcony to the ground below.

The crash reverberated throughout the grounds, echoing like the gongs of a bell. Lilas's heart pitter-pattered in her chest, pounding like a child banging on a locked door.

Splaying her hands across her heaving breasts, she tried to relax, gulping in air. If she had moved a second later…!

The sound of furious knocking came to her ears. Trembling, she went back into the room and over to the door, where she could hear Pierre pounding on it while ordering the servants to bring the master keys.

'I'm all right!' she called.

She unlocked the door and was soon enveloped by her stepbrother, holding her tight and nearly choking her to death.

'Lilas, what happened? I heard a noise, and then you screamed, and—'

'I'm fine,' she said, still a little breathless and shaky as she unlatched Pierre's arms from their death hold around her neck. 'I promise.'

Pierre pulled back. 'What happened?'

Lilas pointed a quivering finger in the direction of the balcony. 'The r-railing. It fell.'

'It fell?'

Lilas nodded and rubbed her arms. 'If I hadn't—'

'I can imagine.'

Pierre went over to the doors and peered out. Lilas followed him, and they took in the sight of the rail-less balcony. Her room was four storeys above the ground.

A hard look came over Pierre's face, and she knew he was thinking the same as she. Had she fallen, she would have done a serious injury to herself, possibly even—

'Let's not dwell on this,' she said, and tugged Pierre back into the room. She locked the doors. 'I'll let Bastien know the balcony will have to be repaired—preferably with a much sturdier rail.'

An hour later she was fully dressed, without further incident. Esme helped her down the stairs, due to the long train of her gown. The slippers underneath were silver and edged with rows of sapphires.

When her eyes lifted from her careful descent down the stairs, she met Bastien's golden gaze.

'Bastien!' she cried out, forgetting everything else but the surge of joy at seeing him after an entire day had gone by. All they had shared the night before flooded through her and she gazed at him with new awareness.

Bastien's eyes remained riveted to her as she descended. 'You're truly exquisite, Lilas.'

His gaze was steady and direct, but he didn't look as she had expected a man to look after he had taken his new wife to bed for the first time. He appeared distant.

'You're looking rather dashing yourself,' she said, wondering if she was imagining this coolness between them. She must be. He wouldn't treat her like that—not after last night.

Her eyes roved over him. His silver waistcoat hugged him well. His plain white shirt was buttoned up to his throat. He'd lightly powdered his hair and drawn it into its usual *queue*, giving it a contrast to his bronze skin and highlighting the deep gold of his eyes.

'*Merci*, Lilas.'

Again that bland tone and uninterested gaze.

She frowned. Why was he acting like this?

'And what about me?' Pierre quipped as he executed a curtsy, using his coat as a dress.

Lilas flinched at the sound of her stepbrother's voice, but she was suddenly glad for it. Bastien had withdrawn his gaze from her and a chill arced down her spine.

'That depends upon whether I pronounce you an ugly woman or a beautiful creature!' Bastien teased.

At any other time she would have relished the banter between her husband and her stepbrother. Not now, though—not while she was staring the truth in the face. She didn't want to believe it, but Bastien's actions were screaming it at her.

Last night hadn't meant anything to him. He didn't love her!

The sound of Pierre's laughter kept Bastien from lingering too long on his wife's appearance. If he did, he'd only be able to think about how much more lovely she'd looked last night, naked and writhing in his arms.

All day long, as he'd gone about his business, Bastien had kept on reliving the night with his wife. Leaving her in bed that morning had been physically painful. He'd wanted nothing more than to stay in her arms all day, waking only to eat and then make love to her again.

With rigid control, he'd dragged himself carefully out of her bed. He'd smiled slightly at the sound of her tiny snores, his eyes roving over her lithe form. They had lingered on the curve of her hip. And a primal, masculine pride had gripped him.

Bastien had worried that he might have taken and used Lilas entirely too enthusiastically, without consideration for her inexperience. But she had met his passion with her own, clearly capable of matching what he'd thought would be his insatiable appetite for her.

If he let it continue.

In the light of day, he'd known he should not have made this a marriage in truth. Now the essence of his wife had crawled beneath his skin and thickened the blood in his veins. Not to mention caused the fierce beating of his heart whenever she was near.

No, he had to stop it from happening again.

Ignoring the sinking feeling in the pit of his stomach, Bastien had forced himself out of her room and back to the business of the day. It had taken every ounce of his willpower to remain focused, and there were times when even that had slipped.

Now she stood before him in an ice-blue gown that flowed about her like a cascading waterfall. The bodice clung to her slender form, revealing the delightful contrast of the cool dress with the warm tone of her skin.

His heart thudded faster when he looked into her eyes, seeing her confusion and dismay at his self-imposed distance. He struggled to hold himself rigid against it.

'I should tell you that you're fortunate. The railing of your wife's balcony fell to the ground while she was leaning on it,' he heard Pierre saying.

A shiver went down his spine. 'Fell? What do you mean?'

Pierre gestured to Lilas, and he listened in growing dismay as she told him as succinctly as possible what had happened.

The idea that someone was still trying to hurt Lilas in his own home made all the demons of hell burst inside his head. An overwhelming sense of possessiveness came over him. The first thing he wanted to do was take her straight to his room and lock her in there. Keep her safe from anyone who would try to take her from him. He forced himself to calm down, but it did nothing to reduce the fear that rocked his soul.

'There is no need to worry about this,' Lilas said evenly.

'No need?' Bastien repeated softly, almost to himself.

Did she have any idea of what was going through his mind? How close had she come to lying in broken pieces on the ground below her room? How could she stand there and say there wasn't a need for him to worry?

I need to protect her, that's all.

He heeded the cool voice of reason, although his heart slammed into his chest until he felt sick at the horrible vision of her broken body on the ground. That must never happen to her.

Slowly he let out a breath and said, as calmly as he could, 'There's every need.'

'No, there isn't. It was a flawed railing—that's all. Nothing more to it than that.'

'There is more to it than that and you know it. You must be more careful. You could have been killed.'

Her eyes finally flared and she spat, 'And I'm sure that wouldn't have bothered you at all, would it?'

She couldn't know the protective instincts coursing through him right now. The rampant desire to haul her into his arms and kiss her. To wrap her in silk and cotton and make sure nothing ever hurt her again. Those feelings were dangerous, and he had to stop them. But his control over them was slipping, especially as that terrible image of her broken form lying on the ground kept flashing in his head like strikes of lightning.

Behind her anger, he saw her pain at his distance, but he knew it was the only way for him to survive.

He could not, *would* not, fall in love with his wife.

The next afternoon found Bastien sitting in his study, going over the ledgers for both his estate and the estate of the Comte de la Baux. Or rather attempting to. Inside he seethed. He'd had little sleep, thinking of the woman who rested on the other side of the connecting door, remembering their night of loving and fighting his body's demand for more.

'Do you have a moment?'

Relieved at the interruption, he set the books away and motioned for Pierre to enter his study. 'I do.'

The other man sauntered in. 'Have you had a chance to look at the railing?'

He nodded. 'I have. It should not have fallen last night. Those rails were installed only a few years ago.'

'That's troubling,' Pierre said, with worry evident in his voice.

'Indeed.' This was the other reason why he seethed inside. Someone had gone out of their way to make that railing unsafe.

'We need to discover if any of the servants saw anyone tampering with it. Or if they heard anything,' said Pierre.

Bastien nodded his agreement.

'I'd like to organise the interviews, if you'll permit me.'

Bastien eyed the man. 'Why?'

'She's my sister in every way that counts. And, further, her father would have wanted me to protect her.'

'Do you love her?' Bastien asked.

Pierre peered at him over the rim of his glasses. 'It would be impossible not to, wouldn't you say, Monsieur le Duc?'

Before he could answer, Pierre left the room, leaving his question ringing in the wake of his departure.

Chapter Thirteen

A week had gone by since the railing had fallen from her balcony, and Lilas couldn't remember a more morose time in her life. Not even when she'd lived in the orphanage had she been this dejected.

Back then, she'd had no idea what it meant to experience the love of family or human kindness. When she'd arrived at Château de Velay she'd soaked up Bastien's friendship with greedy hands. And even when he had betrayed that friendship and left for four years, she hadn't experienced the sort of pain that sliced her in two.

But now she had experienced Bastien's lovemaking and knew she loved him.

If she had known he would act this way afterwards…

She probably still would have given herself to him.

Sighing, she looked at the canvas in front of her. A painting of Château de Velay. She wanted to capture it as she had as a young girl. But instead of ashes, dirt and a single brush, she now had a plethora of colours and brushes to choose from.

So why wasn't she happy with her work? Why did the château reflect her own loneliness?

Glancing at the connecting door of her bedroom, she knew why.

Her passionate lover had retreated once more behind the façade of genteel host. His manner had become more than distant—almost cold. As if she were someone he would rather not spend his time with.

She wanted to be angry with him, and lash out, but her sorrow had overtaken her usual defiance.

Had loving Bastien made her weak?

The doorknob turned just then, and her mouth fell open as Bastien stood in the connecting doorway. For a moment she simply stared at him, drinking in his presence. He looked more detached than before, but that didn't matter. He was still there in her bedchamber.

'What is it, Bastien?'

'I came to tell you something.'

Her breath hitched in her throat. 'Tell me what?'

Bastien said nothing, and the air between them strained with unspoken things. She hated it. Before, if he had sensed this kind of undeniable tension between them, he would have stated his refrain about not keeping secrets and forced her to give up hers.

Now, he didn't say anything like that.

'Pierre and I have been interviewing the servants to see if any of them knew about the balcony railing, but so far no one has admitted to seeing or hearing anything.'

Her shoulders drooped. 'I see.'

'I just wanted you to know. We're doing everything we can to find out who it is that is trying to hurt you, Lilas.'

'I see,' she said. 'Why?'

His brow furrowed. 'What do you mean?'

'Why are you trying to find out who wants me gone?'

'You're my wife. I want to protect you.'

'You haven't treated me as a wife since we married,

Bastien, except for that one night.' The floodgates of her anguish burst open and she stood. 'How can you stand there looking at me as if I am someone you barely know? No one knows me as well as you do, Bastien.'

His eyes narrowed.

'You made love to me in this room,' she forged on, uncaring of how she sounded, or if she revealed her feelings for him or not. 'How can you give me something so wonderful and then treat me this way?'

'It should have never happened. We were supposed to have a marriage of convenience. I shouldn't have taken advantage of you.'

She let out a humorous laugh. 'Advantage of me? I practically begged you to take me, Bastien.'

'Mon Dieu...' he breathed. 'I remember.'

'Do you? If you remember, how can you be so wicked to me now?'

An unexpected tear trailed down her cheek as their gazes held. But Bastien's face hardened. 'I didn't mean to hurt you. Surely you know we can't ever do that again?'

'Why not? Because I am not your ideal?'

A scowl appeared on his face. 'Will you cease your ridiculous talk about my "ideal"?'

'Perhaps you confused me with her that night?'

A warning growl was all she had before he marched over to where she stood and gripped her arms, pulling her against his chest and plundering her mouth without any hint of softness.

She went up in flames, uncaring that this felt more like lust than love. All she knew was that Bastien, her husband, was kissing her again, and she wanted him desperately.

His tongue thrust into her mouth with a dark intimacy, sending her pulses and her senses leaping. His hands left her arms and trembled, revealing his shredded restraint. Letting his long fingers drift over her collarbone, she shivered. It felt like ages since he'd touched her, although it had been only a week.

But almost as soon as he had begun, he thrust her away and left the room, shutting the door behind him.

Lilas stared after him, touching the mouth he'd just kissed and tasting the salt of her tears.

'Lilas, may I talk with you?'

She turned around to see her stepmother gliding towards her from where she stood in the hall.

'What is it Belle-Mère?'

'I've learned something very disturbing that I think you should know about.'

Lilas glanced at her stepmother's face, seeing its usual serene façade. 'What has happened?'

'It's about the railing.'

'What of it?'

'I spoke with one of the servants and he recalled seeing the Duc de Languedoc on the balcony several days before it fell, doing something to its structure.'

Lilas gave a shake of her head. 'That's strange… Bastien told me that when he and Pierre spoke to the servants they hadn't seen anything at all.'

'Don't be so gullible, Lilas,' her stepmother said, in a suddenly high-pitched voice.

The sound of it made Lilas pause. Looking at the woman, she saw a strange expression on her face. 'I'm not.'

'Of course he would say that. He wouldn't want you to know the truth.'

'The truth?'

'He is trying to destroy you. I can prove it to you.'

Her stepmother's eyes grew even colder and fear crawled along Lilas's spine. Something was going on here that she didn't understand.

'Are you saying you don't believe me?'

Lilas chose her words carefully. 'I believe you think it is the truth. But I know my husband wouldn't do something like that.'

'And this because he made love to you?'

'I have known Bastien St Clare my entire life, Belle-Mère. For most of it he has defended me. Why would he suddenly want to hurt me, when he could have done something to me well before now?'

Her stepmother stilled like a statue. 'I was fearful that you would say something like that. It pains me to do so, but I will have to show you the proof of my accusations. Come with me, Lilas.'

'I need to—'

'You must come with me now. Before it's too late. Do you understand?'

Lilas looked down at the small white hand clasping her arm. Slowly she stepped back, letting the hand fall away from her. 'Belle-Mère, this has gone far enough. I have listened to your words many times, but Bastien is my husband now. He could not and would not hurt me in this way. I know it.'

'You're being a fool, Lilas. What can I say to convince you of that?'

'You can't—'

Her stepmother gripped her arm again, tighter this time. 'If I can prove it, beyond any doubt, would you believe me then? Lilas, I am only trying to help you… as any mother would.'

Lilas started. 'Do you see me as…as your daughter, then?'

She lifted her shoulders. 'You are Louis's daughter, and thus mine. Perhaps I have not always articulated this, but it is true. Why do you think I am so insistent on protecting you?'

Lilas wanted to believe it, but years of her stepmother's coolness towards her wouldn't let her. But what was this proof 'beyond any doubt'? Did her stepmother really have such a thing? She didn't think so, but the woman did look anxious. Perhaps Lilas simply needed to humour her.

'As you wish, Belle-Mère. I'll come with you.'

They were walking along the winding path in the gardens behind the château. Lilas strolled along with her stepmother, taking in the sights and sounds all around her, all the while trying to dampen the curious feeling of dread that threatened to overwhelm her.

Her stepmother hadn't said a word ever since they'd left the house. When Lilas had mentioned bringing Esme with her, she'd been told that her maid was spending time with Jacques the driver. Something that pleased Lilas immensely.

This path led to the pavilion in the Chinese garden at the centre, and soon she could see at the edge of the pond the wrought-iron bench she'd found before.

'Shall we sit here, Lilas?' her stepmother asked.

'What is it you have to show me?'

'All in good time, Lilas. Right now I am a little tired. Let us rest for a while.'

As they sat down, a weary sigh escaped the older woman's lips. For the first time since Lilas had known her she looked every inch her forty-plus years. Which was a strange thing to be aware of.

The quiet of the small garden encapsulated them.

'Did you know that I once knew your mother?'

Lilas inhaled sharply. Of all the things she had expected to hear, that wasn't one of them. 'You knew her?' She pursed her lips. 'Pierre told me that you and he came to be with my father after my mother died.'

'I lied.'

How calm she sounded. The Comtesse could have been talking about the weather for all the inflection in her voice. Lilas stared at the woman, feeling her world tilt off its axis.

'As a matter of fact, I knew Atalyia very well. I pretended that I didn't. It brought up too many painful memories. Things I wished I could forget but couldn't.'

'Such as what, Belle-Mère?'

'Such as the fact that Pierre is your half-brother, not your stepbrother.'

The impact of her words erupted like a cannon, leaving a shocked silence in its wake. A lump formed in Lilas's throat as she stared at the woman. Her voice came out in a rasp. 'Are you joking?'

Her stepmother said in a calm voice, 'Why would I joke about something like that?'

Lilas couldn't think of an answer—and she didn't have to.

The Comtesse de la Baux stared out at the pavilion. Dragonflies fluttered above the lily pads and the frogs flung out their stretchy tongues to capture them.

'My first husband was a cruel man—as I told you before. He never loved me, and nor did I love him. We married because it was expected, and my mother was insistent that I marry a man of some status…even if he was an impoverished baron. I met your father before he went abroad. We lived not far from one another. He saw me weeping alone once, and in his gallant fashion he comforted me.'

Her eyes turned misty.

'He was unlike any man I had ever known. Patient, kind…and so considerate. We became lovers shortly afterwards. My husband never knew. When your father went abroad with the Duc de Languedoc, I discovered that I was going to bear his son. I hadn't warmed my husband's bed in some time, so I knew for certain the child was Louis's. Of course my husband was delighted when he discovered I was with child, and when I gave birth to a son. My mother was also pleased, because my son would inherit the Baron's title.'

'But when you eventually married my father, why didn't you tell him that Pierre was his son?' Lilas asked.

'Why does any woman keep a secret? I didn't want to risk Louis not believing me. Further, my husband's baronetcy belonged to Pierre. I wasn't going to let that go. Which it would have if news had got out that Pierre wasn't his son. After the horrible marriage I'd had with him, giving my son his title was the very least my husband could do. Anyway, soon after Pierre's fourth birthday, my husband died. I mourned him as was expected—but not in my heart. I eagerly waited for Louis to return. I knew when he did we would be together again, and I would finally be able to give my son his real father.'

Sadness suffused her face.

'But when your father returned he brought with him his Maroon wife.'

'My mother.'

'I remember I was riding in a carriage when the entourage passed by. My heart lifted in my chest when I saw it was your father, returned safely. It fell to the ground when I saw the dark-skinned woman by his side.'

Her stepmother's face had taken on an introspective

look. Lilas got the impression that she'd even forgotten she was sitting next to her.

'We were invited to a ball to welcome his bride. Everyone from the elite to the commoner—all were invited. It wasn't often one saw a Maroon woman in the region. Not to mention rumours had spread that she was a princess among the Maroon people.'

'My mother wasn't in line for a throne,' Lilas corrected her. 'She was more like a *princesse du sang*, if you will.'

'It didn't matter, Lilas. When word got around, everyone wanted to meet her. And that night I gazed at this strange, lovely woman and wanted to rip her eyes out. She had taken the man I loved, and her child would take the title I wanted for my son.'

Lilas blinked. 'What are you saying?'

The Comtesse de la Baux reached down and plucked a rose from the rosebush near the bench. She pressed it to her nose, closing her eyes and drawing in a deep breath. When she looked at Lilas her pale blue eyes had never looked so cold.

It was then that Lilas realised something she had never known before. The serpent in her *Almost Eve* painting and the asp in the Antony and Cleopatra portrait both had the icy blue eyes of her stepmother. She had subconsciously added that element to her work because somewhere deep inside she'd known she couldn't trust her.

'Imagine when I saw Louis with his wife and the sickening way he adored her. All my dreams and hopes were dashed in that instant.'

The hairs on the back of Lilas's neck lifted. Although her stepmother hadn't moved, a sense of danger was suddenly pervasive. Lilas stayed very still.

'Then I had an idea. If I could get into the household

under some pretence, I'd be able to coax your father back to my bed... But it wasn't meant to be. For one thing, I could see your father had no desire for anyone else but Atalyia. And that hurt worse than anything else, Lilas. How could the man who had given me such comfort in the midst of a cruel marriage not love me? How could our wonderful moments together be erased by that woman?'

'So what did you do?' Lilas asked through numb lips.

'If I couldn't get to Louis, then I knew I had to go through his wife. So I did everything I could to ingratiate myself with Atalyia. And it worked. We became the best of friends...' A sad expression came to her face. 'I can't say all of it was a subterfuge. In some way, I did consider her a friend. She accepted me and treated me like a sister. She loved Pierre almost as if he were her own son.'

Tears swelled in Lilas's eyes. She almost knew what her stepmother would say next.

'When your mother gave birth to you I was there in the birthing room. Louis was away. The delivery was unexpected and very difficult, due to the fact you were born too early. Everyone thought Atalyia hadn't managed to deliver you when she died, so when Louis came back he buried what he thought was his wife and unborn baby. But Soeur Calme smuggled you out, on my instruction, and took you to the orphanage, although neither of us thought you'd survive for long.'

'Please tell me you didn't kill my mother.' The tears flowed down her cheeks in a steady trickle.

'I didn't, Lilas.'

At that, she stilled. 'You didn't?'

Her stepmother shook her head, a haunted look on her face. 'That isn't to say that I wasn't prepared to do what I had to do. But when I went over to her I saw the light had already begun to fade from her eyes. And the last thing she told me was to take care of her daughter. I ran away then. I didn't know until that moment that I had cared about your mother even while I'd wanted her dead. There was no fear in her eyes, no pleas for life. She seemed resigned to her fate.'

'Why would you say that?' The tears burned Lilas's cheeks.

Her stepmother lifted her shoulders. 'I knew it was my chance to get rid of both of you and be in the right place to comfort Louis in his time of grief.'

When she turned to look at Lilas, she felt her blood run cold. A mad light dominated her stepmother's eyes. 'I made a mistake, taking pity on a helpless babe and sending you to the orphanage. But now the chance to rid myself of you has presented itself to me once again.'

Bastien closed the ledger and stretched his hands over his head. He'd been looking over the books for a long time today. Although it wasn't seemly for a man in his position to do something so mundane as study the household accounts, he never felt that way. His father had been knowledgeable about the state of his affairs, never fully trusting other people to do it for him.

It was a practice he intended to keep.

He glanced at the clock and saw it was already two hours past midday.

Getting up, he went over to the paintings of both his parents. Their figures, so boldly depicted, looked down at him from their lofty places.

He had finally come to terms with his guilt. Though he had never reconciled with his father, he knew that his father had loved and forgiven him for his desertion four years ago. And a letter from Guerline had arrived, and she had apologised profusely for her interference.

Sighing, he turned as he heard someone knock on the door. 'Come in.'

Pierre came through it, his eyes filled with wariness. 'Bastien, there's someone here who wants to talk to you.'

He came back towards the table. 'Who is it?'

A slight movement caught his peripheral vision, and he looked past Pierre. Soeur Calme was standing there, her face pensive and uneasy.

'Soeur Calme, what are you doing here?'

The woman had never come to his private office before. Something had to be wrong. The nun walked forward in swift strides until she practically stood under his chin. She opened her mouth.

Pierre and he shared a look. Was she going to speak?

A breath of air erupted from her mouth, but the words were so low he couldn't make them out. 'Soeur Calme… try again.'

The woman's fingers knotted in the material of her habit, and he felt a sense of foreboding worm its way down his spine. When she opened her mouth again, her words slammed into him like fists, although she had still spoken no louder than the fluttering of a butterfly's wings.

'Wife in danger…'

For a moment he could do nothing but stare at the woman. After all, no one had heard her talk for over twenty years. Now here she was, speaking, and her first words were that Lilas was in danger…

'Why is Lilas in danger?'

The woman's face paled, and she worked hard to speak again. He thought back to everything he had learned in the last few weeks whilst trying to find out who it was trying to harm his wife. Only one person could have given those notes to Lilas without her knowing it. A person who moved so silently one could be next to her and yet not aware of her presence.

A vow of silence. Who would take a vow of silence unless they didn't want to hurt someone they were close to? Someone who already had their trust?

The pieces all slid together and his heart plummeted to his feet. 'It's the Comtesse de la Baux, isn't it? She's the one threatening Lilas.'

Tears filled the woman's eyes and her lips quivered as she gave a harried nod.

'My mother?' Pierre looked confused. 'That can't be right. Why would my mother want to hurt Lilas?'

The nun came and pressed her hand to Pierre's heart. 'You…are…her…brother. Louis's…son.'

Pierre's mouth fell open. 'Brother? Lilas's?'

She nodded.

Bastien shook his head. There was more going on here than he'd ever suspected. But now that he knew what he knew it all made sense.

'You were the one to take Lilas to the orphanage, weren't you?'

More tears filled the woman's eyes. 'Afraid…hurt… child.'

'Was it because—?' Pierre's voice broke and he stopped talking for a moment. He took a hard swallow before continuing. 'You suspected she was in danger from my mother?'

Soeur Calme gripped Pierre's hands and squeezed, nodding her head.

'Did my mother kill Lilas's mother?'

Vigorously, the nun shook her head. 'Father.'

Bastien tensed.

Pierre had fallen to his knees. 'She killed my *father*?'

More tears leaked out of the nun's eyes as she also

collapsed to the ground and rocked back and forth, giving the sign of the cross as she did so. All the while not making a sound.

Pierre left the woman to weep on the ground as he stood up once more, turning to Bastien. 'We have to find my mother and Lilas.' Bending down, he asked the nun, 'Where are they now?'

The chilling sound of soft laughter from her stepmother's mouth sent a shaft of fear through Lilas's chest. She was afraid to move the slightest bit. Instead, she listened as her stepmother said, 'Soeur Calme must have been too long burdened by the secret. She sent that letter to Louis, alerting him to your existence and telling him that you'd been taken to the orphanage. I could have strangled her for what she did. It's her fault he's dead, you know. If she hadn't told him about you, I wouldn't have had to get involved.'

Now the madness positively blazed from her stepmother's eyes.

'I had to stop him. He had already agreed to adopt Pierre as his son. He never knew he was really his child anyway. And in the event of his death, my son would finally have received the title of *comte* that he deserved.' The woman snarled. 'I had no idea Louis had changed his will in your favour even before he set out to meet you. That was selfish of him. I'd worked so hard to sabotage his carriage and ensure his death would benefit Pierre. But there was nothing I could do once the will was read, because you are his legitimate daughter and the title will go to your son, not to Pierre.'

'You didn't have to do any of that.'

'I did. I have worked hard for this life of mine. And,

as I said before, I loved your father even when I wasn't free to love him.'

'But you're going to kill me too, aren't you?'

The Comtesse de la Baux stood, a flintlock pistol appearing in her hand as if by magic. 'Yes, I am. But not here. You'll be discovered too soon. So let's go for a walk into the woods.'

Lilas backed away slowly.

'If you run, Lilas, I will shoot you. If you call for help, I will shoot you. If you try to leave a trail for anyone to find, I will kill you. Understood?' She cocked the pistol. 'Your father taught me how to use this and I am a very good shot.'

Her voice sounded pleasant, almost as if she were presiding over afternoon tea. Her hand held the heavy weapon with ease. Lilas knew then that there was nothing she could do. Her stepmother was going to kill her.

For a moment, fear gripped her in its clutches. She was going to be killed by a woman like this! She saw her life flash before her eyes, thinking of all she had gone through. The hardships, the turmoil, the pain.

Bastien's face floated before her. Her lover, her husband. Her friend.

No, she was not going to let this woman take her life. She wanted to spend decades more with Bastien, and she wasn't going to meekly give in to this madwoman's whims.

Sending a prayer upwards to the heavens, she gripped her skirts in her hands and poised herself to lunge at her.

'Don't do it, Lilas. I will shoot you.'

Bastien's heart thumped wildly in his chest as he raced alongside Pierre into the gardens. From what they had gleaned from the nun, the Comtesse de la Baux had every intention of killing Lilas, to give Pierre the title she felt belonged to him, because he would be the only de la Baux left to inherit, despite his illegitimate birth.

'I hope we're not too late,' he heard Pierre say.

That sent a blast of fear ricocheting through him. If anything happened to Lilas, anything at all... How could he have been so blind...so stubborn? He hadn't wanted to fall in love with Lilas. But it was too late; he was already in love with her. Deeply. Madly.

She was his friend, his wife, his lover. More than his ideal, she was the perfect one for him.

His masterpiece.

He should have known it when he'd made love to her that night. When the sensations he'd felt had been unlike anything else he'd ever experienced with a woman. His need and desire had paled in comparison to the love bubbling in his veins.

All this time he could have loved her. Openly. Freely.

But there had been his fear of being controlled by his father. Fear of being a victim of love like his father. Well, there was no more room for that nonsense. He finally understood the pain his father had felt when he'd lost his beloved wife. The St Clares loved with their entire hearts. With every breath they took. With their souls.

If Lilas were to be taken from him he wouldn't have a reason to live.

He had to get to her. Had to tell her that he loved her and always would. Always had!

Pierre's hand slammed into his chest and he brought himself back to the matter at hand. 'What—?'

Swiftly, Pierre covered his mouth and pointed to his ear, indicating that he wanted Bastien to listen. The path was hidden by thick shrubbery almost cocooning the area in silence, but they could still make out the voices.

He inclined his head. The blood turned to ice in his veins as he heard the Comtesse say, 'Don't do it, Lilas. I will shoot you.'

'Why now, Madame la Comtesse? Why this moment?' Lilas asked.

Bastien longed to leap from their hiding place, but a warning squeeze by Pierre kept him from doing that. They had to be careful.

'You gave me no choice, Lilas.'

What was the madwoman talking about?

'When the Duc de Languedoc left to travel around Europe, and you made it clear you had no interest in marriage to anyone else, I knew it was unlikely you'd ever bring forth a child. So I had time on my side. I didn't have to get rid of you straight away, and that might have thrown suspicion on Pierre when he inherited everything.'

They heard a harsh puff of air.

'Then your *duc* came back, and I knew it was imperative I stop you marrying him at any cost. It was I who hired that vagrant to accost you at the dressmaker's. I who put the sleeping draught in your drink on your wedding day. I didn't want to harm you, Lilas. Not then. It was still too soon…too risky for Pierre. I only wanted you to realise how dangerous it was to marry the Duc de Languedoc and put you off consummating your marriage.'

'You were behind the incident with the balcony railing as well?' asked Lilas.

Bastien could hardly believe his ears. Instead of protecting Lilas from danger, he had led her right into the enemy's trap. Her stepmother.

'I was. I went into your bedchamber and sabotaged

it. You should have died then, but fate seems to be in your favour…'

'We have to move now,' he whispered, close to Pierre's ear.

The man turned, his eyes glassy with unshed tears.

'I did everything I could to stop your marriage, Lilas, but nothing worked. And then, when I saw you had finally consummated your vows, I knew it was finally time to get rid of you, in case you'd conceived an heir. My son will have the title and the inheritance that should be his, and there is nothing you can do about it.'

The collected, serene voice frightened Bastien more than anything. He had to go out there now—had to protect his wife. He'd rather die trying to save her than live without her.

Pierre must have had the same thought, because he gave Bastien a silent look that communicated everything.

Then the most wonderful words he'd ever heard came out of Lilas's mouth.

'Whatever you do, then, Madame la Comtesse, don't miss.'

That was his Lilas—his defiant bride! But there was no more time to wait. They had to go now!

He and Pierre ran as fast as their legs would go, hoping the dense shrubbery would muffle the sound of their feet as they raced on.

Then they came to the clearing and shouted.

'Mère!'

'Lilas!'

Bastien and Pierre skidded to a stop, seeing the very steady hand of the Comtesse de la Baux aiming at Lilas.

'Mère, please don't do this…'

At the sound of Pierre's voice, his mother turned to

face him. Even from where he stood, Bastien could see the madness in her eyes.

'I have no choice,' the woman said. Calm, so very calm, her voice without inflection. 'I must.'

'If you harm my wife, I will harm you.'

Lilas heard the deadly threat in Bastien's words as they sent a chill over the clearing. It had more of an effect than the gun in her stepmother's hand.

'Please don't make this any more difficult, Mère. I never wanted a prestigious title, or the de la Baux estate. It doesn't matter to me and it shouldn't to you.'

'You're my son. I want the best for you.'

'This isn't the way to go about getting it!' Pierre's face was flushed red. 'Now, put that gun away. Do you even know what you're doing? You're going to kill an innocent woman! And for what? A title I don't want!'

'Of course!'

Lilas saw Bastien inching closer while Pierre kept his mother talking. She didn't know if she should lunge at the woman or run away.

With the swiftness of a snake, the Comtesse turned the gun on Bastien. 'If you take one more step, I will shoot you where you stand.'

The thought of her husband dying appalled Lilas. She couldn't let that happen. This wasn't a world she wanted to live in if he did not exist. Not now. Not ever.

So what if he didn't love her back? So what if she wasn't his ideal? He had married her, and he wanted her, and she would live with that. If the only thing she could have was his passion, then she would take it. Maybe, after some time, it would turn to love. Even if it didn't, she could not live in this world without him.

She'd rather die.

Pierre cried out again, 'Mère, please don't do this. I don't want to lose you. I love you.'

Tears poured down Pierre's face and Lilas knew they were genuine. The pain he was experiencing as he tried to keep his mother from harming her must be excruciating.

But his mother was trying to kill Lilas's husband.

How often had Bastien come to her rescue? He would not be killed like a dog in the street. Not if she could help it.

The Comtesse de la Baux turned to look at her son, and Lilas took that moment to run and knock the woman to the ground. She used every part of her body in the act. The gun flew out of the woman's hand, the bullet shooting harmlessly as it hit the ground.

Bastien pounced on the woman, grabbing her arms and yanking her to her feet. Pierre came and hugged the woman close and Bastien released her. 'Mère…Mère,' he cried as he took her limp body in his arms.

Lilas jumped into Bastien's arms, showering kisses over his face. 'Are you all right? Please tell me you're all right.'

'I'm all right, Lilas. Are you?'

She couldn't speak because he kissed her then, his lips devouring hers, his arms crushing her so hard to his chest she almost squeaked. She didn't care. None of that mattered. He was alive and so was she!

'Bastien!' She cried out his name, tears trickling down her face. 'Bastien, I thought—I thought—'

'I know…I thought the same,' he breathed, sending them both tumbling to the ground by the pavilion. He lay on top of her and kissed her some more, his lips frantic and hard, as if he was unable to believe she was really there with him.

She met him kiss for kiss, knowing how close she had come to not having him with her. But then, 'Bastien, please…I must say something.'

'You don't have to say anything.'

Behind them, they heard the Comtesse de la Baux start to wail, and Pierre's words, soft and calming, as he might speak to a distraught child. Lilas longed to comfort him, but she knew it would have to wait. She couldn't go another second not telling Bastien how much she loved him.

'Bastien, please listen to me.'

'Whatever it is, it can wait.'

'It can't. Not this.'

He drew back, looking down at her with golden eyes dark with pain and desire. 'What is it?'

'I love you Bastien. With every drop of blood in me, I love you.'

Bastien's eyes widened. 'Lilas, do you mean it?'

She swallowed and smoothed her hands over his shoulders, unable to look into his face. 'It doesn't matter if you don't love me. I'll love you enough for both of us. Please don't push me away any more. I'll accept only your passion if that's all you can give me.'

'Lilas, I can't believe it… You really love me?'

'For such a long time. Maybe from the day when I gave you that ridiculous painting of the château in ash and dirt. When you gave me a *livre*.' She sniffed and gave a watery laugh. 'I don't remember when I fell in love with you. It's always been there. That's why it hurt so terribly when you left four years ago. Before then I knew I could never be in your life. I was your cinder girl, not your equal. But when I found out I was the daughter of a *comte*, suddenly I knew that I could be a part of your world. But then you were searching for your ideal.'

'My ideal?' He let out a harsh laugh. 'My ideal has rainbow-coloured hands, eyes like amethysts and skin the colour of Armagnac. Her lips are plump, like brown berries, and her kisses are just as sweet.'

He took his finger and traced the outline of her mouth. The wailing had subsided, and Lilas knew that Pierre had taken his mother away.

'My ideal did everything she could to fight being away from me. Defying me and luring me in at the same time. She kept me company in my darkest days and gave me light and courage to move on.'

Lilas's heart sped up. That look in his eyes…! That strange note in his voice…!

'My ideal makes me crave her body more than anyone else's. She makes me want to spend my life showing her how I feel with every part of my being. She's my best friend.'

As her eyes started swimming at his sweet words, he captured a tear with his finger and brought it to his mouth.

'I was so afraid of admitting that I love you, Lilas.'

Her heart stopped for a moment, and then pounded on. 'You love me? Truly?'

'I do. But I was so afraid… I saw what loving did to my father. How it devastated him. The idea of being like that repelled me. I thought loving a woman would do the same to me.'

'Is that why you were so cold to me after our night together?'

'It was wrong of me, I know. But you had got into my blood, made my heart beat, my lungs breathe. I couldn't stand it. I didn't want to admit what we shared was more beautiful than anything else I had ever experienced. It was. I took you three times that night, and you matched me kiss for kiss. You were my well, and I was drowning in you.'

Her cheeks warmed as she remembered his passion. 'I didn't mind.'

'I did—more than you realise. My overwhelming need for you frightened me.'

'Is that why you left?'

He gave a slow nod of his head. 'I was in love with you then, but I didn't want to admit it. I told myself I had to break your spell. Keep you away.' Bastien dropped his forehead to hers. 'When I saw that lunatic holding the gun on you, heard what she said to you, I finally understood my father. I simply don't want to live in a world where you don't exist. Where I can't love you.'

'Neither do I. Oh, Bastien, please don't leave me all alone. Don't push me away again.'

'Never again, my love. Never.'

He kissed her once more, and she felt secure in his love. When he drew back, his golden eyes were gleaming.

'I love you, Lilas.'

'I love you, too.'

He held her tight…so tight that she knew then that he would never let her go.

Epilogue

Eighteen months later, Saint Domingue, present-day Haiti

The moonlight flooded the master bedchamber, landing its bluish light on the dark-skinned bodies that were wrapped in each other's arms. Bastien's fingers caressed his wife's shoulder and down her arm, feeling the way goosebumps lifted along her skin and the slight shiver of pleasure she gave at his touch.

How easily this moment might not have been! Though more than a year had passed since the day his wife had been in mortal danger, it remained ever fresh in his mind.

'Do stop thinking about it, Bastien.'

He grinned, not bothering to deny it. They had become even closer, and he wasn't surprised when she knew his thoughts as well as he knew hers.

'I'll try, but it's so difficult.'

'Don't let her control us here, too, Bastien.'

Gathering Lilas closer to him, he kissed the top of her head. 'You're right.'

'Of course, I am.'

He laughed, and then grimaced when a small cry erupted from the crib by the bed.

'I told you to be quiet,' Lilas complained as she turned over and grabbed her dressing gown. 'But I suppose it is time for little Louis to have his feed.'

Unlike most women of their class, Lilas had refused to get a wet nurse. No matter how unpopular or uncommon it was, she didn't want another woman to feed her child.

She lifted the baby from his crib, his tiny eyes squinting in the moonlight. Every time he looked at his son, Bastien couldn't believe how blessed he was.

Lilas settled the child to her breast, and once the boy had latched on, his cries ceased in an instant. Bastien never tired of watching this...seeing little Louis take his nourishment.

They had decided on calling the child Louis Philippe St Clare, Comte de la Baux, although of course he would inherit Bastien's title eventually. Since Lilas had never known her father, she'd wanted some part of him to exist beside her always.

A glint from where she sat with the child caught his eye. It was the *livre* he'd given her years ago. He'd had a hole drilled in the centre so that she could wear it as a necklace. It represented so much for them.

'Do you think she's surviving in the Colonies?'

He scowled. The last thing he wanted to do was think about *her*. They refused to say her name in their house. It was the one thing he was adamant about.

Pierre had not had the heart to make his mother pay for her crimes with her life. Even knowing that his mother was responsible for the death of Louis Moreau was almost too much for him to bear at times.

Bastien had given the woman two choices, and he'd done that for Pierre's sake. She would either find a passage to the New World—the Colonies that were giving England such a difficult time—and make a new life for herself. Or he would take her to the proper authorities and watch her hang from the end of the gallows.

Unsurprisingly, she'd chosen the New World, and had begun her journey the very next day. Lilas had cried, but when he'd tried to discover why she hadn't been able to articulate it. Perhaps she'd cried for everything that had happened.

'I don't care,' he said now. 'She's fortunate to be alive. I wanted to take her to the authorities. But since we are the only ones who know about it, it's enough. The fact she's away from us and we'll never have to see her again doesn't heal the wound, but it gives us peace.'

Lilas stirred under him. 'Bastien, do you think Pierre will be all right?'

Remembering the hollow, shattered look on Pierre's face, Bastien made a sound at the back of his throat. 'Who's to say?'

Pierre had seemed broken by the revelations of his mother, and during the months before they'd left for Saint Domingue Bastien had encouraged the man to visit them regularly.

Learning that he and Lilas were half-siblings had helped somewhat. They had always been close, even when they hadn't known they were related by blood, and despite what his mother had done to her Lilas had refused to let it affect her relationship with Pierre.

Several weeks ago they'd received word that he would be coming to visit them here. He was anxious to meet his nephew and lonely as well, he'd admitted to Lilas in his letter.

They'd moved here because Bastien had wanted to be closer to his mother's side of the family. He felt it was something his father would have wanted. In this way, by learning about his mother's people, he was honouring his father's love for her.

While they were here, he'd generously given Pierre the responsibility of managing both the Languedoc and the de la Baux estates, along with the help of the family solicitors. Pierre had seen the gesture for what it was— Bastien trusting him and letting him know he didn't believe he was guilty for the sins of his mother.

Estienne had also promised to come and visit them before the year was out, but there wasn't any way Bastien would invite his uncle the Comte de Clareville here.

'Are you done, *mon cher*?' She was speaking to Louis, who had a satisfied look on his face that was comical.

'Here, let me hold him.'

Together, they took care of their child, expelling his air and changing him before rocking him back to sleep. It was an unconventional life they led, but it was theirs. He would sleep for another few hours now, and Bastien knew exactly how he wanted to spend them.

He bent his head, sharing with Lilas a deep, soul-stirring kiss that sent healing pulses of love through them both. He gathered her close, knowing that, just like his father, he had married a goddess. All other women were mere mortals.

When they finally broke apart, Lilas reached up and toyed with some strands of his hair. 'I can't believe you're mine,' she said. 'All of you belongs to me. And I to you.'

'Always. Simply always, my love.'

An impish look came into her eyes. 'I can't believe that I was so reluctant to be your bride.' She sighed happily. 'It's because of you that I have this life. Thank you, Bastien.'

'No, it's because of you *I* have this life. From the first

time I saw you as a young girl I knew you were a part of me. You complete me in ways I never thought possible. You make every day the best day of my life. I truly cannot live without you, *ma arc-en-ciel*. I can't.'

Tears welled in her eyes and she gave a little hint of laughter. 'I hope you never do…'

* * * * *

If you enjoyed this story, look out for more great books from Parker J. Cole, coming soon!

Love Harlequin romance?

DISCOVER.

Be the first to find out about promotions, news and exclusive content!

f Facebook.com/HarlequinBooks

**Twitter.com/HarlequinBooks

**Instagram.com/HarlequinBooks

**Pinterest.com/HarlequinBooks

You Tube YouTube.com/HarlequinBooks

ReaderService.com

EXPLORE.

Sign up for the Harlequin e-newsletter and download a free book from any series at
TryHarlequin.com

CONNECT.

Join our Harlequin community to share your thoughts and connect with other romance readers!
Facebook.com/groups/HarlequinConnection

HARLEQUIN

HSOCIAL2021

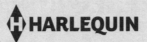

HARLEQUIN

Heartfelt or thrilling, passionate or uplifting—Harlequin is more than just happily-ever-after.

With twelve different series to choose from and new books available every month, you are sure to find stories that will move you, uplift you, inspire and delight you.

HARLEQUIN
PLUS

Announcing a **BRAND-NEW**
multimedia subscription service
for romance fans like you!

Read, Watch and Play.

Experience the easiest way to get
the romance content you crave.

Start your **FREE 7 DAY TRIAL** at
<u>www.harlequinplus.com/freetrial</u>.

Get 4 FREE REWARDS!

We'll send you 2 FREE Books <u>plus</u> 2 FREE Mystery Gifts.

FREE
Value Over
$20

Both the **Harlequin® Desire** and **Harlequin Presents®** series feature compelling novels filled with passion, sensuality and intriguing scandals.

YES! Please send me 2 FREE novels from the Harlequin Desire or Harlequin Presents series and my 2 FREE gifts (gifts are worth about $10 retail). After receiving them, if I don't wish to receive any more books, I can return the shipping statement marked "cancel." If I don't cancel, I will receive 6 brand-new Harlequin Presents Larger-Print books every month and be billed just $6.05 each in the U.S. or $6.24 each in Canada, a savings of at least 10% off the cover price or 6 Harlequin Desire books every month and be billed just $4.80 each in the U.S. or $5.49 each in Canada, a savings of at least 13% off the cover price. It's quite a bargain! Shipping and handling is just 50¢ per book in the U.S. and $1.25 per book in Canada.* I understand that accepting the 2 free books and gifts places me under no obligation to buy anything. I can always return a shipment and cancel at any time by calling the number below. The free books and gifts are mine to keep no matter what I decide.

Choose one: ☐ **Harlequin Desire**
(225/326 HDN GRTW)

☐ **Harlequin Presents Larger-Print**
(176/376 HDN GQ9Z)

Name (please print)

Address   Apt. #

City   State/Province   Zip/Postal Code

Email: Please check this box ☐ if you would like to receive newsletters and promotional emails from Harlequin Enterprises ULC and its affiliates. You can unsubscribe anytime.

Mail to the **Harlequin Reader Service:**
IN U.S.A.: P.O. Box 1341, Buffalo, NY 14240-8531
IN CANADA: P.O. Box 603, Fort Erie, Ontario L2A 5X3

Want to try 2 free books from another series? Call 1-800-873-8635 or visit www.ReaderService.com.

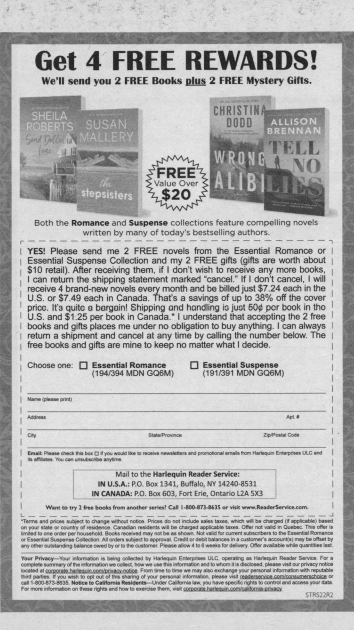